*For Karen*
*With every best wish*

*Steve*

# The Aftermath

## J. Stephen Thompson

A novel of post-war Kosova

This book is written with admiration and affection for my friends in Kosova.

This book is a work of fiction. Names, characters, places and incidents are either products of the author's imagination or are used fictitiously. Every effort has been made to ensure the accuracy of historical events.

# Acknowledgements

Even though writing is thought to be a solitary exercise, no book is ever produced without the involvement of others. I wish to thank many others for their contributions.

Thanks to my friends who read all or part of one or more versions of the manuscript: David Harrington, David Shaw, Fred Cahoon, John Kim, Merv and Andrea Caldwell, Christine Fleming, Alex Thompson, Susan Best and Bob Schmidt.

Thanks also to friends and family who listened to sections read aloud: Andrea and Merv Caldwell, Fred and Trudy Cahoon, David and Elaine Denune, Malcolm Handoll and Rachel DuBois, Alan and Anthea Stephenson, Dan and Katie Ralph, and the members of my Canadian Authors Association, Peterborough and Kawarthas Branch.

Very big thanks to my writing coach and mentor Prim Pemberton and the individuals who attended her workshops, Creative Writing in Cabbagetown. They critiqued and offered suggestions and encouragement along the way: Barb Nahwegahbow, Josie Mounsey, Ilene Cummings, Sylvie Daigneault, Ann Bjorseth, Gobnait McAnoy, Rose Roberts, Asetha Power, Mary Moylan, Leslie Jennings and Nick van Vliet.

My deepest gratitude to everyone I met or worked with in Kosova. The Canadians gave freely of their wisdom and fellowship: Harry Richardson, Andy Hamilton, Christine Fleming, Dick Zoutman, Mike Parry, Sally Maclean, Cathy Ellis.

Harry and Andy appear in this book in roles somewhat similar to the ones they played. That was my way of commemorating their passing and celebrating what they shared with me. Most especially, I dedicate this book to all my Kosovar friends, many who prefer not to be named. They unfolded their stories, interpreted a complex history and acted as ambassadors.

Especially, I wish to thank my wife, Donna, who was there in Kosova and is included in most of the groups above as my greatest friend, supporter, advisor and editor throughout the process of writing this story.

# Dedication

To the memories of Harold Richardson and Andrew Hamilton

To my wife, Donna

To my children, Ondine, Michael, Alex, Bryce and Graham

# The Aftermath

## Organizations encountered

| | |
|---|---|
| CDC | U.S. Centers for Disease Control and Prevention |
| CIDA | Canadian International Development Agency |
| CIPHA* | Canadian Institute of Public Health Associations |
| CLCA | Canadian Landmine Clearing Agency |
| DOW | Doctors of the World |
| IMC | International Medical Corps |
| KLA | Kosova Liberation Army |
| MIN* | Microbiology Intelligence Network |
| OSCE | Organization for Security and Co-operation in Europe |
| UNHCR | UN High Commission for Refugees |
| UNMIK | UN Mission in Kosova |
| WHO | World Health Organization |

*These organizations exist only in the author's imagination

# *Dramatis Personae*

| | |
|---|---|
| Thomas Henry Stephenson | Canadian magazine writer. Agent for MIN |
| Cassandra Agnes Borden | Canadian microbiologist. On assignment in Kosova for CIPHA. Potential MIN operative |
| Fatmir Deliu | Kosovar physician. Ethnic Albanian. Lives in Prishtinë |
| Anthony Petersen | Editor, *The Magazine* |
| Agron Shalla | Forensic epidemiologist. Ethnic Albanian. Lives in Prishtinë. Tom's interpreter |
| Albert Tindall (Bert) | Tom's best friend. Psychiatrist. Lives in Ottawa. Works for Health Canada |
| Shpend Veseli | Kosovar physician. Ethnic Albanian. CIPHA contact in Prishtinë. |
| Willem van der Wal (Willie) | Canadian infectious diseases physician. Infection Control consultant for Kosova project. McGill University. |
| Dennis O'Reilly (Dirk) | Head, Microbiology Intelligence Network. Tom's contact |
| Greg Hanbruz | Project Manager, Kosova Project, CIPHA, Ottawa |
| Karen Borden (kg) | Cassandra's sister. Canadian physician |
| Shelagh Borden | Cassandra's mother |
| Sue McElligott | Cassandra's WHO contact |
| Elvira Kurtz | Kosovar medical microbiologist. Microbiology laboratory supervisor University of Prishtinë Health Centre |
| Sal Maxwell | American physician. Tuberculosis expert. |
| Jordan Siemens | Canadian physician. Medical consultant for Kosova project |
| Andrew Hamilton | Manager, Canadian Support Office, Prishtinë |
| Frank MacGregor | Canadian consular official attached to Canadian Embassy in Vienna. In charge of Canadian Office in Prishtinë |

| | |
|---|---|
| Harold Richardson | Canadian medical microbiologist. Toronto |
| Narong Amranand | Canadian microbiologist. Intelligence role |
| Justine Tachereau | Canadian microbiologist. McGill University. Works with MIN |
| Afërdita | Kosovar medical microbiologist |
| Shpresa | Young Kosovar physician. Gynaecology resident in Switzerland |

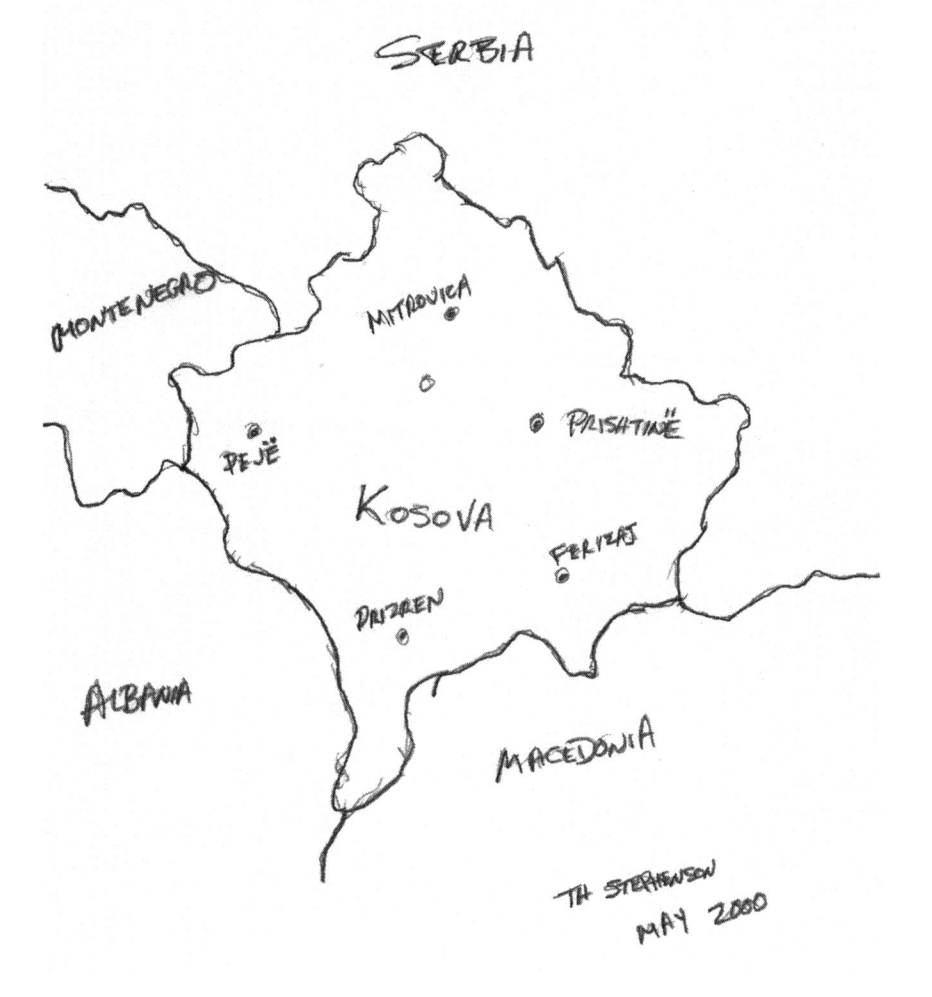

SERBIA

MONTENEGRO

MITROVICA

PRISHTINË

PEJË

KOSOVA

FERIZAJ

DRIZREN

ALBANIA

MACEDONIA

TH STEPHENSON
MAY 2000

# Part 1

# September – December 2000

one

# September 2000
## *Mirëmëngjes*

"What do you want me to say, Thomas? If everything was not mud encrusted, it was shit encrusted. Or both. I would not choose to relive this time." Fatmir Deliu paused to sip some of the sparkling water often served with coffee in Prishtinë cafés. Tom Stephenson tried to encourage Fatmir to elaborate, to describe the refugee camps. "We could not do simple things. We could not change my child's diaper. It was a cesspool. I triaged these people for what? Where could I send them for treatment? Dysentery and depression! It is a deadly mixture. Still today I wake up not certain where I am but relieved to be in my home. Thomas, you know I am reluctant to talk. Not because it is you, my friend, but because I have never talked about this. I know I told you I would tell you something for your story." The right side of Fatmir's mouth twitched. He shrugged his shoulders. "It is hard but I will start with spring 1999. It was very wet. It seemed like it rained every day. I know you have seen mud like that."

"You mean that fine slippery mess like a thin coating of motor oil over the ground?"

Fatmir grinned at Tom, nodded knowingly and waited for Tom to continue.

"Yeah, I know it. I slipped in that stuff trying to avoid a car coming up the hill from Mother Theresa Boulevard. I stepped sideways off the

3

pavement but lost my footing and couldn't recover. Ended up with my leg scraped raw and soaked to the skin instantly. No matter how many times I washed those clothes that mud stain never came out."

"So you know we skidded everywhere. Like the song, slip-sliding away. I listen to classical music now but we always listened to western rock and roll in Yugoslavia. I will also tell you journalists saved us. CNN and BBC saved us. The Serbs would not dare finish us off in front of such witnesses. Okay, the camps..."

Fatmir sat forward. Tom realized he was ready to continue. He switched on his digital recorder so he could focus on Fatmir's story without taking notes.

"Macedonian camps were better. Macedonia has a big Albanian population. Their government was not exactly Serb-friendly but, more likely, Serb-scared."

"Would that Albanian population be the reason they were willing to establish camps?"

"Partly but Macedonia had some autonomy within Yugoslavia. They were allowed to secede peacefully. Yes, they ran better camps but they were careful not to provoke anger from Belgrade."

"Sorry I interrupted your story."

"*S'ka problem*. I welcome the time to think. It is so hard for me to talk about deprivation. Mud was abundant. A few tents were provided by UNHCR. Not much food, no toilet or washing facilities at first. They did not want us comfortable. They did not want permanent refugee camps. I worked eighteen hours each day. I am not a surgeon but I triaged bullet wounds, broken bones. I looked after vomiting, diarrhoea and dysentery. Dysentery! We had one of the best public health systems in the world! Everyone immunized, good hygiene. But total breakdown in society uncovers infectious disease."

Tom shook his head in dismay. "Surely the major purpose in establishing refugee camps is health and safety."

4

"But, Thomas, you know yourself tired and broken people are susceptible to illness."

As Fatmir paused, Tom slumped back into his chair and sipped his cappuccino. This is so far removed from the experiences of my Canadian readers, he thought, but immediately reconsidered that notion. We're a nation of immigrants. Breakdowns like this were often why people emigrated to Canada. Particularly immediately after World War Two.

Fatmir continued to talk. "I cannot say I was motivated. But I was allowed the luxury of having a purpose. Not like other camp residents. For God's sake, we were a modern European country. I was middle-class. A well educated urban person, not much different from you as you know. At the very least, my work with the refugees kept me grounded. Me, a stateless person and *persona non grata* in my own country. Then the NATO bombing forced the Serbs to turn tail and scurry back to Serbia. I joined the long walk home with other refugees. Now, we were needed after more than ten years of... I do not know the words for what happened to us."

"You were disenfranchised."

"Yes but slowly."

"Perhaps insidious. Insidious disenfranchisement."

"Yes, yes," Fatmir agreed then laughed. "But I cannot speak like you, Thomas. My friends would laugh. They would think I am funny," Fatmir chuckled then continued. "I want to tell you why we were now needed. All Serb doctors and Serb administrators ran home. They didn't have balls enough to face us. They destroyed health infrastructure. They looted equipment, computers, files, pharmaceuticals. Everything they could, they disabled. If they could not have it, they did not want us to have it."

"I'm always shocked by things like that even after everything I've been told," Tom said. "You were countrymen." Tom suddenly wondered about his own abilities to make it through such circumstances. He questioned whether he would emerge as whole as Fatmir. Then he asked Fatmir to talk about the future, his vision of his own future and Kosova's.

"We began life anew. I tried to resume my career. I wanted my wife to stay with her family in Macedonia until we knew the NATO victory was permanent. Conditions now are not easy. But I am energized building this new life and new country. We can do this. We need to be free. Depression will continue to haunt me, Thomas, but I no longer suffer those depths of despair. Life in the camps was almost unbearable. One difference now? I told you how proud I was to be Yugoslavian. What a bold experiment to take these little countries, different ethnic origins and create a federation. And it worked. Yes, there has been a long history of ethnic conflict. But we made it work. That is the tragedy of the collapse of Yugoslavia as a federation. Now I have grown to consider myself Albanian. A Kosovar, yes, but first Albanian. We will make this work."

That's the crux, isn't it. Tom realized Fatmir needed to return to work so he thanked him for coming and suggested they meet again soon. He took a moment to look out over the city from the café balcony. A brown haze from the coal-fired power plant to the southwest settled gently over downtown, *Prishtinë Centrum*. This city of half a million people sat on a mountain plateau extending several kilometres in each direction. Looking from this hill to the one across town he envisioned an ancient river valley. Tom smiled as he tried to remember an Albanian saying he'd heard, something like a town without a river is only a village. Offered by some as a slight against Prishtinë, city without a river. He resolved to remember to ask Fatmir for the correct Albanian phrasing. Focussing closer, he noticed just a hint of autumn colour. Not that different from Toronto, he decided.

Tom walked quickly. He punched one fist into the opposite palm in his frustration over Editorial's continued demand for independent corroboration of his stories. He received another message this morning. If he stayed in his apartment he expected he would pull his hair out so he left to walk off his irritation. Corroboration? What about the evidence –bomb damage, the dearth of public health and social programs, collapse of the retail industry, intermittent power and water, no children on the streets or in the parks? He gazed at the small park ahead of him as he walked toward the university. At the moment he realized it was a park in name only. Filled with garbage. He was aware of his growing exasperation. But he knew the danger of undirected annoyance and quickly decided the UN was at fault.

War had been over almost a year. Garbage collection should be a priority by now. His own microbiology background dictated that much. In his neighbourhood, large garbage bins were strategically positioned on several street corners. These were newly added since he was last in Prishtinë. Still no infrastructure for trash collection, though. That, to his mind, was a failing of the UN administration, the *de facto* government of Kosova.

Earlier that morning he'd watched a man approach one of the overfull bins, strike a match and toss it in with a deliberation that suggested he felt obliged to empty the repository. Then the man walked away. Low flame flared across the surface of the garbage within the container before engaging the overflowing rubbish as well. Combustion was slow and incomplete. Now, as Tom passed the same area again, on his way to rendezvous with Fatmir Deliu, the fire continued to smoulder, releasing thick black smoke. An acrid stench assaulted his senses. His eyes stung. He recoiled from the odour of burning plastic. I expect we'll all die of some toxic exposure or other, he thought, then shook his head, steeling himself for journalistic objectivity.

Tom arrived first. Fatmir had suggested they meet again on the coffee patio at the student centre on the main campus of the University of Prishtinë, this austere sidewalk café with its few folding chairs surrounding weather-beaten tables. The temperature was probably twenty degrees Celsius but felt warmer in the direct path of the midmorning sun. The university cafés were always filled with students, faculty, visitors. He grabbed a table newly available, not yet cleared. He sat and prepared to review the transcript of yesterday's interview with Fatmir. As was his habit, he always transcribed his notes and interview tapes while he was still sure of their context. Tom was satisfied with the information he'd gathered so far but today he wanted to hone in on Fatmir's back story.

"*Mirëmëngjes, Thomas.*"

Tom flinched with surprise. He'd been engrossed in his notes and hadn't noticed Fatmir approaching from behind the table. "*Mirëmëngjes, Fatmir. Si jeni?*"

"*Mirë.* A little tired. A late evening. I try to go to bed early before I lecture the next day. It did not work out that way.*"

"*Kafe?*" Tom asked.

"Thank you, Thomas. Cappuccino today, I think. And for you as well?" Fatmir remained standing, didn't wait for an answer but gestured to the waiter. The waiter simply hand signalled two and Fatmir nodded agreement. They'd done this before.

"Is this good for you outside like this?"

He seems disconcerted, Tom thought. Not his usual calm, deliberate self. Maybe anxious about continuing the interview. About feeling forced once more to relive his experiences. Or perhaps he simply needs caffeine today.

As he seated himself, Fatmir explained he'd filled in for a scheduled guest who failed to appear for a TV phone-in program the previous evening.

"You ever watch? It's the local channel. Maybe it is too late for you." He laughed. "Starts at eleven o'clock. Mainly health issues. Pretty fast talk. You might not be able to keep up but it could help your Albanian."

"I understand most of the local news I watch... Well, understand the topic but not necessarily the viewpoint. Funny, eh? Know what it's about but not yes or no. Then I usually switch to BBC." Tom preferred to downplay his facility with the Albanian language. He stopped talking to look at Fatmir. Fatmir would present well on TV, compact form, clean shaven like most Kosovar men, full face and best of all, full head of black hair without a hint of grey. Not lean, but certainly not fat.

"I was ready for bed when the phone rang. The producer apologized for the late hour but explained it was an emergency. Then I got dressed and left for the TV studio. About two blocks walk. You know the place?"

"That low building on Mother Teresa near the Grand Hotel? Surrounded by security fencing?"

"That is it. But closer to Bill Clinton Boulevard than the Grand."

"So that's where you live? I thought you probably lived in Sunny Hill. Sorry, I'm interrupting again."

Fatmir waved away Tom's aside. "*S'ka problem*. My wife asked me what calls I expected. I said 'The usual, sex, drugs and diarrhoea'. I muddled through."

"I can't imagine you muddling through anything. You're always prepared." Tom sipped his coffee then shifted toward the point of this meeting. "Look Fatmir, there's some trouble with *The Magazine*. They want corroboration for events we've talked about."

"Who will do that, Thomas? You think Serbia will admit to ethnic cleansing? Kosova has a population of only two and a half million. More than half were moved outside our borders to refugee camps."

"Actually moved? I have trouble understanding the logistics. How did that work?"

"Some people were loaded onto trucks or buses and driven to the border with Albania or Macedonia, others were simply forced out on foot. As I told you before, myself included."

As Fatmir paused, Tom thought the request for corroboration was bureaucratic nonsense in the face of such horrors.

Fatmir continued, "You think Serbia will acknowledge that? And mass graves. We don't know yet who is buried. Just like in Bosnia and Croatia it will take time."

"I know."

"Sometimes I wonder what was gained with the collapse of communism."

"Why do you say that?"

"I recognize things were not good for everyone. But, you know, in Tito's time, intellectuals, doctors and professors were well paid."

"I thought you might have been undervalued," Tom said.

"No definitely not. We took annual seaside vacations. Attended conferences in Europe regularly. Life was good for professionals. Some memories fade. This stays with me. So does memory of my military training. I'm fifty now. It was my early twenties. Long term memory, yes? They say short term memory is the first to go. Here, we don't have time for memory loss. Life expectancy is too short for that."


The interview continued with digs and quips from Fatmir belying the seriousness of the subject.

"One year of military service was compulsory. Mine was postponed until I finished medical school. After graduation, I went immediately to officer training. Classroom lectures mostly with some field training. I met other doctors from all over Yugoslavia. It was a good time. I did well. Because I was always top of the class, I was released from service after only eleven months. To me, the purpose was a trained militia not a standing army. Yugoslavia was interested in a force available for emergencies like floods. We were not really interested in fighting. We were officially neutral. Like Switzerland."

Tom enjoyed conversing with Fatmir. He had a good command of English. Great sense of humour. Quick with sardonic comments, always teasing but never malicious. Now, he laughed at his own neutrality joke.

"Except for triage training, the rest of my military training was useless to me. And I was never called up because of my poor eyesight. Saved by the eyes, I say."

Tom hadn't been certain how today's interview might proceed. Usually, he preferred to allow his subjects latitude to talk and drift wherever they were comfortable. Today, he'd be happy to avoid the emotion of yesterday. He felt drained by what Fatmir had told him. Now he wanted to focus on background. So he asked Fatmir to explain his Kosovar nationalism.

"I was never a Kosovar patriot. One day, I was a proud Yugoslav. My passport well-respected when I travelled. The next day, I was forced from my home. Serb police seized my apartment. They said we had fifteen minutes to gather personal items. There was no time to collect much other than a few photographs. We left most things behind. We were compelled to walk to the Macedonian border. I don't know now whether that journey was three or four days. Not a great distance I suppose but we had no food, no water, so before long each kilometre was a struggle. We were with thousands of others but strangely I cannot remember recognizing anyone I knew. I now realize Serbia was in a hurry to get rid of us before negotiation for status was forced on them. Many Kosovars do not like the UN now. The UN did nothing for us. NATO finally did. President Clinton did.

They were desperate for physicians to work in the camps in Macedonia. I worked closely with UNHCR. My wife is Macedonian and both of us lived and worked there about twenty years ago. When we moved to Prishtinë, we visited family often when Yugoslavia was still whole. I was surprised how unwelcome we had become. UNHCR staff told me we might never be able to return home. They predicted the conflict would continue for years. I was not comfortable to be a trauma physician but I was willing to work. UNHCR promised to place me quickly somewhere in Europe.

You know Thomas, I will tell you, as a refugee I became so depressed. I no longer knew who I was. I did not know where I belonged. And I did not know if I had options. I am a doctor, so I recognize signs and symptoms. I think I am okay. Now only my dreams bother me."

Not what Tom had expected. From his observations of Fatmir, he would never have suspected depression. He's jovial whenever I see him. He teases his colleagues, especially the females, mercilessly.

"My military training prepared me to care for the sick and wounded. Ironic to me, it was Yugoslav training. Serbia still calls itself Yugoslavia. I was presented with not only the physically sick and wounded in the refugee camps but the incredibly tired and destitute as well. Mental illness was never considered important. The insane were simply locked away. I had no training in that area. And nothing in my life prepared me to live in those conditions. I could not get used to such deprivation."

Tom was distracted by the comment about mental health. He thought of the visit he'd arranged for an interview at the psychiatric hospital on the grounds of the University of Prishtinë Health Centre. Not that the recollection related to the refugee camp situation but it confirmed mental health had not been a priority in Yugoslavia. Bleak had been his first impression. Hopeless his next. *One Flew Over the*

*Cuckoo's Nest* had nothing on this. At least in the movie version, there was a semblance of patient care. Here, family was expected to provide food and bedding. And care. Anything for personal comfort or recovery was not the state's responsibility. A warehouse. A prison.

Back at his apartment that afternoon Tom booted his laptop to transcribe his taped interview. He decided to submit the whole transcript to *The Magazine* as a story proposal for his *Reconstructing Kosova* series. He knew he could finish this piece quickly once Editorial agreed to a publication date.

Looking away from the computer screen and out the window, he contemplated the Prishtinë he'd come to know. There were certainly worse places to be on assignment. Most people he encountered were polite and accommodating, never unfriendly. He was flattered how individuals like Fatmir would now share their wartime experiences with him. This was different since he'd returned. Almost as if he now belonged. No longer considered a here-today, gone-tomorrow correspondent.

Tom himself was convinced his interviews helped flesh out what had happened since 1989. Perhaps one-sided. Because Serbs and ethnic Albanians didn't trust each other, he wouldn't expect an admission of guilt from either. And certainly not simply because a magazine wanted corroboration for his prose. Their legal and ethical responsibility *The Magazine* said. Tom wanted nothing of that. These were narratives of individuals who survived the conflict, best presented as disclosed.

He e-mailed Tony Petersen, his editor, sat a few moments in contemplation, then decided to walk to the market area. He needed to get away from the computer, to clear his head of those images he was determined not to allow to join his growing congregation of personal demons.

Date: Tue, 12 Sep 2000 16:43 EDT
From: Anthony Petersen

Tom, your story will run September 30. Please forward finished piece by the twenty-fourth. I don't understand the insistence on being called Albanian rather than Kosovar. Isn't that akin to fifth generation Canadians identifying as Scots? All the best, Tony

Subject: SECURITY ENCRYPTED MESSAGE
Date: Wed, 13 Sep 2000 10:35 EDT
From: Thomas Stephenson
To: Dirk O'Reilly <doreilly@secure.gov.min.org>

Dirk, please check Fatmir's claims against UNHCR records. We may need his help. I still prefer to use Agron Shalla if I can arrange it. Agron's an epidemiologist with a good understanding of infectious disease. Best, Tom

Cassandra Borden high-fived the air and allowed herself an uncharacteristic whoop. Something she would never do at work, only in the protective seclusion of her home. This was actually happening. A telephone call two months before from her long-ago mentor, Jordan Siemens, was all it had taken to entice her to join the project. Until now, it hadn't seemed possible it would all come together. Now she read Jordan's e-mail for a third time just to confirm all this was real.

Hi Cassie, I realize I haven't thanked you properly for agreeing to help us re-establish public health laboratory services in Kosova. As we discussed about reporting relationships, I will be medical consultant, Greg Hanbruz project director. From my assessment visit this summer, you'll have your work cut out for you to improve competency levels. I see them operating at maybe a 1960s level. But you've never backed away from a challenge. It may require six weeks or so to obtain all clearances necessary for your trip. Best wishes, Jordan

Now she was faced with negotiating a leave-of-absence from the forensics lab, renewing her out-of-date passport, arranging childcare for Jeremy if indeed childcare was what she could call some sort of custodial arrangement for a seventeen year old high school student. As a mother, she needed assurance he had food in the house, his laundry was done and, more importantly, he went to school. She could ask his father but part of the reason for accepting this assignment was to get away from Doug and her continuing sense that he still controlled her even after a year's separation. That Doug also worked at the lab caused her no end of stress. Despite that trepidation, she whooped once again. She anticipated being truly free.

Friday September 15. Tom was once again at the university. This time at the Faculty of Medicine building in the health complex about half a kilometre east and downhill from the main campus. The epidemiology office appeared less hectic than he remembered from his last visit. He hoped Agron would accept his offer.

"How are you, Thomas?" inquired Agron Shalla.

"*Mirë falemnderit, Agron, mirëmëngjes. Si jeni?*"

"*Mirë, mirë.* Thank you for coming to see me again."

"Have you thought about our discussion?"

"Yes, Thomas. It is reasonable. I am not really a translator or driver. But the money you offer is good for me and my family. You see how my girls have grown?" Agron inclined his head toward the photograph on his desk. Tom picked up the framed picture for a closer look. "It is a surprise to me they seem so normal, going through such a problem time as war."

"Of course, they're normal. You and Flora are such good parents. You shielded your girls from the worst."

"Thomas, you always say nice words. You could talk Flora away from me."

"C'mon, she never takes her eyes off you." Tom watched Agron's face to see if his words would qualify as humorous banter. He needed Agron's assistance.

"I know what you do here, Thomas. I know what you look for. We cannot talk in this place, but I know."

"I don't know what you're saying."

"Oh yes, Thomas, you do. I have done something like this before. My country needs me to work with you. Really, I should be head of the Institute. First, it was Serbs kicking me out. Now, it is the UN. Everybody always knows better. I will work with you, Thomas my friend. You are friend of my country and my people. But I mostly need to help because you speak lousy Albanian and need an interpreter."


Subject: SECURITY ENCRYPTED MESSAGE
Date Fri, 22 Sep 2000 14:35 EDT
From: Thomas Stephenson <stephenson@secure.gov.min.org>
To: Dirk O'Reilly <doreilly@secure.gov.min.org>

Dirk, I've arranged to hire Agron Shalla as interpreter and driver. He sends regards. I hadn't realized he was our pre-war contact, our man-on-the-ground, as it were. Was I not supposed to have that info? I look inept when I stumble onto information everyone else seems to know.

Agron doesn't believe the current anthrax cases result from weaponized strains. He thinks they stem from general post-war upheaval, destroyed infrastructure and breakdown in usually good personal hygiene. Probably strains endemic in Kosova. New test organisms would be introduced in an aerosolized format. We're hearing about cutaneous anthrax, not pneumonic. The notion of a breeding ground for bioterrorism-ready anthrax strains is likely unfounded. Some strains may derive from the old Soviet biological warfare development days. Apparently, the Soviets used parts of Kosova as testing areas as late as the 1970s. This may be paranoia on Agron's part but he's shown me documentation of official ethnic cleansing policies toward the Albanian population right from the beginning of Yugoslavia during the late stages of WWI. Not much of a stretch to suggest official complicity in offering a testing ground and test population. After all, anthrax cases aren't really a remarkable occurrence in a farming area. Any collateral cases would have yielded results for either cause – testing or cleansing. Agron says there have been some anthrax hoaxes, though. Tom

"Thomas, I must tell you somebody is trying to scare people about anthrax," Agron had said describing a situation in which three reporters at two Albanian language newspapers received official looking letters from Belgrade in Yugoslavian government envelopes. "As they opened the letters, powder dropped from a folded hand-written note. Each note was the same. It said they were exposed to anthrax."

"Did someone examine the powder?"

"The police. They came, heard the story and laughed. Said it was body powder."

"Did they collect samples to examine?"

"Yes, of course. Said they would send it to the best scientists in Europe."

"Wouldn't they take samples to the public health lab?"

"There is no public health lab, Thomas."

"Wouldn't the hospital lab be able to examine them?"

"No."

"But you told me they admit two dozen anthrax cases a year to the infectious diseases hospital."

"Thomas, the diagnosis is clinical. There is no laboratory confirmation."

"Would the lab have containment facilities like safety cabinets?"

"No."

"So if these powders were tested and actually contained anthrax spores, the organism would spread from the lab through the whole medical complex."

"You are right. Tomorrow, we will visit the hospital laboratories. You will be disappointed."

Date: Sun, 24 Sep 2000 09:50 EST

Tom, there have been about four hundred attempts to scare people with fake samples since 1998. They're regarded as serious attempts to cause panic. That too is terrorism. Dirk

Subject: WHAT ABOUT WOMEN
Date: Sun, 24 Sep 2000 11:40 EST
From: albert.tindall@symplicity.com

Hey Tommy, how are ya? Haven't heard from you lately. Is that because you're busy or is there a love interest you're not telling me about? None of your stories or messages ever mention women. I'm just worried you've lost interest. All the best, Albert (Suzanne sends her love)


Date: Sun, 24 Sep 2000 15:40 EST

Hey Bert, good to hear from you. Thanks for your concerns. It's great to have e-mail access. Though it would be better to be well away from your prying questions. Even filing stories is amazing. I send a draft to *The Magazine* and have editorial corrections and comments usually the next day. Also, questions. It's amazing how someone sitting in an office in Toronto thinks she has a handle on something happening on the ground here.


Tom paused a moment, stretched his arms behind the backless stool that served as a desk chair. He was amazed internet service had been established so quickly post-war. Bodes well for the future, he thought. Information denies opportunity for further repression. He returned to his e-mail:

Okay, women. Today was beautiful, still summery, easily twenty-five Celsius. I spent the afternoon basking in the sun at a sidewalk café on Mother Teresa Boulevard. Watching tall, slim, mini-skirted, wonderful looking women, walking in pairs or threes, often arm-in-arm. I'm generalizing but the Kosovar women are beautiful. There are plenty of other women around at places like Bombay Gardens. There every foreign male patron seems to have an underage companion from Moldavia or one of the 'stans. Reality is the first things back after war – black-market CDs, drugs and women – all in anticipation of a growing number of international aid workers. It's too bad Serbia and Kosova couldn't be as cooperative at the political level as their criminal elements are at the street level. All my best to you and Suzanne, Tom

Tom wondered whether his need to be verbose, even in correspondence, reflected his lack of emotional support. He had friends here but none with whom he could simply shoot the breeze. Does Bert see something? Or are his women questions just Bert being Bert? Strange about e-mail. Once the "Send" button is clicked, there's no opportunity to second guess.

two

# October 2000
*Si jeni?*

When Agron arrived at his apartment, Tom had been about to compose a group e-mail for friends and family back home to explain something about the mix of UN, governmental, non-governmental and other acronymic organizations he encountered daily. Nothing very important, just something to pass time. Agron's interruption was welcome.

"We should meet with Shpend Veseli and Willem van der Wal. They are at Monaco Restaurant," Agron explained. "Do you know Doktor Willem? He is from Canada."

"No, don't think so."

Tom knew Shpend though, one of those very well connected people who could easily navigate the political maze. A Kosovar physician trained in Canada, every Canadian in Prishtinë would eventually gravitate toward Shpend for advice, to find services or curry favour with him as someone who counted government ministers amongst his friends.

"Thomas, good to see you again. You know Willie?" Shpend stood to greet him.

"No... no, we haven't met. Glad to meet you now, though, Willie. What project are you with?"

"I'm looking at possible infection control improvements at the

21

hospital. But, you know, Tom, our paths have crossed. At a weekend seminar on forensic microbiology at McGill."

"That's awhile ago. Your memory's good. I'm surprised you recognize me. I doubt I even had a beard then."

"It's only short-term memory I worry about." Willie laughed then continued, "What're you doing?"

"I'm here writing articles for *The Magazine*."

"A correspondent? You're not with a microbiology project?"

Agron and Shpend had been quietly conversing but now Shpend said, "The articles Thomas writes are very much respected in Kosova."

"Okay, yeah. Do you write as T. S. Stephenson?"

"That's me but it's T. H. not T. S. You may have been thinking of Eliot."

"Sure." Willie laughed then said, "That's quite a change from forensics."

"Maybe so, but I've always written."

"Thomas, you and Agron have a beer with us." Shpend waved a waiter over to the table.

"How long you been here?" Willie continued.

"I came in with NATO. Been back and forth since then."

"So you must be used to the power outages?"

"Oh, this is nothing. The on:off ratio's manageable now. In the spring it was four hours off, one on."

"I'm only here a week or ten days each trip so I never have the chance to get used to those things. I'm leaving Wednesday but I'll be back in six weeks."

"*Gezuar!*" Shpend raised his glass after the round of beer arrived. Agron and Tom responded in Albanian. Willie proffered, "Cheers!"

As Tom recalled, armed with the confidence of several beers, the four of them walked the few blocks to the Grand Hotel in an attempt to run into the Minister of Health. As Willie had explained to Tom he was frustrated dealing with administrative officials and wanted to explain his latest proposals to someone at the top before he headed back home. The minister was a personal friend of Shpend, so it was no coincidence he would know where to expect to bump into him. But, no dice, no minister. Tom and Agron left Willie and Shpend with the promise of *nëser* – tomorrow.

Back at his apartment Tom took time to reflect and record some of his thoughts for story ideas in his journal. He'd become concerned about issues other than the growth and sustainability of democracy. He was troubled about practical things such as the shortage of water in reservoirs because of lack of snow the previous winter and the shortage of food and medical supplies because of the frequent closure of the Macedonian border because of skirmishes happening in that country. These were sources of his apprehension – issues affecting the daily lives of the Kosovars.

# three

# November 2000
## *Mirëdita!*

When her flight landed, Cassandra was taken aback by the level of military presence at Prishtinë International Airport. No, maybe not so much surprised, she thought, disconcerted. A ring of soldiers in combat fatigues encircled the Austrian Airways flight. Machine guns ready! Armed personnel carriers backed them up. Jeez, who were they expecting? She realized all this should make her feel safe but instead it added to her doubts. Especially when she deplaned directly onto the tarmac into blowing snow. She was glad Greg was there to hurry her along. He was obviously more familiar with international air travel than she.

She met Greg Hanbruz for the first time the previous day in Toronto at the airport check-in. They had been in e-mail contact, however, for the several weeks since she'd accepted the invitation to work in Kosova. Initially she'd found his attitude cavalier especially when she tried to pin him down on travel arrangements.

Date: Mon, 27 Nov 2000 11:46 EST

Cassandra, attached are your flight details. Sorry for the delay in finalizing. Just a clerical slip-up. We're really pleased you decided to come on-board with CIPHA. Don't hesitate to contact me if you have any questions.

Let's meet at the airport before the flight Wednesday. I have no plan to wear anything in my lapel for recognition purposes. My connecting flight from Ottawa arrives about three hours before flight time so I'll go directly to the Air Canada check-in counter for Frankfurt. Meet you there.

It's a three stage journey – Toronto-Frankfurt, Frankfurt-Vienna, Vienna-Prishtina. Not much time between flights, but I'll guide you through those airports. When everything works, it's quite smooth. About fourteen hours from boarding in Toronto. See you Wednesday. Regards, Greg

Now in Prishtinë, Greg placed his hand on her elbow to steer her toward the dreary, grey terminal building. With his help they cleared customs and immigration, using the shorter designated UN employees queue to complete the formalities quickly. Their suitcases awaited them in the small baggage area.

"Cassie, come meet Shpend." Greg hurried her into the parking area.

"Welcome, Cassandra. *Mirë ditë!*"

Introductions were made. Shpend was younger than she'd expected, maybe early thirties. Probably six feet tall. Professionally styled dark brown hair. And those deep brown eyes that welcomed her.

"Hello, Spend."

"We're working together, so let me start with pronouncing my name. *Sh*, got it? Then *pend*. Sh pend. But slide it into one syllable."

"Sh pend. Sh pend. Shpend!"

"Yes, that is good. Friends must be able to say each other's names."

"Thanks, Shpend. Please call me Cassie."

"We do not have many Cassandras in Kosova. Maybe a few

Kassandras with a 'K'. Are you Greek?"

"Canadian."

"I know but your family. I am Albanian but my family has been more than five generations in Kosova."

"Sorry. I wasn't thinking. Just tired from travelling. My grandparents were from Scotland, all four of them. My parents were both born in Canada. But my father was working in Scotland after the war so I was born there. We returned to Canada soon after so I never really lived in Scotland." Stop. I've just met the man. Sure he's good looking but I don't need to lay out my whole history.

"But a Greek name?"

"I think we just like nice names in North America."

"Okay, tired, nice name lady. I will take you to your apartment."


The next afternoon, as she walked toward the Canadian Support Office, Cassie's legs felt heavy, still jet-lagged. She had the sensation every direction in Prishtinë was uphill. It was great, though, to see the Canadian flag billowing outside the Support Office. Her sense of pride robbed the biting wind of its sting as she paused for a moment to appreciate the maple leaf.

"*Mirëdita,* Cassie. *Si jeni*? How are you?"

Shpend met her at the door and guided her through the reception area, pausing to introduce her to local staff. The polished walnut panelling in the old house was enticing, a great place to have an office, she thought. But it was outdated by Canadian standards and quickly lost it's allure as Cassie realised how dark the house was with its very few lights. And maybe just a little cool and damp as well. A slight musty odour, almost hidden, but detectable.

"I'm fine, thanks, Shpend. I slept okay. I'm not so tired now." She didn't really wish to explain her tormented night in a strange apartment, wondering about her decision to come here, hoping her mother was okay staying with Jeremy. Add to that her apartment mate was Greg, until yesterday a stranger.

"That is good, Cassie. I want you to know you can use the computer in my office as well as this one here. Please feel you are free to do so. There is my office, upstairs, first door on right." Shpend pointed. "This computer is used by so many people, I think. Mine has good virus software for when you are working on something important. My computer is much faster than this one and the one at the lab. The hook-up there is not proper, divided with other offices. How is your family?"

"Everything's fine at home, thank you. I came from the hospital to do some e-mailing. So thank you for your offer."

"Was the walk to the hospital okay for you? I can arrange a driver each morning, if you like that better."

"It was good to walk. Only about forty-five minutes. And I was with Greg. Will it be safe for me to walk alone?"

"Yes, Cassie, it will be safe in daytime. And please walk along Mother Teresa Boulevard not on back streets. The street is wide and sidewalks are good. You will not be harmed. Do not walk alone at night, better to call me or take a taxi."

"Thank you. How do you say thank you?"

"*Të falemnderit* or, thank you very much, *falemnderit shumë.* So Sunday you will come to maternity hospital?"

"Yes. That should be interesting." She was pleased to be asked. Certainly much better than spending Sunday alone. I'm a minority, easily recognizable on the street, she thought. She'd noticed people staring at her. We're all Caucasian. What makes me different?

"Okay, Cassandra with a 'C'," said Shpend. "*Ditën e mirë!*"

Subject: ARRIVED SAFE
Date: Thu, 30 Nov 2000 10:08 EST

Hello sis. I'm at the Canadian Support office with Shpend, my contact here. Life is a bit of a blur. I'm almost spaced out with so little sleep. Already I'm thankful for all I have, for not ever having known the ravages and malevolence of war. Our flights were fine but Greg's luggage didn't arrive. Luckily, it wasn't the one wrapped in yellow Lufthansa tape binding together miscellaneous contents into what was left of a bag. Apartment's adequate. Very busy part of Prishtina, downtown, close to UN headquarters and their fleet of white Toyota 4Runners lining both sides of the road. Weather is almost balmy here so I may have overdone packing warm clothing. Thank you for all your help, sis. Bye for now, Cassie


Date: Thu, 30 Nov 2000 10:06 EST

Hi Cassie, hope your trip was good! Jeremy went to school – he's much better today but not really one hundred percent. I told him I'd be home today and he could call if he had trouble. I'm sure he'd just love to have his grandma picking him up from school. Love, Mom


Pushing back from the computer desk, Cassandra stood, flexed her tight shoulders and stretched her back. Too tired to continue with e-mail. My lord, isn't that exactly what I need now? A sick kid. She hoped her mother was competent to do this. She smiled. Her mom had raised Cassie and Karen more or less by herself. I'm the incompetent. Unable to do anything from Prishtinë but fret. Besides, I can hardly stay awake.

Good thing I hadn't worried about contingencies. Likely I'd never have come. She was pleased Greg had arranged to fly with her to introduce her to this foreign place. Traversing Frankfurt airport with only an hour between flights was challenging enough. What would happen if, no not if, when a flight's delayed? What's that smell? Here in the office and on the street as well. She felt so bushed! But she intended to follow the travel advice she got at home. Resist going to sleep when you're travelling until normal local bedtime. Normal time! I'm five time zones from, no wait, six time zones from normal time...

# four

# December 2000
## *Ditën  e mirë!*

Date: Fri, 01 Dec 2000 03:48 EST

Hi sis, I'm delighted we're able to communicate this easily. I don't know what I was expecting but it didn't occur to me I'd have e-mail available.

Last night we went to dinner with two people Greg knows from his years of this international stuff. That really made me feel like a novice. The restaurant was good. I had risotto marinara. Lots of garlic and full of seafood.

Went to bed around ten p.m. and then woke about eleven thirty – frightened and wide awake. I was a bit cold, the kind of cold you get when you're alone in a very strange place. Pulled on socks and found my book. Read but don't remember the content – only kept focussing on words appropriate to my experiences of the day. Was tempted to write in my journal but wasn't sure I actually wanted to reflect that intently in the night. Then slept well until about six thirty.

I was warned not to always expect running water in the morning. However, the shower worked and felt good. Day was off to a good start. Today is sunny with moderate temperature. I'm going to the hospital to meet Sue McElligott from WHO.

The apartment will be good accommodation with a few things added for cooking. Greg fried eggs (brought home six in a small paper bag) without so much as a flipper. That was a feat! Maybe that's the original scrambled eggs. Those are small things in the big picture. Much love, Cassie

Date: Sat, 02 Dec 2000 08:41 EST

Hi sister kg, Saturday afternoon now. Needed to meet with Sue McElligott again to talk more about the lab. Just walked back from there. Saturday seems to be a full workday. Not sure if that's widespread or just the internationals.

Greg and Shpend are waiting for me now so I won't spend too much more time. They just picked up two Canadians from the airport, Willem van der Wal and George Michaelis. They'll be my new roommates until Saturday.

So last night Greg and I were out for dinner again. A seafood restaurant this time – nice place. We had some good Italian wine. Wrote down the name for future reference but I've already misplaced my note. I bet all this sounds glamorous. It's how everyone stays connected. There's such a large international presence the restaurants sometimes seem like home. Was in bed by eleven.

Phone rang twice at two a.m. and that was it for sleeping. Couldn't understand the person so just said wrong number and hung up but you know how upsetting that can be in the middle of the night.

The visit to the lab was useful in getting perspective. I can now laugh at my doubts about whether I'd have anything to offer. Of course even though things so obviously need to change I need to navigate carefully to help rather than impose myself. They really don't seem busy considering the lab serves a twenty-three hundred bed hospital complex. There's more to tell but I'd rather share that when I get home. The day is nice and mild and sunny – snow has all melted. Love, Cassie

Saturday evening, Tom sat in the bar at the Grand Hotel. He watched Aleksandër come in, pause to survey the room, then, as if he had given himself an *all clear*, stride in youthful confidence toward his table.

"Hey, Aleks."

"Hey there, Tom. What's up?" Aleks tried to emulate "Wazzup?" but missed slightly.

"How's the old translation business going?"

"Pays a helluva lot better than teaching. They've offered me assistant professor in the Anthrop department."

"Sounds good. I assume you'll accept?" Such a conundrum for these young professionals. Aleksandër now worked as a UN translator. He and Tom got together occasionally for coffee, lunch or, sometimes, a beer after work. This time a beer, maybe two, then likely they'd move a few blocks for pizza. Maybe a Vullkano special tonight, peppers, prosciutto and mushrooms in a double-crusted masterpiece, steaming like a volcano through an opening in the puffed up top crust.

"I know I should accept but I can't give up this UN money," Aleks said. "These translation jobs won't last forever but I make four times a professor's salary. And they pay me danger pay."

"Danger pay?" Tom raised his eyebrows.

"Crazy, yes. Five hundred deutschmarks every month. Enough to pay for my *benzinë* for most of the year. You understand? Gasoline or, as the Brits say, petrol. Crazy language yours."

"Why danger pay? I don't understand."

"All UN personnel get it. This is a war zone. The UN cannot discriminate. So all employees get it. I don't know why local translators should be given danger pay. But we are. You should tell your magazine this is still a war zone. You should get danger pay. For when you walk from your apartment to *Il Passatore* restaurant or, worse, here to Grand Hotel. That's at least a hundred metres," Aleks teased.

"Sure, danger pay. They'd love that." Tom never complained to anyone about pay in Kosova. No matter how little he might think he was being compensated, he knew it was far in excess of what Kosovars were paid.

"I've heard, though, danger pay will be eliminated for Prishtinë soon."

"Why?"

Aleks shrugged. "The new UN Chief of Mission won't be allowed to move his family to Prishtinë if it's still classified war zone."

"Really? That sounds pretty crass."

"I don't know crass."

"Insensitive, ridiculous."

"A friend of mine has an important position in the Kosova Joint Administration," Aleks said. "He told me some UN and WHO officials are making one hundred fifty thousand or two hundred thousand US dollars for this assignment along with housing and expense allowances. And danger pay on top of that."

"Interesting." Tom was not incensed with this revelation. We need to pay for good people. "Have you got time to explain more about the parallel system? I've decided to write about it," Tom continued after a pause.

"Of course, Tom."

"Let's do it then. Can I get you a beer?"

"We already talked about moving classrooms from house to house almost every night when I began teaching. That was 1998. We held classes at night so we could keep schools secret from the police. Even primary school kids. Right under the noses of Serb administrators. Very few Albanians attended their officially sanctioned school system. We kept our mouths shut."

"Do you really believe they didn't know?"

"I honestly don't know. How could they not? It went on for ten years. They probably didn't understand we had our own tax system. Or how organized we were. They likely thought it was like home schooling. Let me tell you about an incident during one class. Funny now, but scary at the time." Aleks described how he was delivering an anthropology lecture in the basement of a store. At one point, two students signalled him to stop talking. Mostly, his students were serious about learning, he explained, but there were a few jokers, funny guys, always horsing around. As he continued his lecture he spoke even louder to counter the joke he still didn't comprehend. Then the whole class started to point at the window behind him. Seeing their expressions of fear, he turned and stared right into the back of the legs of two Serb policemen stopped in front of the store, not two metres from him. He quickly stopped talking and froze where he stood. Eventually, the police officers moved on and class resumed with a decidedly quieter tenor.

Aleksandër signalled the waiter for another round of *birrë e Pejë* to sustain them until he and Tom were ready for the two block walk to Vullkano Pizza.

Subject: THE PARALLEL SYSTEM
Date: Sun, 3 Dec 2000 06:14 EDT
To: Anthony Petersen <petersen@themagazine.ca>

Hi Tony, I almost have my parallel system article ready. I have the gist of it now but I'm still fact checking with other contacts. I want to have it ready before I leave for home.

I'm booked to fly Tuesday. It'll be a welcome break. Regards, Tom

Shpend's driver picked Cassie up from her apartment Sunday morning and drove her to the Maternity Building on the University of Prishtinë Hospital Campus. She was glad to be included in the hospital visit rather than being left on her own but as they were looking at structural changes, she had no real reference point. The trip down into the basement and up onto the roof and into reconstructed rooms with nothing but concrete walls and doorways to look at wasn't very useful to her. She was surprised at the number of people in the entourage. All these people to do what? Look at walls and ceilings?

"Willie, who is everybody? Will there be introductions?"

"Not likely." Willie answered Cassie's question as they walked through a maze of corridors. "Stay with me. I'll show you the infection control issues. This hospital delivers a thousand babies a month."

"Sounds like a lot."

"Well, compare that to Mount Sinai in Toronto, about six hundred a month. Similar number for McGill Health Centre. So, yeah, that's a pile of deliveries."

Cassandra stood transfixed, staring at broken or missing windows. She noticed one young woman, post-delivery she assumed, in slippers and a winter coat huddled in the corridor with two others for warmth.

"You may never get used to it, Cassie. Believe it or not, this is greatly improved from what we first saw." Willie laughed. "You really needed to be here. No water, no heat, holes in the roof. Still don't have heat but the roof's repaired. You know, I was brought to Prishtinë to implement an infection control program."

George Michaelis joined them in the corridor. "That was really like the cart before the horse for me," he said.

"For sure. No one can control infections without soap and water. So far, we have water."

George picked up the story. "After that trip Willie came back to Montreal and convinced me to sign on. The two of us suggested to CIDA that structural change was needed before we could accomplish infection control improvements. I was surprised we got the funding after Willie muttered something about careless use of tax dollars if we proceeded with the program without first improving infrastructure. But they listened and we got it. Anything you need help with, Cassie? You understanding all this?"

"Thanks, George, I'm fine."

"Good, I'm off to join the local architect to inspect the roof."

Willie continued, "We can talk more later but a good microbiology lab is essential to any program I set up. The lab staff and medical microbiologists are absolutely important to infection control. They're the ones who can recognize trends and tip us off."

Cassie thought about that. This is the sort of thing Tom Stephenson was good at. Teaching people to recognize trends. "First thing, Willie, the lab must be able to recognize an anomaly."

"You're not being funny are you, Cassie?"

"No, unfortunately, to me the lab's stalled in the nineteen-fifties. Today's infection control is much different. What are the washrooms like?"

"Two on this ward. I hope you're not thinking of using one?"

"No, just wondering. How can you control infection with communal washrooms on a maternity ward?"

"You can't. Don't inspect them too critically. I can tell you one's been missing a toilet seat ever since I've been coming here. The women stand on the edge of the toilet and squat. Cleaning's not frequent and when it is done, a wet mop just spreads the filth around evenly. The toilet at the other end of the ward is a Turkish toilet. That's a whole other form of squatting."

"And we worry about biowarfare!"

Date: Sun, 03 Dec 2000 14:20 EST

Hi again, sis, Sunday afternoon. I'm doing e-mail while the others meet with a local architect they'd like to hire. Lots of interesting dynamics, not least of which is the need for translation. Also, the requirement to be comfortable with constant changes. Greg Hanbruz is looking like my best friend yet I've known him less than five days. Last night we all went to a restaurant within walking distance of the apartment. Tonight we're invited to the office where Andy will cook for us. He lives upstairs there so he's never away from the job.

Judging from the little I saw of the actual functioning part of this maternity hospital the needs are dire. Mortality in newborns is conservatively five percent overall. On top of that, Willie told me that of the babies who have difficult births, thirty percent die. The hospital is cold, hygiene questionable. Actually everywhere hygiene is questionable.

Cassie knew that, being a physician, Karen would appreciate this detail. She found it calming to record the day's events. She was meticulous about journaling even at home. Especially since she separated from Doug. It was therapeutic in her loneliness maybe even cathartic. Funny thinking about Tom, she thought. His name just popped into my mind. I probably wouldn't even be here if Chicago had worked out.

> I'm meeting Monday morning with the Director of Public Health. After that I'll work in the lab. I don't remember if I told you I spent time yesterday with Sue McElligott. We talked about the public health service.

Sue had talked about staffing and other administrative concerns between gulps of coffee. "Hard night last night. I really need my drug this morning. It's tough all this eating and drinking. But all in the line of duty, I assure you."

Cassie reached to accept the sheaf of papers Sue was extending toward her, "There's a lot of background here. I photocopied some generic policy and procedure stuff from other missions. Elvira could use this as reference material but they must develop their own guidelines for their local situation. Of course, they need *written* documentation."

"Other than overseeing the lab project, what else are you involved with?"

"Well... let me say first how happy I am to hand this stuff over to you. Now I can get to establishing water and food quality standards for Kosova. That's my primary WHO function. The lab's been a time-consuming sideshow."

Cassandra sipped her coffee and waited for Sue to continue. To expound. Something she'd come to realize Sue was always prepared to do. "The Kosovars want to view themselves as having strict standards. But there's little thought about what's feasible. Until now the benchmarks they use are from Yugoslavia. The rub is they don't want to use any regulation they consider Serbian."

"They should develop their own measures anyway." Cassie

shrugged her shoulders.

"But they're contemplating measures way beyond their abilities and some totally unnecessary."

"Like what?"

"Like cured meats and pickled products for example. I'm trying to argue them out of looking for the whole gamut of food poisoning organisms and spoilage organisms in foods prepared for long shelf-life."

"I know what you mean. Poor use of limited resources."

"This is high level political stuff. Maybe you can influence Elvira on the practical level. It's a funny place this. Everybody knows everybody. If you impress Elvira with your logic, word will reach the minister's office *tout de suite*."

"Okay."

Willie shepherded me through much of the meeting today. But when he was occupied, I had side conversations with Greg's UK counterpart. His background is Public Health in the UK. He was a very cynical character. I'm not sure why he made so many comments to me. Love, Cassie

She thought about yesterday after Willie and George arrived. Shpend had taken them all to a place outside the city for a drink. Just into the hills, a log place, a restaurant. The setting was so picturesque it provided her an entirely different perspective. Comforting. Not so different from home after all. Rolling, fully treed hills. Most of the deciduous foliage gone but some trees still held their leaves tightly. The remnants of fall colour looked more subdued than at home, but it was December. Now she thought she'd like to see more of the outlying areas. She realized Shpend was working hard to make her comfortable.

That she appreciated.

> Date: Mon, 04 Dec 2000 06:22 EST
>
> Hi mom, please tell Jeremy not to bother getting his father to co-sign his passport application. There's no point in him coming here. A day or two would be quite an eye opener but to stay longer than that would not be useful.

Cassie knew Jeremy was no longer a child. This city must have thousands of children but I sure haven't seen many. What do kids do without green areas? Nothing much to do even for adults as far as I can tell. One cinema. Would the movies even be current?

Greg had told her he would make the apartment available to her if Jeremy came to Prishtinë. He would find alternate housing for other project people who were here less often than Cassandra. But in her estimation it'd be no place for Jeremy, just a recipe for trouble. She knew she was being over-protective. She returned to her e-mail:

> By the way, I know I left in a hurry, but I'm eternally grateful you're doing this for me. I know a teenager is tough to deal with anywhere, Prishtina or Church Hill. Love, Cassie

A couple of days later Cassandra sat at the computer in Sue

McElligott's office composing another message to her sister. After a good weekend, Monday didn't seem to be going smoothly. She'd met the Director of Public Health in his office first thing that morning as a courtesy. He didn't seem interested in her name and didn't offer his. He showed even less interest in who Cassie represented or why she was in his department. He did ask, however, whether she had project money attached to her. Not certain if this was some kind of joke, she replied only what she had in her purse. He glared at her, told her when she had some money to come talk with him.

"But I am offering my expertise to help the lab, sir."

"I have own experts," he replied, waving her off dismissively. That surprised Cassie, her first encounter with arrogance.

Date: Tue, 05 Dec 2000 06:11 EST

Hi again sis. Today I'm spinning my wheels. Missing home. Even missing Doug. I can't even make overseas phone calls. Just can't connect today although somehow I accessed three other people's webmail accounts. Talk about privacy, security and anonymity! I sure hope Mom doesn't get tired of looking after my kid. I couldn't do this without her support and yours, sis. Love, Cassie

Date: Tue, 05 Dec 2000 10:57 EST

Whoa there, sister! Rein in those thoughts! Give yourself a shake! I know you must be incredibly lonely, but thinking about Doug? Remember, one of your main reasons for accepting this assignment – to steer clear of Doug. It doesn't sound like you're lacking male company. Maybe you're missing intimacy.

41

By the way, you may also be missing the signs. The Brit at the hospital meeting was doing everything he could to pick you up, Ms "I'm not sure why he made so many comments to me". Buck up! Do something for yourself for a change. But who am I to give advice, huh! Love, kg


Of course Karen's right. In the light of day Cassie remembered exactly why she wasn't with Doug!!! She wondered why she'd even written that. That's what sisters are for, she thought. A sounding board for stupidity. Better than looking foolish generally. There'd only been one woman who'd asked about her husband. Cassie didn't know her name. Others asked about her children. Maybe a husband is simply assumed. Or possibly Sue McElligott briefed the lab people with my personal details.


Date: Tue, 05 Dec 2000 12:20 EST

Hey Cass. Your friend Natasha asked me to say hi and to remind you how different the system is over there and you will not change things in a couple of weeks. I'm paraphrasing but that captures her message. Not to be discouraged – Natasha grew up in a corrupt and repressive society in Odessa. The Kosovars may not be receptive to or want change. Try to shrug it off. Natasha would really like to get together to talk about things when you're home. And, you know, she turned out fine, ambitious and productive in her endeavours. Bye for now, kg


Wednesday morning Cassie arrived at the microbiology laboratory early. She squinted down the corridor to determine who Elvira was talking with. That Elvira was using hand gestures meant she was likely speaking English. Therefore, Cassie deduced it was probably Sal Maxwell, who they'd been expecting. The lighting for the narrow hallway was a series of single bulbs, some lit, some burnt out, each hanging from the curved twelve foot ceiling by a long thin electrical cord that looked to be bare copper wire. Cassie thought that was improbable; however, she didn't dismiss her observation completely. What did she know of electricity. She thought it was odd she hadn't noticed how dim the lighting was until she actually needed to see. If it was indeed Dr Maxwell, she wanted to speak with him about his program. I don't want to be teaching a different approach, she thought. We're all here to help. But there's so little coordination. A French consultant says do this, an Italian, no, no, no, not the French way, my way, the Kosovars left with their heads spinning. She hoped she'd be able to harmonize techniques with Sal Maxwell. She'd heard only good things about him. That he had a practical approach to tuberculosis control.

As she walked toward the two of them, she realized Elvira was shouting, delivering her message even louder than she usually did.

"We have big problem and you was not here," Cassie heard Elvira say.

"You can always call my cell phone. If I can't answer, it will…"

"We cannot telephone from this place. We not to use long distance."

"Then e-mail…"

Again Elvira cut him off. "E-mail do not work so good," she said.

"I have projects all over Eastern Europe. I'm more than willing to help but you already know I spend as much time in Kosova as I can. You need to take ownership of your own day-to-day process." With a hint of exasperation in his voice, he turned away from Elvira and, for the first time, noticed Cassie standing there, a respectful distance away.

"Maybe your answer is right here." He spoke to Elvira but swept his hand to indicate Cassie. "Dr Borden, I presume."

"Yes, I'm Cassandra Borden and I assume you're Dr Maxwell..."

"Good to meet you, Cassandra. And it's Sal, please. I heard you were here. I was surprised to learn your background isn't public health."

"Actually, I come from forensics."

"Forensics? That's interesting. How'd you come to be working in public health?" Sal regarded her quizzically, furrowing his bushy eyebrows.

"Oh, I needed a change, partly for personal reasons. Jordan Siemens recruited me."

"I know Jordan. So you must have a clinical background."

"I did my master's in Jordan's lab. But that's awhile back." Cassie thought she should ask Sal to explain his work before Elvira ushered him off somewhere. "If you have a moment, I'd like to learn about the tuberculosis lab training you're doing."

"I'm sure you've seen what we're doing here in Prishtinë but how'd you like to observe a regional operation up close."

"I'd love that."

"Well, young lady, pack up and come with me." Sal imitated a John Wayne swagger. "I'm off to visit the clinic in Gjakovë this afternoon."

"Well, I..."

"Don't say no. I'll have you back here before dinner."


Sal's driver chauffeured them out of the city. "Boy, I'm glad to get out of there," Sal said. "I like Elvira a lot but lately she's becoming a pain in the ass."

Cassandra hesitated to defend Elvira but couldn't help saying, "She's ambitious for her lab. But you know, I think she's as frustrated as the rest of us with the slow pace of things."

"Yeah, I guess," Sal replied then carried on with his explanation of what Cassie could expect to see when they arrived in Gjakovë. He emphasized his approach was tailored to local facilities and technical competence. Smaller clinics in places like Gjakovë and Gjilani were expected to prepare microscope slides, stain and examine them for TB organisms. Only as a preliminary screening procedure. More complete diagnosis including all culturing was performed at the larger diagnostic labs in Prishtinë or Pejë.

They entered Gjakovë through the old market area. Cassie knew these shops had been destroyed by the Serbs during the war. She was surprised by the speed of redevelopment as she looked at freshly poured concrete buttresses and what she would describe as post-and-beam store fronts. All this building activity so recent the wood was still unweathered and as yet unpainted.

"I'm impressed," she said to Sal.

"They keep look of old Turkish market," their driver explained. "Only two floor high. Is that correct?"

"We would say two storeys," Sal said.

"Story like newspaper?"

"Sounds the same but spelled differently."

The driver laughed. "New shops is very modern," he said.

They continued a few blocks to the new free-standing TB clinic building on the grounds of the local hospital. A two storey structure with gable ends, a steep-pitched clay-tile roof, exterior walls finished, as was customary, with an off-white stucco. Although the foyer entrance with a door at each end did not provide an air-lock, Cassandra was pleased to see the efforts to contain the organism to the clinic building.

Inside they were greeted by three of the clinic staff who obviously knew Sal.

"It is so good you come back, Dr Sal," said Lorenc, the clinic physician.

Cassie realized the room to the right with access from the foyer was a waiting room. Six people sat on folding chairs. Sindi, the lab tech, steered her past two examination rooms to her own area, the rudimentary lab. "I know you are at Prishtinë," she said. "I am glad you come in Gjakovë. Maybe you help me too."

"I'd be happy to help," Cassie replied. The room contained a safety-shielded bench centrifuge and a small laminar-flow safety cabinet but otherwise was almost empty. Cassie was impressed to see the one piece seamless stainless steel double sink and lab counter. And a new Leitz microscope with a teaching screen.

"I'm amazed," she said to Sal when he joined them in the room. "You must have an in with UN purchasing to acquire these things."

"Oh, I'm afraid we did an end-run around the UN. This whole building and the other rapid response clinics were equipped directly by the Egyptian government. That's how we got what we wanted. Well, at least what we needed."

Sindi led Cassie back to the waiting room where she announced in English, "*Doktor* Cassandra. From Canada."

Several patients nodded knowingly, repeated *Ka-na-da*. It became apparent as Sindi continued to speak, they didn't comprehend English.

"Are these people waiting for the Dr Lorenc?"

"Oh no, see already. Wait for result."

"So they've come back for results and follow-up visit?"

"Oh no, they wait."

"For how long?"

"Maybe one hour."

"Really?"

"*Doktor* Sal want thirty minute only."

Once again, Sal took over and explained that patients waited for results at the clinic. Then the clinic doc dispensed the first two week's meds immediately to those presumptively infected, aiming to arrest spread to close contacts.

"It's a pretty remarkable process. Able to react so quickly," Cassie said.

"We call these small clinic labs rapid response centres. The staff here is impressive and dedicated. It's always different in regional facilities away from the centre. Not to slight Prishtinë. Their TB competence is excellent."

Cassie asked Sal about the incidence of tuberculosis in Kosova.

"Well, WHO estimates almost fifteen hundred new cases annually." Sal explained it was one of the highest rates in the world. "Hence our emphasis on immediate results," he continued. "We know these rapid response centres can make a huge difference when they follow established protocol."

They thanked their hosts and went back out to the car.

"I know I promised we'd be back to Prishtinë before dinnertime but since it's almost dark now would you object to having dinner down the road in Prizren?"

Cassie didn't hesitate. She'd enjoyed her afternoon with Sal. "No objection from me. That'd be fine."

"Prizren's a beautiful old city. You won't see much tonight but we'll stop at a *qebapa* restaurant."

The driver knew some of the locals in the restaurant so he excused himself to join three men at another table. Cassandra was comfortable to be free to talk frankly with Sal about what she'd seen. While they waited for their kebobs and salads, they each enjoyed a pint of Efes beer.

"How long will you continue your involvement here?" she asked.

"Indefinitely. I come back to Kosova about four times a year usually when I'm in Eastern Europe for other projects. Tuberculosis is a major problem for former Soviet republics as well as former Yugoslav republics. So I can usually spend only about a week here each visit." Sal was expansive in his replies. Cassie liked that.

"What do you do about quality assurance?"

"It might surprise you but all Kosova labs are in the top tier in external quality assessment compared with Pennsylvania labs and others in North America."

"You must be proud of that!"

"You bet. I'm guardedly optimistic though because things in this part of the world can change rapidly. You need to be cautious about expectations in this work."

The waiter served their dinners. *Salat Shope* came first, a salad to share - cucumbers, tomatoes and onion slices laid out individually on a small platter accompanied by feta cheese slices and a small flagon of herbed olive oil. Then four kebobs of lamb, a basket of grilled pita bread and *hajvar* red pepper sauce condiment appeared as soon as they'd finished the salad.

"Speaking of quality assurance, you must know Harry Richardson?" Sal picked up the conversation.

Harry. She hadn't crossed paths with him in quite a while. "Yes, of course, I know Harry. I served on several committees with the Quality Management Program."

"We used Harry's expertise to get our Pennsylvania program set up. I'd love to have him involved here in Kosova."

"That'd be nice." She paused a moment then asked, "Anything I can do for you while I'm here?"

"Yes, indeed. Keep an eye on the labs. I'll leave you a set of procedure manuals. If you can ensure adherence, I'd be grateful. Especially since you're here for longer periods than I am."

"I'm more than willing. But just so you know, I'm not sure I'll be back."

"You disappointed with things, Cassie?"

"No, it's personal. I'm lonely here. I have two kids. Marianne is finished school but Jeremy's at home, his final year of high school. He's seventeen. That's a hard age for a mother to be away from home."

"Your husband?"

"We're divorced. My mother's staying with Jeremy and looking after him as much as anyone can look after a seventeen year old."

"Been there, done that. All of it, divorce included. But I'd bet you'll be back. This work grows on you. You see the result of your interventions every day. Your advice is actually valued."

"Thanks very much for this, Sal. Thanks for your confidence." But Cassie was not yet sure about her continued involvement.


Subject: PHONE CONTACT TONIGHT
Date: Wed, 06 Dec 2000 11:17 EST

Hi sis. I met with Dr. Sal Maxwell from Philadelphia today. He's here doing tuberculosis lab training. He was very helpful and has a true perspective on the limitations – both technical and administrative.

And yes, before you ask, we had dinner. Hardly a date because his driver was in the room. Sal's an interesting man. Divorced. And at least ten years younger than me. I'd make him to be early forties. On top of that, I caught my reflection in a store window on my way to the support office just now. There's been no water to wash my hair for two days. And the grey's already showing through my colour job. Not an enticing picture!

I'll make sure to be home for your phone call tonight. If you call after five o'clock your time you should be able to make a connection. Normally, international traffic has subsided by then. I'd love to hear a voice from home. Most people use cell phones and it's really funny because they all have them set with all that musical ringing stuff – really elaborate and distracting. Apparently mobile service is better than land lines but there's a moratorium on issuing new cell phone numbers. Tomorrow night we're going to Shpend's to meet his family and then to another UN friend of Greg's for dinner. I know you think this is just a barrel of parties!!! Your party hearty sister, Cassie

"Cassie, are you cold?" Andy Hamilton asked. Cassandra was seated at one of the Canadian Support Office computers Saturday afternoon. "We use these portable electric heaters. The whole central system doesn't work very well."

Cassie shivered in response. "Sure, a little warmer would be good. Thanks, Andy."

"You know the city's centrally heated?"

Centrally heated? I assumed nothing could be done about being chilled in this old building. Doug used to insist on setting the thermostat at fifteen degrees. Just put on another sweater he'd respond when I complained. But, Prishtinë's centrally heated?

"Hot water is piped through underground mains. You must've seen those smokestacks near the airport?"

"Yeah, I know the ones you mean."

"Belch black smoke, they do. Worse than Manchester. It's a coal-fired heating plant."

"Are these heaters an efficient use of hydro?" Cassie asked.

"Actually, they're oil filled, some sort of neutral oil. They store heat, so they're good even when the power's off. Alternative is to freeze,"

Andy explained.

"More efficient than I thought. I find I jump to conclusions these days."

"You'll be fine. By the way, nobody will understand if you ask about hydro. It's electricity here. To change the subject, I hope you're coming to our get-together tonight?"

"I don't really know anybody."

"I hate socializing myself but Michèle Lesage is leaving for home and she's one of my favourites. You'd like her. She has an interesting story. Besides, it's a good time to meet people. We call it a Christmas party. Even though all the local staff's Muslim, nobody cares. I mean nobody's offended. They love a party, any gathering, for any reason."

Date: Sat, 09 Dec 2000 08:30 EST

Hi sis. There's incredible rebuilding going on here. However, it seems totally unplanned, no building code, no infrastructure. We've been without water most of the day. Shpend tells me they take advantage of weekends to save water when people can be more flexible, not having to go to work. Also it's a good time to repair water system problems. Power still goes off often but it's much improved because of enormous efforts by foreign agencies and the Kosovar desire to restore order. Prishtinë is not very pleasant, though. Garbage and sanitation are huge problems. But I haven't met anyone here who's anything but agreeable and kind. We could learn a lot. Imagine the number of grouchy people with an opinion and/or attitude we encounter every day at home. Perhaps we all need a Kosova reality check. Oh, oh, retraction – I forgot the money-grubbing Director of Public Health. Love, Cassie

"So, Cassie, it's been great to be with you this last ten days." Willie grabbed Cassandra in a friendly hug. "Shpend's coming around noon. Our flight's at one-thirty."

"I can't believe it's been ten days. I feel like I've known you and George forever. Where is George, by the way?"

"Ah, you know George. Working 'til the last moment. He wanted to go over some things with the local contractor. Again!" Willie extended his palms upward and shrugged his shoulders to express mock exasperation. "You're going to be alone here now. Will you be okay?"

"Sure, I'll be fine. Never thought I'd want to share an apartment with other adults but it's been good. I feel like I'm losing my best friends with you two leaving."

"I'm glad we went to the gathering last night. Felt like it was a send-off for us, not Michèle."

The previous evening they'd gone to the Canadian Liaison office, the local branch office of the embassy in Skopë. Cassie had assumed it was a gathering for the support office staff. But it was the whole Canadian contingent as well as local employees. Andy was right, I'm glad I attended. She hadn't felt much like schmoozing with a bunch of people she didn't know, even if they were Canadian. George and Willie were easy to be with. She was pleased they'd accompanied her. She felt safe with them. And because there were two of them, she hadn't felt awkward. Shpend and his wife were also there. Drita didn't speak much English but she and Cassie understood each other and were able to laugh at their attempt to converse in an English, French and Albanian *mélange*. Funny, thought Cassie, when the people you feel most comfortable with are the Albanians and other folks you've known for only a couple of weeks.

Date: Sun, 10 Dec 2000 09:46 EST

Dear sis, at the party last night, they acknowledged Michèle, a young woman who's going home to another project. I've seen her around the support office. When she was cited for bravery I started to pay attention. Know what surprised me? She defused and cleared landmines. I'd just assumed she was some type of office worker. Oh, those stereotypes!!! While I was walking today, it was almost a relief to see more usual human activity – lots of people about on foot, walking, running, shopping. Finally I've started to see some children and teenagers. Guess the weekends are more leisurely and "normal". Love, Cassie

Michèle Lesage waited outside the Canadian Support Office for Cassandra to reach the porch before she opened the outer door. "Hello, Cassandra. Nice to see you."

"Hello Michèle. I didn't know you'd be here."

"I haven't come for Sunday dinner in quite a while." They climbed the stairs to Andy's third floor apartment.

"Hello you two." Andy paused from his chicken curry preparations to greet the women. Then he gave Michèle a hug. "You've been avoiding me, my dear," he continued.

"*Non, ce n'est pas vrai.* Just busy," Michèle replied.

"Well I'm glad they gave you such a good send-off the other night."

"I was pleased to see you, *mon ami*. You're not usually at such events." Before Andy could reply, Michèle saved herself the embarrassment of praise by quickly changing the subject. "I'll grab some beer. I assume it's still in the office fridge, Andy? One for you, Cassie? It's Efes, from Turkey. Quite good. I need to warn you though, Andy makes a mean martini. Martinis on the menu tonight?"

"Whatever. You're my guests." Andy shrugged, then grinned.

When Michèle returned with the beer, Cassandra said, "So Michèle, satisfy my curiosity. How'd you get into the landmine detection business?"

"How'd I become a sapper?"

"Sapper. That's a funny word."

"Technically a sapper's a combat engineer but that's what we call landmine clearers. It's from the French *sapeur*. You remember *The English Patient*? Kip was a sapper, a mine clearer."

"Clearing mines. That has to be dangerous."

"I studied mining engineering at *École Polytechnique* in Montreal. Gravitated to explosives, I guess. It was quite a rush dismantling failed charges, understanding why they didn't explode. Then, after graduation, I joined the army."

"*École Polytechnique*. You're too young to have been there…"

"*Moi*, too young? Thank you for that. But no, the massacre happened my first year. I was away from school December sixth, but my best friend Nathalie was wounded and I knew the fourteen who were killed. The school was in turmoil for months. But during second semester we women found new resolve." Michèle continued to explain she'd been an introverted kid, from Thetford Mines, smart enough but uninspired and very provincial. Her life plan was simple, to return home for a good job at the asbestos mines, in engineering. Her dad was an mining engineer.

"But you went into the military."

"Much as I hate to acknowledge it, the massacre was pivotal in my life. My eyes were opened and my perspective changed enormously the next three years. I became a feminist – a right-wing feminist."

"Law and order?"

"Yes."

"We're terrible guests," Cassie suddenly said. "We've abandoned Andy!" Their host was busily cooking, the aroma of roasted curry wafting through the room.

"It's okay. I'm listening," Andy said. "Michèle," he continued. "Were you ever interviewed by Tom Stephenson?"

Tom Stephenson? Cassie was shocked to hear Tom's name. Interviewed by Tom? Andy continued, "The writer with *The Magazine.*"

They're talking about a different Tom Stephenson, she thought.

"Cassie, are you okay?" Andy's voice penetrated her thoughts.

"Oh, fine. Something just triggered a memory." She remembered the Chicago fiasco. That Tom.

"That's good. Wouldn't want it to be us making you sick, eh Michèle?" Andy kidded. "I just asked Michèle if she's still considered military."

Michèle looks tired. Cassie was now fully aware of her surroundings. Is she remembering events or is she just worn down by her mission?

"I was telling Andy I served my five years, then left," Michèle answered. "My final posting was in Croatia. Peacekeeping. Ordinance officer. But when we shipped home, for me it was premature. I wanted the opportunity to see the fruits of the mission. So I joined CLCA."

"CLCA?" Cassie asked.

"Canadian Landmine Clearing Agency. NGO with major government support through CIDA. But we also depend on private donations. So I'm headed home to fundraise. The lecture circuit. I need a break. You can only live so long on adrenaline rushes." After the speaking circuit, she was scheduled to be trained by Canine Mine Clearing. She'd already met her dog, a Malinois named Blaze, already in the first phase of his training. She explained it took about a year to train a mine detecting dog to work with a handler. Next assignment, she'd be in charge of the mission.

I can't even relate. I don't even know anybody in the military. I don't even know enough to talk about it. Cassie's academic life had been simple. She hadn't even needed to job search. She did a post-doc at the forensics lab. They then approached her with a good offer for a permanent position. Would I even have continued studying if I'd encountered the Montreal massacre? "The bravery citation last night? What'd you do?"

"We just do our jobs. We build teams. Everybody in this work is courageous. Or foolhardy." Michèle gave a Gallic shrug.

"Well, I thought being singled out was impressive. Will you be back in Kosova?"

"Sorry, Cassie, I can't say. Classified, you know. I can tell you we've cleared more than ninety percent of the mines. That's public record. The lecture circuit will certainly be different for me," she said changing the subject. "I've never done anything remotely like fundraising. They need a face to present. I know I provide more mileage because I'm a woman. I've decided I'm okay with that."

"How many women in your field?"

"It's about fifty/fifty."

Andy's voice broke in. "Okay, you two, dinner's almost ready. Cassie could you open that wine? I found a good Montenegro Vranac Red at the market."

Cassie felt awkward uncorking the wine. Poor quality cork? An unfamiliar corkscrew? Maybe, but mostly she realized she was preoccupied with how the *Polytechnique* massacre had shaped Michèle's life. And the memory of Chicago. And Tom.

Cassie had begun to notice her training efforts were producing what she considered positive results. Not earth-shattering, but positive. She'd asked the Medical Microbiologist examining cultures to comment on any difference he'd noticed since she'd introduced changes into the method for culturing specimens. He smiled and said they were very good and much easier to interpret.

When she'd looked over at Pashko, the technician who had actually worked with her, he beamed. He expressed his pleasure without struggling with the English he neither spoke nor understood. He smiled, pointed and said "Cassie – Pashko" and gave her a high five.

The day before, Cassie worked for a while in the enteric lab and revamped preliminary culturing there as well. She was concerned she might not have an opportunity to examine those cultures properly. She tried to establish whether the weekend routine included refrigerating cultures so they'd be kept in good condition to examine Monday. She wasn't really certain how to interpret the answer she received but guessed it was probably *no*. Alas one must crawl, she thought.


Wednesday afternoon, Cassie returned to the Canadian Support Office. As she punched in her secure entry code to unlock the door she realized how important this office had become to her. She assumed it was as appreciated by other Canadians as well. Somewhere for e-mail access or maybe just to have a beer with Andy and catch up on news from home. Now she nodded an acknowledgement to a woman sitting on one of the worn overstuffed leather couches. She looks familiar. About my age.

"Hi, Cassie. I'm Sonja. Sonja Wright. We met the other night at the Liaison Office." Sonja stood up, smoothed the front of her slacks and moved toward Cassie extending her hand in greeting.

"Of course. Good to see you Sonja. I forget. You're with CIPHA?" Not sure we were actually introduced. Being the new kid I guess I'm easily recognized.

"For sure. I'm the infectious diseases nurse. Attached directly to the ministry. Advisor to the Health Coordinator."

"Okay, I heard about you from Jordan Siemens."

"Hope he wasn't telling lies." Sonja laughed.

"No, no. Only flattering comments."

"Now I report directly to Greg Hanbruz. There are a couple things I wanted to say. Greg tells me you're not sure you want to commit to continuing with this mission."

"That's right, I'm not sure." Cassie wondered where this conversation was headed.

"Any particular reason?"

"I'm feeling pretty isolated. My daughter is finished school and away working but my son is still at home in his final year of high school. Guess I miss my kids." Is this really a major topic of conversation in the Balkans? Have you heard, Cassandra Borden's undecided? Undecided is she? She some kind of wimp?

"Well Cassie, I'm involved in infection control meetings so I already see improvements in reports from the hospital lab. You're gaining quite a reputation in those quarters. Saw Elvira Kurtz in action at a recent nosocomial infections meeting. She's a live wire to say the least. Elvira tore a major strip off everyone, physicians, nurses, ward staff for their lax attitude toward infection control and, just to step it up a notch, quality standards of care. I've been in meetings before where she's just one of the crowd, the old-boys network. You've given her confidence."

"I haven't been here long enough to have that impact."

"Believe me, you gave her the ammo and the shotgun to scatter it. She hit everyone."

"I would've liked to have seen that! I'd like to attend those meetings."

"So you should, Cassandra. WHO attends but you're delivering their program. They're only administrators."

"You said a couple of things?"

"Yeah, I don't want to forget. Greg is considering leasing a house for the CIPHA project staff. There could be as many as five or six in town at any one time. Most would only stay four or five days. Then there's at least you, me and Claire who're on varying length stays. Occasionally some of the financial people will come for a week or two."

"Sounds better than living alone if you're thinking of including me."

"It's being done for you. Greg Hanbruz's doing this to keep you. Don't worry about us. We want to be here. We applied, we weren't wooed."

"Is that a problem?"

"No. We can hang our hats on your star. We just wonder why you're special, why you're chosen for special treatment. Surely microbiologists can't be that hard to find."

"Well, just to clarify, I'm not sleeping with anybody, if that's what you're wondering." Cassandra laughed as she watched a shocked expression develop on Sonja's face.


Date: Sun, 17 Dec 2000 09:27 EST

Hey sis, tried to buy tea at the grocery store today. Every kind of herbal tea imaginable but I wanted just plain old tea – Orange Pekoe, English Breakfast – I'm not so fussy. Just want my tea! On the plus side, I was able to buy chicken stock, potatoes and leeks to make a soup. The selection and quality of fresh produce is astounding. Prices are cheap. And they tell me there's a huge outdoor market I haven't even seen yet.

Yesterday Shpend told me he has friends who live in my building. He told me to contact them if I need anything or if something goes wrong. He says they'll know who I am. So as I've said before people are very thoughtful. Love, Cassie

Subject: POTATO LEEK SOUP
Date: Sun, 17 Dec 2000 09:45 EST

Dear Cassie, Karen told me you were making one of my favourite comfort foods. I'm making some today also. I think we may be eating at quite different times. The time's not so important but there is some comfort in family members preparing food together, even at a distance. By the way, Brenda asked me if I thought Jeremy's violin might be for sale. A friend of hers is looking for one for her son. Love, Mom

Cassandra sighed forcefully. Violin? As if I have time. Jeez, mother. C'mon Cassandra, a simple question. Don't be rattled just because it's out of the blue. I should get Mom to ask Doug. He's the one who insisted both kids take violin lessons. Then left it to me to buy the instruments. Then forced me to return one. Not up to his peculiar specifications. As if he knew anything about music let alone instruments. Whoa there girl. Slow those horses down. Bring them to a stop. Damn that Doug! Don't need to crank up. Don't follow that tangent. Yes, just sell the damn thing. Jeremy hasn't looked at it for years. It's lost its cool.

Date: Tue, 19 Dec 2000 08:25 EST

Dear sis, I'm greatly disappointed today. They're backsliding to old methods even though everyone seems to realise those ways are wrong. So many consultant's reports on what's needed it's almost a waste. The potential for good work is there because patient specimens are delivered almost immediately after collection; however, the way specimens are handled is unbelievable. I picked up some culture plates to see how they were inoculated and found one without any growth medium yet the empty Petri dish had been swabbed with a specimen. Go figure! How do you rationalize this? Elvira asked me to accompany her to hear her challenge (in Albanian) the contractor who through donor funding is upgrading the tuberculosis lab. He's used kitchen counters instead of standard one-piece lab counters. Better than nothing I guess but they won't stand up to harsh disinfecting solutions. I understood him to say there was no money to do things differently. Sorry to bore you with technical details but you and I've discussed lab problems so often I'm sure you get the drift. Besides I need to vent or my exasperation will build to an explosion. Thanks for "listening" kg. Love, Cassie


Subject: SNOWDAY DECEMBER 12
Date: Tue, 19 Dec 2000 10:13 EST

Dear Cassie. Well, we got dumped on. School buses are not running. Jeremy got dressed into snow pants, parka and toque and started searching for snow boots as soon as he realized he'd have the day off. He's now crawling around the backyard and making angels. Nothing like a good snowfall to get one's eyes sparkling. And to bring the inner child back to life. Hard to believe he'll be at university next year. Love, Mom


Cassie stopped reading. She suddenly felt sad, almost a sense of loss. She should be the one watching Jeremy make snow angels, not her mother. But then, she couldn't help but smile at the image of that big kid playing. He always seemed so serious to her. She thought back to her own childhood in Toronto when they still had real winters. A snow angel could be quite an artistic accomplishment. Important not to contaminate the area with footprints. Jump into deep snow as far as possible from the path. Almost an athletic endeavour, long jump. Then of course, stretch arms and legs to appear as tall as possible, move them in just the right arc to form wings with the arms and a gown with the legs. With mathematical precision. But the *pièce de résistance*, to extricate one's self, to get up from the impression without leaving signs of a struggle in the snow and to jump back to the path without leaving tell-tale footprints. Cassandra smiled, surprised at the calm she now felt, the pleasure of remembering moments from her joy-filled childhood.

Date: Wed, 20 Dec 2000 08:50 EST

Hey Karen Gabriella, this is my third attempt. I've been trying to tell you about going to Valentines late yesterday afternoon. Ordered a delicious vegetarian lasagne. So, in the restaurant, as they do so often here, they were playing North American popular songs and I was moved almost to tears. It's like they saw me coming! When I'm home I may never listen to Bryan Adams, Shania Twain or Celine Dion but here it's comforting.

Also, this morning there was water to shower. A nice day again for walking. So things are looking up! I went out with Sue for a bite…

"To be honest," Cassie said, "I feel very alone here. I miss my kids."

"Well, I won't say I know how you feel. I don't have kids," Sue replied.

"I'm considering strategies to continue the work I've got underway but…"

"I'm getting together with some friends tonight. Nothing fancy. Just at a friend's apartment. Come with me."

"Are you sure it's okay?"

"I'll make a phone call. But yes it's okay. The phone call's just a courtesy."

"I hope this isn't a pity thing. I don't want anyone feeling sorry for me."

"Cassandra! Stop it! You should know I never do anything I don't want to."


I enjoyed last night visiting Sue's epidemiologist friend. Her boss Roberto was there and Patrick from the UK. Anton shared Austrian delicacies like special cheeses and roasted chestnuts and a Christmas loaf, something like our Christmas pudding. And mulled wine with liqueur added!!! Feeling much calmer now.

Sue wants me to come back – even for a month, she says. Shpend also said he hopes I'll come back. Frankly, I'm ambivalent. I'd like to continue what I've started. No matter what, I've decided to continue my leave from the forensics lab. I don't know if I'm simply trying to avoid contact with Doug, in which case, I'm probably better off over here than consulting at home.

Elvira was really on a high today because she made some in-roads with the physicians in the Maternity hospital. Things can happen with amazing speed here when there's a will.

Well, sis, my last night here. I take off for home at noon tomorrow. That can't come soon enough. See you soon, Cassie

# Part 2

# March – December 2001

# one

# March 2001
## *Shumës si jeni*

About three months after he'd left for home, Tom was back in Prishtinë. This morning he walked toward the Uphill Café in *Velania*. A degree or two below freezing with the sun low above the south-eastern hills, he found this March day particularly energizing. Prishtinë looks good in morning light, cleaner, no overt signs of air pollution, no foul smells in the air, he thought. Should hike in Gërmia later now the snow's melted. He was always happier to use the hills for recreation than spend time in the musty gym. Fitness centre they call it. No windows, no natural light, no ventilation. He needed to pick up the pace. Agron would be waiting at the café. Uphill Café, well named. The hill on Bill Clinton Boulevard was always intimidating, especially carrying a laptop. Only five pounds the salesperson had said. Only five pounds. Everything in Prishtinë seemed uphill to Tom. It appeared to affect his breathing. He didn't think it was an altitude effect, although Prishtinë was five hundred metres higher than Toronto. He'd checked. Gotta be particulate air pollution. Particulate pollution. Pollution particles. Polyparticulate pollution problem.

Agron was waiting on the café patio. It's not warm enough to sit outside. Why don't we just go to City Park across the road? It's deserted and equally as cold.

"Thomas, it is so funny to be interviewed by you. I think my story is not unique. Something like this happened to many doctors and professors."

"Maybe, but I want to record as many stories as possible."

"People know these stories."

"Albanians, yes. But Agron, we need to tell the world. Tell Serbs who've heard only their government's story. It's important. You and I discussed this as a form of genocide."

"Genocide is such a terrible word, Thomas. It tears at my heart. But for a long time ethnic cleansing was official policy. Our people were here many generations but, somehow, we were inconvenient."

"I don't understand. You'll say ethnic cleansing but you think genocide is too strong a term."

"The words are similar, I think. To me, genocide means to kill a whole population or as many people as possible. I prefer to think it was only expulsion they wanted."

"It's semantics. Either way is destructive."

"Many Albanians are Muslim, Thomas, but only because the Turks forced us to be. It was easier to be Muslim than be tortured or killed."

"I still don't get it. Your people are secular. How can this be a religious thing?"

"It is not religious. Religious conflict is terrible but easy to understand. Albanians always see themselves as Albanian, same as Serbs as Serb. No matter how long they live outside Albania or Serbia. Bad feelings can last without end when propaganda is used to exaggerate historic grievances."

Tom began recording the conversation by stating the date, time and place, then nodded to Agron to continue talking.

"I am happy to work with you, Thomas. I do not yet know whether it is such a good choice for you to have me as driver. But," he laughed, "we are both still alive."

Tom thought Agron seemed uncharacteristically nervous being

interviewed. Tom was amused by his self-deprecation of his driving skills. Actually, Agron had proved to be a skilful driver. Streets had not been maintained. Most drivers took evasive action to save themselves from being swallowed by potholes without considering the presence of other vehicles on the roadway as they dipsy doodled into oncoming traffic.

"I like to be your interpreter, translator and friend. I am a realist. My family is young. I am certain you must realize what you pay me is four times my salary as a forensic epidemiologist. Of course, I am no longer Director of the Institute. Just a simple staff epidemiologist reporting to a UN boss. Forensic site work is done by Europeans and North Americans. UN does not understand we had good forensic people in Yugoslavia."

"Do you remember when I first came to see you?"

"Of course. You were new in Prishtinë. You asked me for background information about forensics in the Balkans. There were about ten or twelve people in my office celebrating a staff birthday."

"Before you even asked why I was there we ate cake and drank coffee."

Agron smiled at Tom's recollection. "Normal hospitality. But I was happy to slip away with you to discuss outbreaks of tularaemia and Crimean Congo haemorrhagic fever. In 1990 I was removed from my job. Me, the only professor of forensic epidemiology at University of Prishtinë. There were very few forensic epidemiologists in the Balkans."

"Then, why would that happen?"

"Because I am Albanian. That would be reason enough for Milosevic to fire me. Belgrade sent someone as the new director."

"Someone you knew?"

"I knew him, of course. We few formed a close community. We worked together on difficult cases, but, as I recall, he always needed my advice not *vice versa*. My colleague offered no explanation. I will not name him now. I hope we will work together again after everything settles down. It is so important to solve puzzles and identify victims. We must know everything we can. Families need to know what happened to fathers, mothers, sisters and brothers."

"What did he say? It must have been difficult for both of you."

"He asked politely at first, then ordered me to leave. I ignored him. Then finally four police officers wearing protective equipment removed me from the office and off university grounds at gunpoint. Riot gear! Can you imagine how that was? I have always worked with the police. Was I now on the other side? They arrested me five more times in the next nine years."

Tom paused the tape. Agron rubbed his temples and gazed seemingly vacantly past other patrons. After a moment he shrugged his shoulders and signalled for more coffee. The waiter responded immediately bringing them a cafetière and two clean mugs.

"I wasn't aware of any of this," Tom eventually said.

"I have not told many people," Agron replied. "Except of course my wife and a few colleagues. I remember that day so clearly. I began to work with Mother Teresa organization, MC, Missionaries of Charity. After the fall of communism, MC was active in the southern Balkans. In 1990, I became their voice."

"That's interesting… you, a Muslim."

"Don't be surprised, Thomas. We are Albanian. Muslim and Catholic Albanians work together. *Nënë Teresë* was Albanian. Born in Skopë. That is Macedonia now. When she was born, it was the Ottoman Province of Kosova. I know it was because of my work with the Missionaries of Charity they arrested me. Sometimes, they said I was planning insurrection against Belgrade. Other times, gathering intelligence for somebody unnamed. But the Serbs were careful not to offend the Mother Teresa group even if they did not like me. So, usually they released me after a few hours, physically unharmed. It was not a serious issue, only harassment."

"Did the police know who you were?" Tom asked.

"Yes, of course, the police knew who I was. And always who and where I visited. Who I talked to. They insisted I explain my visits and conversations. I would say I am a humanist and a doctor. I am not a politician. I serve Serbs as well as Albanians, Roma, Bosnians and other groups who need humanitarian or medical assistance. So I would suggest they look at my staff and see how many Serbs worked with me."

"Did that make any difference?"

"It was well known who worked for MC. Then in 1997, I was invited to United Nations in New York to share my perspective as physician and aid worker. I met there with thirty-two ambassadors. I spoke only Serbian in New York so there would be no misunderstanding when I returned home. I was careful. My purpose was to discuss humanitarian problems.

I met also with US congressmen and some senators. After that, I visited Ottawa and Toronto to meet with Parliament and foreign service people.

In Toronto, I was a guest of Kosovar Albanians living there. My hosts took me to visit many tourist sites around the city. Of course, we also went to Niagara Falls. In Kosova we know about Niagara Falls. That is what they ask about when someone comes back from Canada. We also visited neighbourhoods in the city. This impressed me greatly. We visited Albanian and Greek restaurants. I saw Greek flags, Italian flags and others I do not recognize. Many customers in the Greek area are not Greek. People of other cultures enjoying Greek culture and hospitality. Why are we not able to do that and get along with each other in the Balkans?

When I came back in Kosova, it was my longest interrogation. I explained my visit was to arrange humanitarian and medical support. It was not political. After a while I was tired of answering questions about the UN meeting. I said ask the Yugoslav UN ambassador because he attended every meeting. Of course, they already had his report. They just wanted to continue to harass me. I repeated I am a humanist and a doctor.

My final arrest was in 1999 after NATO started bombing. The question was the same. My answer was the same, humanist and physician, not politician. Before, the other officers had been calm and polite. This man was agitated. Serbs knew they would soon be gone from Kosova. He pulled a gun to threaten me when I said I had no more information."

Tom paused the tape and discontinued his note-taking. This time for himself. Agron remained composed. A gun. I can't even picture that. Agron attempted some humorous comments to put Tom at ease. Then Agron nodded he wanted to continue.

"It is impossible not to remember. I live that moment again and again. Time stood still. It seemed very long. The officer glared and pointed his gun at me. Suddenly, he shoved the gun into my mouth. Broke two teeth and ripped the roof of my mouth... he pulled the trigger. It only clicked. The cylinder was empty. I collapsed to the floor, quivering and shaking. There was no time to be terrorized until later. The Serb laughed. Then I was released. My final arrest."

"Jesus, Agron. I had no idea." Tom stopped taping. Agron was grave and silent, slowly drinking coffee, gathering his thoughts. Several minutes passed in silence. Tom decided it was time to conclude the interview. He wanted to get away. He didn't want to hear more details. Didn't want to spend any more time with Agron.

"No, Thomas. I want to tell this story."

"Let's just wrap up. You've told me plenty. I had no idea this happened to you. I'm truly sorry."

"Thomas, I am strong now. My will brought me through these times. You asked me earlier when things will normalize, I think that was your word."

"Yeah, normalize."

"Well, as an intellectual, as soon as possible for the economy, for peace. I know it is the right thing. But in my gut, I hope never. I never want to tell my neighbour whose family was dragged to the street and shot in the head... executed. I never want to tell him it is time to kiss and make up."

two

# April 2001
## *Mirë, falemnderit*

Saturday morning Tom met Agron near the Grand Hotel as planned, a routine they'd established to share the week's information and new observations. Mother Teresa Boulevard teemed with pedestrians and cars. An amazingly warm day for early April. Too nice for Prishtinë to stay indoors. Agron steered Tom toward the patio area already packed with coffee drinkers. Maybe not just coffee drinkers. Plenty of beer mugs and shot glasses on the tables as well as coffee cups. The two of them could easily spend an hour or more drinking coffee, sitting in the sun, watching the world, or the women, go by. Mini-skirts had replaced winter drab. Springtime in Prishtinë!

"Thanks for the list, Agron."

"*S'ka problem.*"

"You read this?"

"*Po*. Of course," he answered.

"Can you find out more about this one?" Tom pointed to a name.

"Sure, Thomas. Cassandra Borden?"

"I may know her."

"That is good, no? A woman from home? I have met her. She worked at the hospital in Elvira Kurtz's lab."

"Microbiology lab?"

"Yes, Microbiology. You met Elvira. Cassandra seemed nice. You have trouble with her?"

"No, no trouble. I'm just surprised she's here."

"She worked at the lab last year, maybe November. She is not here now."

"Why would she still be on the list?"

"Sometimes it is not up to date. Elvira wants her to come back. Sue McElligott, also."

"Sue McElligott 's with World Health?"

"*Po.*"

"By the way, do you have a secure e-mail address?"

"Yes, with MIN."

"We could use that to communicate when you're away from Prishtinë."

"I would need to ask Dirk O'Reilly. He explained it was only to contact him."

Tom smirked. "Yeah, old Divide and Control O'Reilly. Ignore him. Let's just do it."


Date: Sat, 07 Apr 2001 14:35 EDT
To: Dirk O'Reilly <doreilly@secure.gov.min.org>

Dirk, were you aware Cassandra Borden was here last Nov/Dec? Maybe with a CIPHA project at the hospital microbiology lab. Could also be WHO. She's on the list of Canadians known to be in Prishtina. If this is an on-going project, I need to know. I'm surprised we didn't cross paths in December. Best, Tom


Date: Wed, 11 Apr 2001 20:16 EDT
To: Anthony Petersen <petersen@themagazine.ca>

Hi Tony. I'm relieved that Editorial agrees with changing Agron's identity and circumstances in the article. Please consider whether I can make a practice of changing identifiers. All the best, Tom

Sunday afternoon. Tom felt good. Beautiful spring day. For the first time since he'd been coming to Prishtinë he realized he was able to see mountains from downtown. Sky's so unusually clear today, must be a low pollution index day. He anticipated Agron's laughter when he considered asking him whether they measure and report pollution indices.

He wondered who he might encounter at Vullkano Pizza, his customary Sunday night spot. Won't be Cassandra Borden if she's not in town. Wouldn't that be a can absolutely full of worms. I'd have to come up with some explanation why I didn't show up in Chicago. If she would even talk to me. I'm sure she's an excellent resource here, though.

He wondered whether she was still married to Doug Goode. He always considered that a tense situation. Doug so jealous and proprietary Tom could never understand Cassie being with him. He didn't like me at all. Good thing Doug's a biochemist so I had little reason to run into him. Don't remember him being on Agron's consulate list. Can't imagine Doug being happy to have Cassie in Kosova alone.

In the end he decided to follow his routine. He knew he couldn't afford to dwell on Cassandra Borden, trying to stay out of her way. He decided he'd worry about Vullkano later and spend the rest of the afternoon writing. He was developing a story based on the experience of a young couple he'd recently interviewed:

Kristofor Troshani escaped Kosova by walking to the Macedonian border. Accompanied by his pregnant wife, Kaltrina, and their four year old son, Rami, this was a planned escape. An opportunity for Kristofor to ensure his family was safely across the Macedonian border to stay with relatives until they could be airlifted to France. The escape plan was devised because Kristofor's work with Doctors of the World brought him to the attention of CNN News and thereby, Serb authorities. He had become a target of harassment because of his steadfast refusal to be stopped from providing medical services to the villages of Kosova, his refusal to be deterred by roadblocks. He believed no harm would come to him personally from the Serbs as long as he remained a person of interest to Western media. But he did not believe the same degree of safety necessarily extended to his family. He wanted them in Europe, far removed from the conflict.

Kristofor, Kaltrina and Rami walked four days to reach the Macedonian border. Once there, because both Kristofor and Kaltrina were physicians, they had less trouble than most escapees since they had crucial skills to provide medical assistance in the refugee camps on either side of the border.

But Kristofor was having none of that. He wanted his family safe in France. Once he knew Kaltrina and Rami were secure, he returned to Kosova and continued to provide medical aid to several villages.

Because of Kristofor's high profile, the three of them had not taken the more travelled routes with endless lines of other refugees. Instead, they hiked deep into the woods, over hills and through mountains. They followed well worn trails, probably sheep or goat tracks that had been used for centuries, always with the fear the Serbs may have land-mined the paths. Quite a frightening experience for two adults but they were frightened for four-year old Rami and wanted to downplay the gravity of the situation for him.

To allay any fears Rami might have, Kristofor explained to him they were on an adventure, looking for rabbits, that they must stay quiet so they would not frighten the rabbits. Four days and three nights of the hunt!

Once at the border, Kristofor managed to telephone Kaltrina's father in Prizren to assure him they were safe. Rami wanted to speak with his grandfather who he adored. On the phone, Rami said, "Grandpa, grandpa, we walked in the woods and we were very quiet because we were always hiding from men with guns."


Date: Sun, 25 Apr 2001 10:40 EST

Hey, Bert. Sometimes lately, I have this nagging doubt about writing personal stories. If anything were to happen to someone I'd written about, I doubt I could sleep with clear conscience. Yet that's my role, what I'm paid for, personal stories from post-conflict situations. It worries me. All the best to both you and Suzanne, Tom


Date: Mon, 26 Apr 2001 14:35 EDT

Tom, re Cassandra Borden. The feds want intelligence services to keep away from NGOs and federally financed projects. CIPHA's funding comes from CIDA. Seems Cassandra's on indefinite leave from the forensics lab to assist WHO with public health infrastructure rebuilding. She's slated to spend about three years travelling back and forth to Prishtina. It may not be feasible for you to avoid encountering her. At least since, you're using your own identity you don't need to worry about being outed. Take care, Dirk

# three

# June 2001
## *Të falemnderit*

Rumours came into the restaurant, at first whispered then the subsequent buzz erupted into loud excited talk and changed the tone of the get-together, the quiet celebratory gathering at Ballantine's Restaurant. Fellow Canadians came to show appreciation and support for two compatriot midwives who were returning home after spending six months training Kosovar obstetric nurses, pouring their energies into trying to improve life for women and babies. However, the complexion of the evening was altered by the news that Slobodan Milosevic had been spirited away to The Hague from the Belgrade prison where he had been incarcerated since late March.

"What d'ya think, Agron? You must be happy," Tom said.

"We will see." Agron waved his hand dismissively, not caught up in the excitement.

"What about the massacres? Incidents that were independently verified." This is a breakthrough, Tom thought.

"We will see. The UN is the government since the war. Two years. Where is the improvement? Why can't we govern ourself now? We will see." Agron was clearly not impressed.

"But I'd expect celebration. When Bill Clinton announced NATO was going to start bombing, the streets filled with defiant happy people."

"Thomas, we are tired of being excited about nothing. Yes, it is good Milosevic will go to The Hague. What should we be excited about?"

"Isn't the arrest a good start?"

"Yes, yes. Please understand. It is very important. Serbia gave him up. There must be an angle, there must be something in it for them. We do not trust them. We lived with Serbia as part of Yugoslavia for more than eighty years."

"What about proven massacres?" Tom asked again. "*Shtime* and *Gjakovë*? And the other validated ones?"

"We will see," Agron turned away.


Agron had already ordered coffee when Tom arrived the following Tuesday at the Hotel Drenica in *Fushë Kosovë*.

"Why'd you pick this place?" Tom asked.

"This place is important to Serbs and Albanians. Serbs call it *Kosovo Polje*. Maybe you have heard that name?"

Tom nodded. "Yeah."

Agron continued, "I thought you should see where it started. It was April 1987 when Belgrade sent Slobodan Milosevic to calm an angry Serb mob at City Hall. They were protesting what they thought were anti-Serb policies. Instead of settling the crowd he fired them up like Hitler. He told militants he would never again allow others to push Serbian people around. That was not the first time this place started things. It is the site of the Battle of Kosova in 1389, *Beteja e Kosovës*. Serbs fought the Ottoman Empire. Turks say they won, Serbs say they won."

"I don't understand why this village is so important to Serbia."

"Here Turks captured and beheaded Prince Lazar. After his death he became St. Lazar. He built many new Serbian churches and monasteries. His body and relics are buried in Serbia at Ravanica monastery. Many pilgrims visit each year."

"You're a Muslim!"

"Ah, Thomas, my friends say I am Muslim light. The truth is most of us are not serious about religion. When this was Yugoslavia, the history of all Yugoslav peoples was important to me. This village is sacred to Serbs the same way Jerusalem is for Christians, Jews and Muslims. Serbs want all of Kosova's farmland, museums, art galleries. They say Albanians came here during the world wars. Albanians have been here for much longer than a century. Serbs and Albanians married each other. My great-grandmother was Serbian. So it is my culture, also."

"Oh, really!"

"Yes but, Thomas, I must tell you that is a family secret. I have told only my wife. Now I must kill you." Agron laughed and punched Tom's shoulder.

Tom feigned recoiling in pain. "Hey."

"Thomas, we, you and me, are similar. We work for the people. I know rich governments try to help us. But they do not like to spend money for simple things. We need simple things. As well as big infrastructure. Let us go back in Prishtinë now."

# four

# September 2001
## *Gjithçka punon*

Damn it! It's killing me. Tom had agreed to meet Agron at the corner of Mother Teresa and Bill Clinton Boulevard. But faced with the powerful symbolism, he walked instead into a schoolyard just short of the intersection. He chose to sit on a backless wooden bench in the north-east corner of the yard, hoping the small cluster of immature chestnut trees not meant to be anything but a windbreak would effectively conceal him. He needed a few moments of quiet. He was in tears and desperate to compose himself. Overnight in Prishtinë billboards had been erected of the New York skyline with two burning candles in place of the twin towers of the World Trade Center. The image hit him hard. He sobbed involuntarily and gasped for breathe, his energy suddenly sapped. He had been walking quickly along Mother Teresa Boulevard, pleased that Agron planned to take him to a couple of the Health Houses he'd heard so much about. He noticed the billboard from about half a block away. The candles he assumed symbolized some celebration or other. Then as he got closer, the full import shocked him. His eyes welled with tears. Tom understood how important America was for the Kosovars. Bill Clinton was a hero here. Everyone listened to Clinton's speech in the spring of 1999 as he insisted NATO would not stand by, that NATO would take decisive action to end ethnic cleansing. Everyone still remembered the exact moment the first bomb dropped. The streets filled with people within minutes. The celebration began. The US was their saviour. So now, an attack on America was devastating.

He knew where he'd been on September eleventh. Still in Canada, he had met Bert at his Ottawa office just after nine that morning. They were headed to Cornwall for the funeral of a boyhood friend. They'd allowed enough time for a leisurely drive, a chance to catch up with each other, that beautiful cloudless morning.

"Ever been to a Jewish funeral?" Bert asked as they headed toward the highway.

"No, this is my first." Tom suddenly remembered what he'd heard on the radio. "Just before I picked you up I heard a report from New York about a small plane crashing into one of the World Trade Centre buildings."

"Really? A traffic reporter or something?"

"I don't know. Shouldn't be a visibility issue if it's as clear as it is here."

Bert's cell phone rang. He checked the display. "It's Suzanne. I should answer," he said to Tom. "What? You're kidding. That can't be," he exclaimed. "Tommy, the Trade Centre thing's a disaster. It wasn't a small plane. It was a seven-sixty-seven."

"No way!"

"Probably engine trouble. That's why I hate airports so close to residential areas."

Before long, Bert's phone rang again. "Two, Suzanne? What do you mean? Tommy, turn on the radio. This is bad."

As the story unfolded on CBC Radio, they spoke of how strange this event seemed. At one point Bert described it as surreal. "That's not a word I like to use," he said. "It's so overused. This must be like hearing Orson Welles do *War of the Worlds*."

Tom froze.

"You okay Tommy? We don't have to go, you know."

"I want to go. For Drew's kids. For Lena. You know it's been tough for her these last few years. How could she watch Drew deteriorate and still be okay? I wouldn't want to put anybody through that."

"C'mon Tommy, they had some good days. They even travelled almost 'til the end."

"Yeah."

"Sure you're okay?"

"I just feel so bad for Lena and the kids."

Now, in the schoolyard in Prishtinë, he once again struggled with his feelings. He got up from the bench and walked back out of the schoolyard toward his rendezvous with Agron. I know also where I was for John and Robert Kennedy. And Martin Luther King.


Tom and Agron drove west from Prishtinë to a Heath House in the village of Gllogoc. Agron explained to Tom how the Health Houses, these remnants of the parallel system, had become important symbols of rebellion and were now integrated into the medical community as family clinics.

"There is a physician here who knows our interest in anthrax and other bugs," Agron explained. "Today he wants us to see a young patient with lymphadenopathy."

"Us? You mean me too? Why? What does he know about me?"

"Relax, Thomas. We have a network. I cannot do this medical intelligence by myself."

"But does he know I'm a microbiologist?"

"Relax, relax, relax. He thinks you are researching a story. There is no medical information system. We have informal network to share interesting findings."

"What about confidentiality?"

"It's okay, Thomas. That is a concept that has not been important here."

Although he'd been enthusiastically anticipating this visit, Tom was still distressed. The billboard image continued to trouble him. He hadn't discussed his thoughts with Agron but he was certain Agron sensed his discomfort. It was an unusually quiet drive.

"Thomas, this is Dr Taulant," Agron introduced the physician in charge who was smoking outside the clinic door.

"Welcome, Mr Thomas. I wait for you. I have smoke. I know you Canadian not like smoke inside. I tell Dr Agron about case. He want to see patient result. It is very interest. I have see ten case like this since two month. Maybe you write about interest case in West?"

"Yes, I sometimes write medical articles."

"Come."

As they stepped inside, Tom noticed the floors were clean, the walls whitewashed. An old monocular microscope sat on a high wooden bench that also held a stack of file folders and looked to serve as a desk. Lower wooden benches lined three walls. This seemed to be a waiting room. Two doors opened from the fourth wall. Taulant led them through the door on the right into a primitive examining room. A young, dark-haired woman stood against the wall in the tiny room suddenly crowded with three more bodies. Taulant smiled kindly at the woman and spoke to her in Albanian. The introduction was too quick for Tom to grasp the patient's name but he did catch a phrase that sounded like *expert from the West*.

Taulant asked the woman to sweep her long hair back to expose a fist-sized asymmetric reddened distension of the left side of her upper throat and neck. Tom leaned closer to look for suppuration but there was no leakage of pus. Agron glanced quickly at Tom moving his head almost imperceptibly sideways toward the woman tacitly suggesting he begin the discussion.

"Have you done microbiology testing?" Tom asked. Agron interpreted the dialogue into Albanian for the benefit of the young

86

patient.

"No, only thyroid testing."

"Where was that done?"

"Prizren hospital. It was normal."

I won't even ask about methodology. It's right to rule out thyroid imbalance but it would not be my first consideration. "There are so many things it could be. To me, the degree of inflammation means infection."

"They don't have access to microbiology lab, Thomas."


As they drove past Prizren toward Gjilani and the other Health House Agron wanted to visit, Tom discussed what they'd seen. "There are so many possible causes from infected teeth or sinuses or even tonsillitis. Or a whole variety of tumours."

"But those are not likely, Thomas. Not if there are ten similar cases."

"That's what I was thinking. It seems more like infectious mononucleosis if the age range is primarily youth as Taulant suggested. Can Taulant access serology testing to rule out mono?"

"Those tests cannot be done here. They must be sent to Germany. The Health House and the patient cannot afford to pay for that."

At the second Health House, Agron introduced Rovena, the young physician in charge. She immediately raised her concern about the onset of arthritis in a number of young people. Tom and Agron spoke with one young man, well dressed, well educated.

"Do you work in the country?" Tom asked through Agron's translation.

"I know what you ask," the young man replied. "I speak English."

"Good."

"In school, I have choice to learn English or German. I think

English be better."

"So, where do you work?"

"I study at University for English teacher. I never work in country with hands." He stretched his arm toward Tom. He displayed enlarged knuckles more likely to be those of a much older labourer than a man in his early twenties. He pulled his pant leg up to expose his right knee, swollen, reddened and distorted. He winced with pain when Rovena asked him to step forward.

"I have seen many cases like this," she said. "This arthritis-like presentation. I believe it is infectious cause."

They discussed her concerns and promised to try to help establish a diagnosis and improve information sharing especially for such highly unusual cases.

On the drive back to Prishtinë, they talked about what they'd seen.

"Thomas, you know there is no information system. We do this in old way. We talk to each other like old days. *Doktors* keep notes and remember patients they see. There is not yet public health system for epidemiology. We have that in Yugoslavia but no one wants to use Serb system now."

"What do you think we're looking at?"

"I do not know but I think we must look for more than anthrax."

"Yeah, I agree. We could start with a few of the notorious organisms of known biowarfare potential."

"But, Thomas, we do not know if this is only overactive immune responses to post-war condition."

"Well, let's not limit ourselves to the usual nasties. I know testing options are close to nil. I'd still like to be able to access the University of Prishtinë microbiology facilities."

"We'll see," Agron replied. They drove into Prishtinë on Bill

Clinton Boulevard. As they approached Mother Teresa, Agron pointed at the billboard. "Do you feel better now?" he asked.

Tom was surprised by Agron's insight and contemplated sharing his visceral reaction. But he simply said, "Much better now, thanks."

A few days later, Agron with uncharacteristic seriousness told Tom that workers excavating nearby caves just outside Prishtinë had uncovered human bones.

"Workers say it looks like mass grave but maybe from older time. Not this conflict. A friend asked me to go there to offer my opinion."

"Could I go along with you?"

"I can take you there tomorrow. I have been myself but I must go back. We have not yet told the UN. We think Serbs never knew about these *shpella*."

"Should you interfere if it could be a mass grave? Don't such suspicions need to be reported?"

They travelled the next day to Gedima, south-east of Prishtinë. Two older local men wearing the *qeleshe,* the traditional Albanian felted white wool skull cap, met them. Their greeting was warm and Tom realized they knew and trusted Agron. The men led them up the hill away from the regular visitor entrance. They walked back a hundred meters or so along the ridge to a small vertical opening hidden by dense shrubbery.

We're going in through there? Tom tried to focus his breathing to distract his thoughts from claustrophobia. I can do this. I won't panic. He looked over the valley and the dry river bed below. He focussed briefly on a hill opposite where a man tended a herd of about a dozen goats. Tom knew that was his occupation, goatherd. He internalized his glimpse into an enduring twenty-first century reality as if this was to be the last event he would ever see above ground.

"It will not collapse, Thomas. It is very solid. *Mermerna.* Marble you call it. I will go first, then you follow."

Tom reluctantly squeezed his tall body through the narrow opening. Agron handed Tom their only flashlight as a peace offering for forcing him to confront his fears and proceeded to direct Tom's attention to the piles of bones. Tom could think only of the confined, dimly illuminated chamber. We'll run out of air with two of us in here. I'll go back up. The space was cool but not cold and surprisingly dry. No particular smell. Must be a fresh air source. Maybe we will survive.

Agron directed Tom to shine the light on the specific bones he wanted to examine.

"Whadda ya make of them?" Tom asked, distracted by the bones, less concerned with survival.

"I don't know, Thomas. I cannot age them properly. The UN could do that. But I think we need to get as much information as possible before we notify anybody."

"Why do you say that?"

"If UN forensics comes, they will excavate the caves, maybe destroy them. First, I want to be sure for myself this is a crime scene. Local people are working hard to make this an historic site and visitor centre. They have jobs reconstructing. Even the guides are from this area. They deserve to be allowed to complete their project."

"What else?"

"I have interviewed many villagers. I truly believe they know nothing. They might not tell Serbs or the UN anything but this is near my home village. They know me. My grandparents are from this area. That counts."

"Even though you've never lived here?"

"It is like your Tahir Domi. He was born in Canada but all Kosovars say he is from Gjakovë, town of his parents. You look puzzled,

Thomas… Tie Domi. You know, the hockey player."

Tom laughed. "I know who you're talking about."

Agron showed Tom a skull. "This is my concern. I am an epidemiologist not a pathologist. But these are bones from a young person. Look at the lower jaw. Third molars have erupted but surfaces are not worn. Some decay between teeth. It is difficult to examine properly in the cave. Tooth decay in young persons means they were born before we had universal dental care in Yugoslavia."

"Could the bodies be brought from somewhere else?"

"That is possible. Look at this joint, Thomas. Very worn like arthritis. Not usual in youth. It is not a single observation. It is here in each body."

"Could they be bones from different people?"

"No. These are full skeletons. All bones have correct orientation."

Tom realized Agron was right. What he'd seen as piles of bones in his initial panic were actually well organized.

"Look at the rest of this leg. Look at the hip epiphysis."

"Maybe hard working rural people wear their joints out prematurely?" Tom suggested.

"No, Thomas. People look after their dead in Kosova. A mass grave means someone else is involved. Soil compaction, decay of bones makes me think thirty or forty years past. Serbs wanted to get rid of Albanians but not actively during Tito's time."

"Okay. Thanks."

"*S'ka persë*, my friend. Before we go back in Prishtinë, I have something more to tell. Last week in Pejë, Fisnik at the Health House told me he thinks the mysterious lymphadenopathy may be tularaemia."

"Is there a lab capable of handling class three organisms? Maybe the forensics lab?"

"No labs. Forensic lab is not yet ready."

# five

# November 2001
## *Falemnderit*

Back in Prishtinë about eleven months since she'd left, Cassandra met Claire and Sonja and walked with them the four kilometres to Gërmia Park for Sunday brunch at Freskia restaurant. She was reassured by familiar surroundings. Her mushroom omelette tasted fine but really was a little greasy for her liking. Side salad was good. When she saw Claire's tomato basil soup she was reminded how many local restaurants made great soups. She was surprised it was not busy but there was still plenty of staff.

"We should have dinner at *Il Passatore* to properly celebrate your return," Claire suggested.

"Good with me," Cassie replied. "Of course, I'll be there but not to celebrate my foolishness. It'll be in honour of your trip home."

"Okay. Tuesday then. Are you available, Sonja?" Sonja nodded she could make it.

"I will need to be back by eleven because my sister's going to phone that night," Cassie added.

"We'll be early. We all need our beauty sleep these days," Claire teased. "Besides, I leave the following day."

Cassie realized how much she liked the restaurant setting within Gërmia Park. Reminds me of home, so heavily wooded, a mixed forest with plenty of conifers. Just like my property. Nice to be welcomed back so heartily by Claire and Sonja. Her mind drifted to another welcome, much more of a surprise, the previous day at the Canadian Support Office.

"Hello there, Cassie. So good to see you. Welcome back." Sue McElligott had poked her head into the doorway of the small office Cassie was using to organize her instructional material into file folders.

"It's good to see you, Sue," she'd replied.

"I've a meeting with Shpend but couldn't pass up the opportunity to pop my head in. I hoped you'd come back. It wasn't the pressure WHO put on the Canadian government, was it?" Sue laughed.

"No just the psychological pressure you exerted directly on me. Making me feel indispensable. That wasn't at all fair," Cassandra joked in return.

"Oh but it worked. We'll get together for lunch. I'll give you a couple days to settle back in. How's Wednesday?"

"Good for me."

"I'll come to the lab to collect you. We can just walk over to the Baci Hotel if you like. They always have a good lunch special and cold beer."

Subject: HERE OKAY
Date: Sun, 18 Nov 2001 18:53 EST
From: cassandra.borden@symplicity.com
To: brenda3@nexium.ca

Hi Brenda. Just wanted you to know my travel was smooth, flights connecting like clockwork. I met a man I knew on the Toronto- Frankfurt flight so that helped pass the time. Funny, when I wrote my mother and sister, I said I'd met a woman I'd known. Don't know what I was thinking but probably felt guilty for thinking it was too bad he had to fly on to Cairo. That we weren't both stopping over in Frankfurt. Unfortunately or fortunately for me, I guess.

This is not a great place to be alone. Luckily, I'm with Claire, the infectious diseases nurse I know from my last visit but she's leaving Wednesday and it'll be just me at the house.

Riding in from the airport and then walking downtown, things look to have changed for the better – lots of building projects and generally less garbage evident. However, power blackouts are still the norm and water availability is not reliable. Apparently, the house was very cold last week before I arrived but it's been fine for me so far. I'm looking forward to going to work tomorrow and seeing my friends at the lab. Bye for now, Cassie

Prishtinë University Hospital, Microbiology Laboratory, Monday morning. As Cassandra climbed the stairs to the second floor laboratory, she glanced up to the landing, surprised to see a welcoming committee of Elvira, Afërdita, and several technologists.

"*Mirëmëngjes*, Cassie. Welcome back. It make me happy to see you."

"Thank you, Elvira. It's good to see you, too."

"*Mirëmëngjes*, Cassandra."

"*Mirëmëngjes*, Afërdita." A quick hug, then a kiss to each cheek.

"*Mirëmëngjes*, Dr Cassie."

"*Mirëmëngjes*, Cassie."

After the morning greetings, Cassie realized Elvira had not gone to her office but stood waiting to talk with her. They hadn't seen each other for almost a year and even though they'd pledged to maintain e-mail contact, it proved to be less than satisfactory for someone whose first language wasn't English. Elvira conversed well but had trouble committing Albanian thoughts to English words via keyboard. Cassandra's Albanian fluency was minimal. Besides, Cassie thought, Elvira's such a people person regardless of language. She communicates with body language and eye contact, things e-mail does not offer.

"Cassandra, how is your family?" Elvira touched both of Cassandra's forearms with her hands.

"Everyone's well thanks. My mother and my sister are fine. Marianne is studying hard. Jeremy is… well, you know… he's nineteen like your son. Good kid."

"Yes, Cassandra. Now, I want to talk. You just came in Prishtinë. But much happen. You have time now?"

"Elvira, I always have time for you."

Elvira grabbed Cassie's hand. "Thank you. You understand I want to make lab for zoonosis. I return from CDC excited, ready to start. I know how reference laboratory should look like."

"Good."

"But they want to move public health microbiology from hospital. I must go in meeting tomorrow for discuss. You come with me."

"Oh, okay. Who will be there?"

"Hospital administrator, chief medical officer, WHO. WHO want to do this, to make separate public health. There are translator because WHO is at meeting, so it is easy for you for understand."

"We could ask to delay discussion to another time. Tell them we're getting an expert opinion from Jordan Siemens. I can write Jordan for assistance."

"I think Dr Siemens is also in favour."

"Yes, he is but only when the time is right. The microbiology lab is not strong enough yet."

"Hospital don't want pay for infectious disease surveillance.

Government pay for hospital. Government pay for public health. Administrator don't want public health on hospital budget. I leave if this happen."

"Leave? But what would you do?" Cassie asked.

"I must continue work. There is not yet pension. I would start private lab."

"Maybe the hospital docs think the lab is too busy with public health to give them the service they want."

"They complain always. I know older ones. We all go in school together. Now we drink coffee and talk about problems. Young ones, they want more. They want thing we cannot give." Elvira shrugged her shoulders. "We start to work Saturday for them."

"Let's tell them we're willing to consider changes like longer hours to accommodate specimens collected at the end of the day. I'm sure there's more we could do as well."

"But, Cassie," Elvira emphatically slapped her palms together. "Staff don't want change work hours."

"It's gotta happen."


Subject: SUPPORT FOR MICROBIOLOGY
Date: Mon, 19 Nov 2001 11:34 EST

Hi Jordan. Arrived Saturday. What a welcome my first day at the lab! I'm exhilarated to feel a part of this rebirth.

Elvira is just back from spending a month at CDC Atlanta with another doctor and a technician. Molecular techniques do not intimidate her and she is a change maker. With support, she can make things happen. But she has other problems. The oft discussed proposal to separate public health and hospital microbiology is on the table again, apparently with some urgency. Public health micro has no chance for survival on its own. To take this barely functioning laboratory and break it into smaller pieces would be its death knell. If this lab has not achieved the basics of microbiology, what chance is there for smaller laboratories to perform in this environment? They must be able to detect all organisms of communicable disease significance endemic – to develop capabilities for hepatitis and HIV screening and discontinue outdated tests.

I'm asking for your support in fashioning an argument for delaying these decisions to a more appropriate time. Your word remains very influential here. Warmest regards, Cassie


Date: Sun, 25 Nov 2001 07:21 EST

Hi Cass. Just thought I'd tell you I had a drunken (him, not me) phone conversation with Doug last night. Seems he's unhappy with you being in Kosova. I told him it was none of his business. I'll write you again later, kg


The next Monday morning before Cassie had a chance to hang her coat, Elvira was bearing down on her. She nodded a greeting and beckoned Cassie to follow her into the water testing lab. So much for morning niceties. Cassie usually enjoyed Turkish coffee with the other microbiologists before tackling the day's problems.

Water's not my expertise, she thought, but let's see what she's after. The lab looks so different from last year. New flooring, new workbenches, new microbiology incubators, new lighting. They're using kitchen counter tops but I'm okay with that now. Everything is clean. It is possible.

"Cassandra, Italian consultant say test *Clostridium perfringens.* For sample from municipal supply system."

"But, Elvira, you told me yourself water is shut off at night because they cannot control leakage."

"Yes, all day most of water is used. At night it leaks out from pipe. Everything is so old."

"I'm not an environmental microbiologist, but to me it makes no sense to test for all these organisms when the system is not intact. If water leaks out, it leaks in as well. It's probably always contaminated."

"Tell me what to test."

"Coliforms and faecal coliforms."

"We use membrane filter but now there is no more supplies so we use MPN dilution tube."

"You know, we need to develop an inventory system so you won't run out of supplies. How often do you place an order?"

"UN do not allow order except each six months," Elvira replied.

"How fast are your orders filled?"

"About four month after UN approve."

Cassandra raised and dropped her hands in exasperation. "My God, Elvira! UN purchasing must think you're an office ordering pencils and photocopy paper. You're hamstrung if you're unable..."

"What is hamstring? You mean muscle?"

"Sorry. Plain English. A lab needs to order perishable lab supplies far more frequently. Every week or two. It doesn't work any other way."

Date: Mon, 26 Nov 2001 11:34 EST

Hi Jordan, now I need help with Clostridia in water. They do a lot of testing that doesn't make sense to me. They're paying an atrocious price for the chromatic compound derivatives someone advised them to use.

I'm starting to think it might actually be advisable to build a public health laboratory service outside the hospital lab environment after all. It's the proverbial individual health vs. the common good argument. The mindset is so different. Thanks, Cassandra

Date: Mon, 26 Nov 2001 14:36 EST

Hi Cassandra, I referred your water question to Harry Richardson. By the way, WHO has asked Sue McElligott to facilitate segregating clinical microbiology from public health microbiology. It should still be possible to strengthen both clinical and public health microbiology within the hospital lab setting with expanded services based on needs assessments. Not easy without strong political support for such a mandate. I've also heard WHO is ready to downsize their mission in Kosova. A new lab would be part of their legacy. That's the likely reason for pushing this. Great for progress reports but they won't be there to deal with the aftermath. Please let me know if there is anything more any of us can do. Regards, Jordan

Subject: re: WATER MICROBIOLOGY
Date: Mon, 26 Nov 2001 19:18 EST
From: richardson@qms.gov.ca

Hi Cassandra. Long time, no see! Jordan filled me in on your activities in Kosova. Sounds exciting. If there is anything I can do to help, please contact me. And, that does not preclude a visit over there. As for water microbiology, anything more than coliforms and E. coli is a waste of resources. Sophisticated testing can be added as the system improves. But minimal testing for now. I know we could find suppliers for reasonably priced products. Given the rebuilding circumstances I think there should be good price breaks available from NATO countries. All the best to you, Harry six

# December 2001
## *Më takon*

Date: Tue, 11 Dec 2001 14:43 EST

Tom, Greg Hanbruz tells me Cassandra Borden was stuck in Canada post nine-eleven. They decided to rearrange her work period. Greg expects her to be in-country until Christmas break. Please do not try to manipulate her to gain access to a micro lab. There would be hell to pay if Foreign Affairs discovered us using an NGO to gather intel contrary to their specific orders. I know you're friends but please stay away from her. Maybe it'd be a good time for you to visit one of the regional cities. She will be leaving before Christmas. Dirk

Cassandra headed home from the laboratory about three-thirty Wednesday afternoon into the deepening December twilight. She found it hard to get used to early darkness. Shpend explained to her that Kosova was close to the eastern edge of the time zone. In fact, Greece, due south, followed Eastern European Time but all of former Yugoslavia had been included in the Central European Time zone. Earlier evenings and earlier mornings, thought Cassie. She'd prefer more daylight in the afternoon.

As she walked along Mother Teresa Boulevard toward downtown, she noticed a man standing on the crowded sidewalk gazing at a store window display. It *is* Tom, she thought. The beard's new but, for sure, that's Tom – tall and slim. Still looks good. She hesitated, aware her pulse rate had increased and her heart was beating hard, surely audible to the people around her, she thought. She took several deep breaths to steady herself. What's he doing here, she wondered, then hurried toward him.

"Hello, Thomas Stephenson," she said.

"Hey… Cassandra Borden," Tom replied, caught off guard. "Good to see you." He paused. "I.. uh.. I knew you'd been here but I didn't realize you were in Prishtinë now."

"I thought I saw you on the street the other day."

"Really?"

"What do you mean you knew I'd been here?" Cassie continued.

"Your name was on last year's list at the Canadian Office of who's in town. It's something I use for scheduling interviews and finding interesting stories."

"Stories …?"

"Well, you know, human interest. What Canadians are doing here to help."

"Like what I'm doing here?" What does he mean – interviews, stories?

"Of course. Just like that."

"So you're not here as a microbiologist?"

"No. You got time for coffee?" Tom indicated a coffee shop with a quick head gesture. "I'll explain what I'm doing."

"Sure," Cassandra replied. As they walked into the small shop, she looked for a place to sit. She'd prefer a table near the woodstove but other patrons had the same notion. Tom touched her elbow to steer her toward a small empty table. She flinched, drawing her arm into her side. Tom looked startled and stepped away. His cheeks started to redden above his beard. She smiled in an effort to reduce the tension but it felt forced, false, too broad. Then she asked, "Have you been here before?"

Tom's tight facial expression eased. He shrugged. "Couple times. It's a warm, casual place for an interview. Helps people relax. How's your family? Your kids must be grown." Tom didn't wait for a reply but signalled a waiter to take their order. "You still fond of cappuccino, Cass?"

Cassie paused then nodded. "Marianne's qualifying in accountancy and working full time. Jeremy's in his first year at the University of Ottawa."

"You must be proud of them."

"They're great."

"How about ..." he said then didn't want to ask. "Where are you staying?"

Cassie told him about her apartment. She knew he'd been going to ask about Doug. He had no right. He hadn't even shown up in Chicago. No wonder he seems anxious, she thought. I hope he doesn't know I stayed an extra day after the conference hoping beyond hope he was still coming. When I got back to Toronto, he was gone.

"You know Cassie, I'm sorry. I didn't..." she heard Tom say as if replying to her thoughts. She didn't hear what else he said because she was thinking how she intended to tell Doug she was leaving him, but instead returned home feeling stupid and betrayed. Did Tom really think she would get involved with him and stay married? She jostled her cup spilling foam over the lip. She blotted the table with her serviette. Then she sipped her cappuccino, pleased she hadn't blurted out what she'd been mentally rehearsing in anticipation of bumping into Tom since first catching sight of him a few days before. Now looking at him again, she laughed when he seemed to have once again heard her unspoken outburst.

"Cass, I'm really glad to see you."

"It's good to see you, too." Then she said, "I was supposed to fly home next week. Austrian Airlines was overbooked so they offered me a free upgrade to change bookings. Now I'm going a week Monday."

"I'll be leaving that Wednesday. But no upgrades."

"Actually it's only to London. Crossing the Atlantic, it's back to cattle car."

"So you're going via Heathrow. They've got me through Frankfurt."

"Are you going to the Canadian Office tomorrow night?" Cassie asked.

"For what?"

"There's a small gathering. Most projects are already wound down for Christmas."

"Really? So soon?"

"I think it's just a get-together for the few of us left behind. The airline bumpees, I mean."

"No, I hadn't heard about it. You know me, I usually avoid cocktail parties."

"I'd think it'd be a great place for you to contact people. You know, for your stories."

"You think?"


Subject: WHAT ABOUT WOMEN PART TWO
Date: Wed, 12 Dec 2001 15:40 EST

Hey Bert. Remember I used to work with Cassandra Borden? Haven't seen her for years so did a bit of a double-take when she appeared on Mother Theresa Boulevard in downtown Prishtinë. Cassie's here with CIPHA (Canadian Institute of Public Health Associations) helping WHO rebuild a public health capacity.

It was good to have someone upbeat (read female) to talk with. And to get away from that overwhelming sadness amongst the internationals and the Kosovars since September eleven. Still hard for them to comprehend America being vulnerable to attack. All the best, Tom

Subject: SECURITY ENCRYPTED MESSAGE
Date: Thu, 13 Dec 2001 03:35 EST
Dirk. Cassie Borden and I met for coffee. She seemed to accept my identity as a writer. Christmas may give us time to strengthen my cover. Actually, as long as I submit regular articles, it's reality, hardly a cover. Tom

Thursday evening hadn't come quickly for Cassandra. She spent the endless afternoon in nervous apprehension, repeatedly sorting through her limited wardrobe, looking for something more dressy than her usual Kosova attire. She tried all her blouses and three skirts. She discarded the lot onto the bedroom floor. She needed to scrutinize everything again. Oh, she knew it was all good stuff. It just lacked pizzazz. At least she could accessorize. She had colourful scarves and the chain she bought at the gold shop at the top of the street. It was meant for a gift but she would use it. She didn't want to be business grey.

Tom said he'd meet her at the reception but she wasn't convinced he'd show. So she was pleased when he arrived shortly after she did. As she looked around, she realized how few of the Canadians serving in Prishtinë she actually knew. Sonja and Claire had gone home for a Christmas break as had others she knew only casually. Brian Castleman was the host that night. He introduced himself immediately when she arrived at the beautiful old house.

"Oh, Cassandra Borden. I recognize your name from my list."

"Your list?" she asked.

"The list of Canadians in Kosova. You were registered with Foreign Affairs when you began work here."

"Is that the same list you told me about?" She turned to face Tom as he waited his turn to be welcomed.

"Probably." Tom smiled, scanned the room, asked if he could get her a glass of wine, then headed off as if that was his mission. Cassie was surprised he didn't wait for the server making her way around the room. She watched him detour around the bar then walk straight toward a tall man apparently holding court at the edge of the room.


"Hey Frank."

"Tom! Good to see you again." Frank MacGregor thrust out his hand, grabbed Tom and pulled him into a hug. "I thought it was you. Who's the woman you were talking to?" They were out of earshot of others as Frank, diplomatic hand that he was, steered Tom quickly into an unoccupied corner.

"What're you doing here, Frank?"

"I'm at the embassy in Vienna but I oversee the Prishtinë office."

"Still science officer?"

"No... Political and Public Affairs. Promotion, you know. If you ever get to Vienna we could have a great night on the town. For old times sake. But enough about me. Who is she?"

"Cassandra Borden, she's..."

"Ah yes, the microbiologist. I suppose I should've realized you'd know her."

"I... Well, I... we're old friends. I ran into her the other day."

"You should introduce me. She keeps glancing this way." Frank nodded and smiled toward Cassie. "She's assessing me."

"She's not your type but I'll introduce you anyway."

"You know me. I'm easy."


"You and Tom obviously know each other. Has he interviewed you?" Cassie asked Frank after introductions were made.

Frank laughed. "Not yet."

"I thought Tom didn't have much to do with this office."

"I'm new here myself," Frank continued. "In charge actually. I'm gonna be here a couple times a month. You leaving for Christmas?"

"Yeah, I'm going to spend Christmas with my kids."

"Hmm, that's good. Tom, something more... talk with you later, Cassandra?" Tom followed Frank into one of the offices adjacent to the reception room.

"I like her, Tom. I'd be hitting on her myself if she wasn't with you." Tom tried to object but Frank continued. "You're a lucky guy," he went on, annoying Tom. "Look, I want you to know that Narong spends time in Prishtinë."

"What's he doing here?"

"Can't say. That's classified..." Frank laughed. "Actually, I'm kidding. I have no idea. Apparently, his brother has a restaurant here, the Thai something or other."

"I don't know any Thai restaurants."

"We should have dinner, Tom."

"When I'm back from home in March. We can talk then."


Tom and Cassie left shortly after, deciding to walk back to the city centre from the hilly Arberia location of the office. As they walked,

Cassie said, "I know this isn't an embassy but is it a consular office?"

"I don't know," Tom replied, wondering about Frank's presence in Kosova. "I've only heard it referred to as the office. Look, I apologize for spending so much time with Frank."

"That's okay. That's what these gatherings are for."

Tom smiled. Cassie looked around at the large houses, each with a view overlooking the city. Buildings, dusted with fresh snow, hanging onto the side of the hill gave a very European alpine appearance to that section of the city. Quite different from what she'd usually experienced of Prishtinë.

Date: Fri, 14 Dec 2001 11:53 EST

Dirk, I need to touch base with Narong. Is he currently in Europe? Tom

Saturday evening, Tom met Cassie for dinner at a restaurant she'd suggested. He didn't know *Il Passatore,* couldn't really place it by Cassie's directions, so he took a taxi rather than walk. The driver assured Tom he knew where it was. In fact, once they arrived Tom realized he could have walked and arrived easily before the taxi. This was the road to Gërmia Park. The driver followed a circuitous route through narrow roadways winding gently uphill, around poorly placed garbage bins, erratically parked vehicles and deep, unfenced construction craters.

As Tom walked through the doorway into the reception area, Cassandra stood near the poorly lit bar, talking with a small, slightly built woman with light brown hair. He thought Cassie looked good.

Maybe a little thinner, just a trace of grey in her hair. She didn't appear to realize Tom had arrived. The other woman didn't look Kosovar. She wore a long white apron almost to her ankles. Like a baker might wear, Tom thought.

This anteroom reminded Tom of a Scottish bothy, dimly lit, though the two men seated at the bar were better dressed than most fishermen. Tom assessed them as locals. They regarded his arrival expressionlessly, unimpressed. He wasn't whomever they were expecting. Along the wall opposite the bar was a woodstove, stovepipe jerry-rigged and placement peculiar. A dog lay passively beside the stove, unaware its precarious positioning on loose bricks wouldn't be acceptable if local building code enforcement or restaurant inspection was functional. The dog's presence surprised Tom. Any dogs he'd encountered in Prishtinë were feral, skulking things, wandering the streets around dusk and during the night, lurking around garbage bins. Tom started to wonder why Cassie chose this place when the woman, Antonella, the restaurant owner, greeted Tom excitedly, then looked back at Cassie.

"Oh, is good. You bring your man tonight." She grabbed Cassie's shoulders, kissed both her cheeks and nodded her approval.

Antonella escorted them up a few stairs into a large spacious room, the lighting level again low but with a starkly different feeling from the entranceway. Light orange stucco walls and well spaced tables gave a Mediterranean ambiance. In one corner was a woodstove, this one properly installed. As they were being seated at their table, a smart-looking waiter in white shirt and black tie appeared to explain the antipasto bar, the evening's menu and to take drink orders.

Dinner started with Tom and Cassie making selections from the antipasto bar – interesting salads, shellfish, roasted eggplant, dips and condiments. Then, when they were ready, seafood linguine was served at their table.

"You seem to know this restaurant," Tom said.

"I've come to know Antonella," Cassie replied. "She's from Italy but she has another restaurant in Albania, in Tirana. Now she says she prefers to live in Prishtinë. *Il Passatore* is my favourite in Prishtinë. I've been a few times… with friends."

"Dates?"

"Is this a date, Tom?" Cassie spoke abruptly. We need to deal with Chicago, she thought. Maybe not now. Maybe this isn't the right time.

"Sorry, just curious. A good looking woman like you…"

"In her fifties!"

"Nothing wrong with that. You look good."

"A lot of men working here act as if they're single. I'm not interested. You know me better than that."

"Of course I do. I'm sorry."

"You picked a nice wine, Tom," said Cassie.

"Yeah, I'm surprised at the wine selections here. Good Italian and Greek varieties at the grocery store. Even a few French and Aussie. Some good local ones, too. Kosova Red from Gjakovë. Sells for two euros at the fruit market near your place."

"Is Gjakovë agricultural?"

"Oh, absolutely. Not yet back on its feet. It'll be the major farming area eventually. Most of the landmines have been cleared."

"Did you ever meet Michèle Lesage? The mine clearer?"

"No, she was on my list. I thought landmine clearing would make a good article. When I tried to contact her, she'd been assigned back to Canada. I've made another interview appointment with CLCA for when I come back in March."

"You said you'd be leaving soon."

"Yeah. I've accumulated enough material to write from home for a while. Will your kids be home for Christmas?"

"For sure. I'm looking forward to being with them."

"I'll catch up with family myself – my parents, my brother Keith in Ottawa. Course when I'm in Ottawa I'll spend time with my friend Bert as well."

"So you won't be that far from my new place."

"New place? You're not still in Toronto?"

"Church Hill. About an hour from Ottawa."

"How do you handle work?"

"I've taken a long leave-of-absence. You might come over some time." Cassie smiled at him.

"I'd like that!"

"My mother'll be there… And my kids, of course. Maybe even my sister. You remember Karen?"

"Of course. I'd love to see Karen again."

"Please come. And don't be nervous. Doug won't be there." Good, I got that out. I'm sure Tom's been wondering.

"Oh, I …"

"It's okay."

"Cass…"

"My kids had their father around until I just couldn't stand another day. We shared custody, if you're wondering."

"I'm sorry, Cass…"

"Don't be. Doug and I weren't compatible. I don't know why we were ever attracted to each other. Oh, it worked for a time, but… I'm actually here to escape… to escape Doug…" And to escape you, my memories. Then she said, "Let's get out of here, Tommy…"

"I'm sorry, I didn't mean…"

"No, no, Tommy. Come back to my place for coffee and dessert. We can walk past the bakery on my corner. It's early. They'll still be open. They have the best baklava. And…" she hesitated. "You could get us a bottle of Kosova Red from the fruit market."

He smiled at her. "That'd be great."

They shared the best part of two bottles of Kosova Red at Cassie's apartment, sitting around her kitchen table. Talked comfortably about everything except Chicago. After a while, Tom leaned from his chair, lifted her chin with his hand and kissed her. To his delight, she answered.

He thought what followed had been wonderful. She responded to his every touch. Eventually she turned away from him and he fell asleep hugging her from behind, his hands tenderly cupping her breasts. When he awoke an hour or so later, he reached for her. She wasn't there. He pulled on his clothing, walked out to the living/dining area. She was seated at the table in her housecoat, her arms wrapped across her body as if she was cold. She appeared to be staring at the wall opposite her in the darkened room.

"You okay?" he asked.

She smiled weakly, as if she were a videophone image from another continent. "I'm fine," she said. "Just thinking. I didn't want to disturb your sleep." She didn't object when Tom gently massaged her shoulders but she didn't respond or encourage him to continue.

"Maybe I should go home now," he said more as a question than a statement. When she simply nodded he asked, "Anything you need to do before your flight?"

"I'd like to spend a few hours Monday at the lab. Maybe I could show you around."

"I need to meet Agron tomorrow to plan my schedule for when I'm back. Maybe I can meet you at the lab Monday."

Date: Sat, 15 Dec 2001 12:09 EST

Hello Thomas. We will meet for kafe Sunday afternoon at Freskia. Go for a hike at Gërmia. Stay on the path, ha, ha! We will meet by accident at the restaurant. No hiking buddies please. Agron

Agron told Tom the locals he interviewed were surprised by the discovery of a mass grave at Gedima. He suggested the site could be far older than they first suspected. Maybe far more nefarious also. Bodies from another area was his best guess. Someone had knowledge of the caves... burying evidence of an outbreak ... or biological testing? Tom decided to withhold speculation about the Gedima caves from Dirk for now since they didn't know if real evidence would emerge.

Date: Sun, 16 Dec 2001 18:36 EST

Dirk, I'll be flying home the twenty-first. Loose ends need to be tidied up before I leave. Agron's been to Pejë again because of the cases of cervical and submandibular lymphadenopathies. This week, Agron's friend Fisnik examined one patient with a necrotic ulceration – could be an inoculation point, possibly a tick bite. And bingo, differential diagnosis changed from hypothyroidism to tularaemia. Clinical only, none of this lab confirmed. There's no ability to culture class three organisms. No containment facilities. I'm not attaching particular import since tularaemia's endemic. Unusual presentation, though. Best, Tom

They met at the lab Monday afternoon. Cassie introduced Tom to the staff members working that day. Afterward, they walked downtown.

"I couldn't change my flight," Cassie said as they approached where Tom's apartment lay south of Mother Teresa Boulevard and Cassie's was still three blocks west. In the fervour of the weekend, they'd discussed trying to fly home together. But she didn't contact Austrian Airlines as she promised she would. "It's a time of year thing. All flights are fully booked." She thought that sounded reasonable.

"Yeah, I know." Tom looked away. He shivered involuntarily. The damp December cold pierced his jacket and sweater. The drab, grey buildings failed to hold his interest. Time to go home, he thought.

Christmas Day, Tom drove about an hour from Keith's house in Ottawa to Cassie's in Church Hill. He'd been nervous before he arrived, uncertain about her family dynamics and his introduction into that *milieu*. He'd met Karen on a number of occasions over the years. Jeremy and Marianne he'd last seen as much younger kids at a lab party or picnic. Now he'd be meeting Cassie's mother for the first time. He got there mid-afternoon, still daylight but with the December sun slipping toward the horizon. Enough light, though, to be impressed with the log and post-and-beam structure. She'd called it a cottage, he remembered from Prishtinë, her log cabin in the woods. Must be over two thousand square feet. In the woods was right, though. He was always surprised how much of the land this close to the capital was rural. Farms, bush, villages. Inside he was impressed by the beautiful, naturally finished pine ceilings, the tasteful mix of natural wood and calming colours. When Cassie opened the door in response to his knock, the welcoming fragrance of cooking floated toward him. This place is really Cassie, he thought. He wondered how she was able to decorate for Christmas when she'd only arrived home from Kosova a couple of days before. Arriving into Pearson airport late evening and grabbing the last shuttle flight to Ottawa. She must be tired.

Cassie's mother, Shelagh, greeted him politely, but even after he'd been there several hours, he felt she regarded him suspiciously. She's not sure she wants to like me. She's wondering about my status with Cass. What I'm doing here.

Cassandra had welcomed him warmly with an embrace and a quick brush on the lips, then seemed to stiffen and pull back as he tried to prolong the hug. That confused him at first. Then, she introduced him as an old friend from the forensics lab but said nothing about their shared experience of Kosova. She wasn't ready to acknowledge Prishtinë. He almost missed the puzzled look Karen shot her sister before Karen took over hosting duties and offered Tom a drink. Tom knew her well enough to make small talk easy. He was surprised, though, when she asked nothing about Kosova or his writing career.

At the dinner table, Cassie asked Jeremy to carve the turkey. Cassie, her mother and Karen had teamed up to produce what they called a country kitchen Christmas dinner – turkey, mashed potatoes, dressing, broccoli, cauliflower, green beans, cranberry sauce and what Cassie called her *pièce de résistance*, a sweet potato casserole topped with ground pecans and decorated with pecan halves. Actually she jokingly called it her piece of resistance.

"It's a recipe I got from *Canadian Living* magazine in the nineties," she explained for Tom's benefit. "It was an issue where celebrities donated favourite holiday feast recipes. Remember the Blue Jays catcher Pat Borders? This was his contribution. It's become such a family favourite I wouldn't dare not make it for Christmas or Thanksgiving."

"I like it a lot," Tom said. "It's great."

"Now we just refer to it as the Pat Borders."

The dinner table was set in Cassie's dining room for the six of them. There was little conversation at the table until Jeremy started to tease his sister about something Tom missed the significance of. Cassie and Tom conversed very little. He really didn't know how to talk with her under these different circumstances. Cassie had told him enough that he was able to engage with Marianne about her accounting studies, her job and her specialization.

Tom turned to Cassie when Marianne got up to start clearing away dinner plates. "She's sure grown up since I last saw her," he said. "I see a lot of you in her." I don't recognize anything of Doug, at all.

"I'll take that as a compliment."

"She's beautiful, of course, but I also see some of your mannerisms."

"Really?" Cassie expressed surprise. "I've never thought we're particularly alike."

"I think so but maybe I just see you in a new light."

Cassie smiled briefly, then frowned and excused herself to help with the table clearing.

After dinner, in the living room, Karen offered Tom a *liqueur.* He was tempted but declined her suggestion.

"It's good to see you again, Tom," Karen said quietly. "I'm glad you were able to come." Karen didn't say anything more. Tom realized she stopped talking because Cassie came into the living room.

"Tommy, I'm really glad you came. Will you stay?" Cassie asked.

"Thanks, Cass. I really think I should go back to Keith's tonight. I'll call you about getting together in Ottawa."

"I'd like that a lot." Tom believed Cassie's words were genuine. But he sensed a sadness in her demeanour and interpreted a mixture of excitement and relief on her face. She doesn't know where we're headed. And with good reason. We have to deal with Chicago. He missed the euphoria of their last weekend in Prishtinë.

"So, when are we going to meet her?" Bert asked on the phone. He had already asked Tom about how Christmas dinner had gone at Cassie's. Tom said everything went well. He would have welcomed Bert's advice – they had talked about each other's relationships since they were teenagers – but he thought he needed to sort it out himself.

"I was planning to make reservations for the four of us at Vittoria Trattoria for Sunday dinner. That work for you?" Tom said.

"Sounds good. Let me check with Suzanne and I'll get back to you."

"Okay. Good."

"Plan to come here first as an icebreaker. We'll have a drink. It'll be more comfortable here than a restaurant for meeting the first time," Bert offered.

"Yeah, good idea. Then we can relax."

"I'm looking forward to this. Meeting your new *femme*."

"It's been awhile since I've been to Vittoria's. Not since you and I were there in the summer. I'm really looking forward to this."

# Part 3

# January – October  2002

# one

# January 2002
## *Mirëpo, nesër*

"Maybe we could talk about a few days skiing," he said. "Maybe at Mont Tremblant."

"Sure, Tommy, I'd like you to come," she replied, surprised to perceive an anxious note in Tom's voice.

"I've got an article to finish but I can be there before noon."

Cassie was pleased to hear from Tom. She'd enjoyed dinner with Bert and Suzanne. She found them an easy couple to be with. No demanding questions but able to talk about almost anything. Interested in whatever she and Tom were willing to share. She was able to be herself. And being with Tom for the first time since Christmas dinner was easier than she anticipated. She didn't regret inviting him as much as she regretted her own uneasiness around her family. She'd frozen. Not able to explain Tom. Suddenly ashamed, no not that. Just reluctant to admit to what she frighteningly realized might only have been a fling. Admit in front of her family to being impulsive. To her kids and mother. Karen understood, she thought. And both Jeremy and Marianne liked him. But, she'd overheard her mother talking quietly with Karen. Something about Tom being easier to get along with than Doug but she wouldn't trust him. Something about recognizing a con man. C'mon mother, what would you know of con men?

Then, Tom phoned to ask about coming up to her place from Toronto Saturday. This was so much different from Prishtinë. Asking permission to visit. She missed just dropping in on friends. She knew Tom took writing as seriously as he'd taken his role at the forensics lab. In Prishtinë, he didn't talk much about his interviews though he did mention Agron had introduced him to the President of Kosova.

"Did you have much of a chance to talk?" she asked him then.

"Sure, we talked for about an hour."

"Are you planning an article?"

"Mm..." he said. "Not really. It was deep background." Then Tom changed the subject. She was okay with that. She'd worked with him at the forensics lab where information was shared on a need-to-know basis. Sometimes she consulted Tom when she needed someone to take a fresh look at her results. And he did the same with her. Until he left with no explanation.


Tom arrived late Saturday morning in time for lunch. Jeremy talked with them awhile but was off to Ottawa with some friends to skate on the Rideau Canal. Tom and Jeremy chatted easily about his course load at the University of Ottawa.

"Where do you see yourself in five years?" Tom asked then tried to retract immediately. "Sorry about that. I hate being asked that myself."

"It's okay. I've thought about it a lot. My goal is a PhD like Mom and Dad."

"That's a lot of pressure."

"Yeah, maybe. But it's what I'm aiming for. Do you have a PhD?"

"I have. In microbiology. From McGill."

Cassie busied herself with clearing away the lunch dishes while Tom and Jeremy were talking, then she sat back down after Jeremy had left. "His friends wanted to head out earlier but he talked them into waiting a bit when he knew you were coming," she said. She felt thankful for that.

"That's nice," Tom said. He smiled at Cassie.

Tom and Cassie lingered comfortably over coffee. After a while, Tom shifted around in his chair as if unable to find a comfortable position. He lifted his coffee cup and immediately replaced it on the tabletop.

"Cass," Tom began. "I'd like to explain what I can about Chicago."

Cassie looked at him but said nothing.

"I know you must have been upset when I didn't contact you," Tom continued. "I thought you might not understand."

"What was I supposed to understand?"

"I didn't really know what was happening myself until the last minute. I worked with *The Magazine* off and on. Now they wanted me full time."

"That's the reason? Is that what you're saying?"

"I wasn't coming back to the lab. I thought if I showed up in Chicago then left, you'd feel taken for granted."

"Taken for granted? You think? Maybe I could've dealt with that."

"I'm sorry, Cass. I didn't intend…"

"I felt abandoned. Dumped. Discarded."

"I'm sorry, Cass. Maybe this isn't such a great idea. I don't know how to deal with it. I'm uneasy and I'm sure you are too. I've seen it in your eyes."

"My eyes? What have you seen there?"

"Doubt."

"Doubt?"

"And Bert's always told me…"

"Bert? You've discussed our relationship with Bert?"

"No… no. I was just…"

"You discussed me with Bert!"

"No, Cass, let me..."

"So he was assessing me at the restaurant?"

"No, Cass..."

"What'd he do? Report back to you?"

"Of course not."

"But you needed his support to deal with me. I thought we were friends. Why couldn't you have just picked up the fucking phone?"

"Dammit Cassie, I'm sorry. Don't you understand that? I'm trying to tell you I'm sorry."

"No, what I don't understand is why you didn't call me. You humiliated me. Destroyed my marriage. And on top of that, you weren't even there for me. And now you've got nothing to offer except this nonsense."

"Cassie, please let's..."

"Please leave, Tom. Just leave."

"You've gotta be kidding! I just got here..."

"Tom..."

"I'm trying to explain. You really want me to leave?"

"Yes!" she shouted.

"Fine."

After he left, she leaned against the door, visualizing Chicago, her anticipation of a wonderful weekend, a wonderful future, then the jolting realization he wasn't coming. She'd hoped he was okay. Hadn't had an accident. Maybe it was simpler, something beyond his control – his flight delayed. But this was Tom, logistics expert. He knew how to contact her. He would phone as soon as he could. When he didn't, she knew he'd have a tale of missed connections, dead phone batteries, emergency response to an outbreak of Lassa fever. They'd laugh at it Monday at the lab. But she was left with a feeling of dread. And the biggest insult? When she got home, self-consciously aware her face probably showed her distress, it was Doug who told her Tom had resigned and left the lab, was gone the day after she left for Chicago. Doug seemed to enjoy her disquiet. What had he known?

She watched Tom walk purposely toward his car. He didn't look back. Not even to see if she was watching. Before opening the car door, he raised his palms in exasperation and quickly dropped them in a gesture of frustration. Then as he slipped into the driver's seat, she thought he seemed to slump momentarily. She couldn't see his face but his shoulders showed defeat, exactly what she herself was feeling. Defeat. Anguish. She watched him drive slowly out her laneway without once looking back.

Damn him. She sat back down at the table but knew she didn't want more coffee. She picked up her phone but didn't really know why. It was no longer Tom she wanted to talk to. She had such high hopes for today. Damn him. She realized even if she wanted to call him she didn't know Tom's cell number, or indeed, if he even owned a mobile phone. She was confused by her sudden awareness of how little she actually knew of Tom's life. She pressed Marianne's speed-dial number. When Doug answered she almost hung up.

"Hello?" he said a second time.

"Oh, hello Doug, it's Cassie. Sorry, I thought I called Marianne." Why do I have his number on speed-dial?

"She's just cleaning up so she asked me to answer. I can get her."

"No, it's okay. I just wanted to make sure... you know... to make sure she got back home from my place okay."

"Home? From Christmas? That was almost two weeks ago."

"No, no. I know that. I mean I wanted to say hello. See how work's going. That stuff, you know."

"She's waving hello. Says she'll call you back later."

"Fine then. I'll just..."

"It's good to talk to you, Cassie. Glad you're back home. You're not thinking of going back there are you? Surely you've had enough of that crap by now..."

She let Doug continue as she gently replaced her handset in its cradle. I'm glad he's never called me Cass. That's so special with Tommy. Dammit Tommy, why couldn't you be straight with me.

The second call she made was to Karen.

Tom drove about ten kilometres from Cassie's before he pulled over onto the shoulder of the highway. He wasn't really sure how the mood had changed that quickly. Cassandra was so angry. He wanted to turn around and head back. He grabbed his phone but immediately replaced it into its holder. It's too soon to call. It'll add fuel to the fire. I was so wrong but how could I have said it differently – I couldn't come to Chicago because they wanted me to go to Thailand, infiltrate the national lab and steal some viruses?

It all happened so fast that afternoon in 1996.

"Everything's ready," Dirk O'Reilly had said. "You leave tonight for Kuala Lumpur."

"Tonight? I didn't expect things would happen that fast."

"We've got you accredited as a journalist for the APEC meeting in Malaysia. Things are moving. We need you there."

"What about the Thailand plan?"

"You'll fly to Bangkok right after APEC. Actually, you're attending only some preliminary meetings. You'll be gone by the time the bigwigs get there."

"Why?"

"You'll be there to observe the planning sessions for the

management of displaced persons and refugees. That'll be your focus for *The Magazine*."

"I thought I'd start by writing general scientific articles."

"No time for that. Things in the Balkans are not going to quiet down. We need you to establish credibility as a writer before you go to Bosnia. You'll be there about six months unless something else develops. We expect Serbia will put down the unrest in Kosova. There'll be no story there."

"If I leave tonight I need to go back to the forensics lab."

"You've already resigned."

"What?"

"You're using vacation time in lieu of giving a month's notice."

"How do you do this?"

"They've agreed to maintain your pension and benefit contributions."

"Huh!" Tom responded. "Anything else?"

"When you meet Narong Amranand in Bangkok, he'll fill you in on some suspicious anthrax deaths near the Cambodian border."

"Suspicious? How so? It's farmland."

"Just practical experience for the Balkans."

"So, tonight? Can't it wait 'til next week?"

"No, it's tonight." Dirk's tone was insistent.

"What's my itinerary, then?"

"Pearson, O'Hare, Los Angeles…"

"O'Hare? You mean I'll be in Chicago."

"Just to change planes."

"What about a stop-over?" I could still meet Cassie.

"Like I said, you'll change planes."

"One night even?" I need to explain to Cassie. I can't just not show up, he thought.

They had been friends and colleagues for close to thirty years. They occupied adjacent labs in Toronto. An association based on professional respect quickly developed into an at work friendship. They genuinely liked each other yet, for several years, knew nothing of each other's personal lives. Something they avoided discussing. Tom was single at the time, having been through a cascade of short-term relationships. Somehow, unintentionally, Cassie became his gold standard, especially after they began to, as she called it, date. It began innocently.

"I'm stuck with an extra ticket for *Cats*," she'd said as they took a late coffee break together. "Nobody I've called can make it on short notice."

"When's the performance?" Then, knowing Cassie was a theatre subscriber, he suggested, "Can you exchange for another time?"

"There's no point – Doug doesn't want to go anyway."

Tom laughed. "I'd love to see *Cats*," he said.

"You'd go with me?"

"When is it?"

"Tonight. Eight o'clock."

Tom glanced at his watch. "Well, I guess we'd better hurry."

They enjoyed being together for something other than a work function. Over the next year, Cassie seemed to be able to line up friends to accompany her to other theatre events. Then, she asked Tom again and again and they became theatre buddies. They never talked about whether Doug minded. Eventually, Cassie telephoned one night to say she was coming over to Tom's condo, a place she'd never visited. She brought an Australian Shiraz with her.

After some preliminary banter, Cassie delicately manoeuvred the conversation. "Tommy, I think you know I'm attending the FMS meeting in Chicago as the lab delegate."

Tom waited for her to continue.

"And I know you're going as a member of the executive." Laboratory policy allowed only one senior microbiologist to attend any professional meeting or conference. They'd never attended the same event together. "There're so many things I'd like to do in Chicago," she said. "Art galleries, theatres, restaurants – and I'd like to do them with you." She surprised herself with her boldness.

They sipped wine, laughed, looked at the tourist pamphlets Cassie brought with her, and agreed to extend their trips by two days.

"Would you be comfortable if we shared a room?" Tom asked.

Cassie touched Tom on the arm, laughed, and kissed him.


"C'mon Tom. What's special about Chicago?" Dirk said.

"Forensic Microbiology Society meeting. I'd planned a couple days there."

"You're not still on the executive?"

"No, no, I resigned everything so I'd be ready to disappear like you suggested."

"Your itinerary's set. We need you in Malaysia *tout de suite*."

Dirk really didn't need to conscript me, I was keen. I should've known how upset Cassie would be. I should have called her. I should have followed my instincts in Kosova. Found a way to avoid her completely. She deserves better. I can't call her now – maybe tomorrow or Monday.


"Hey, sis," Karen let herself in the door and walked into Cassie's foyer.

"Hey, kg. Thanks for coming." Cassie hugged her sister.

"You look good. Better than I imagined from the phone call."

"Can you stay over? Jeremy's decided to stay in Ottawa tonight."

"Sure. You know I'm always ready to stay."

"Do you think I should look for a condo in Ottawa?"

"Pardon me?"

"You know, for Jeremy while he's a student. We could rent the extra rooms to other students. Should be tax benefits there. Whadda ya think?"

"Cassie, you didn't ask me here for a real estate consultation."

"No, of course not. It's something I just thought of. Jeremy's going to continue living in Ottawa."

"What do you really want to talk about?"

"We had a fight, a big one that..."

"Okay. You and..."

"Tom. There's nobody else." Cassie's tone showed her irritation with Karen's question.

"Okay. Just trying to figure out the parameters here."

"Don't you start with the professional talk. Parameters, indeed. Bad enough one of us had professional help."

"What in the world are you talking about?" Karen asked.

"That's what galls me most. Tommy was talking with Bert and Bert must've told him something about dealing with unfinished business. Well, it's finished now. He needed Bert to tell him to talk to me. I'm sounding crazy, aren't I? I'm hurting and it's Tom's fault."

"Tell me who Bert is."

"Tom's friend, Albert Tindall."

"The psychiatrist?"

"Yeah. He's Tom's best friend. We had dinner with him and his wife."

Karen waited for Cassie to continue.

"Maybe I blew everything out of proportion."

"Wanna tell me about it?"

Karen was a good listener, touching Cassie's hands gently, giving her a hug during the most emotional elements and never laughing at angry retorts Cassie herself was beginning to see as irrational. "And the worst part," Cassie laughed for the first time. "Now I feel like I'm the one to blame."

"So you were planning to have an affair and leave Doug. I wish I'd known."

"What?"

"I would've sent flowers."

"It didn't happen, kg."

"I know and I'm sorry. But look at the bright side. Maybe that eventually helped you leave. It's never easy. Listen to me, doling out relationship advice as if I ever kept one together. You got any good red wine, Cass? I mean really good."

"I had a little cognac before you came. But what the heck." Cassie chose a *Côtes du Rhône*. "How's this?" She read from the label, "Grenache, syrah and mourvèdre." She knew it would have been Tom's choice to share with her. Ironically comforting, she thought.

"Until Tom, I'd never been with a man other than Doug."

Karen started to protest she didn't need to hear these intimacies when she stopped and fixed Cassie with a quizzical stare. "What?"

Cassie started then realized her sister's point. "Oh, Benjamin, I almost forgot. And then Gerald. But that was before Doug. Remember how we used to refer to them as Ben and Jerry and roar with laughter. But I'm talking serious stuff now."

"You know what happens between a couple is no one else's business," Karen said. "But you're on a roll, kid. Keep talking – as long as it doesn't become my turn to disclose my brilliant disasters."

Cassie laughed, feeling much better now. Lately, the two sisters enjoyed each other's company in a way they hadn't since their student days. Since then relationships, real or imagined seemed to get in the way. Then family and professional responsibilities. After they talked awhile, Cassie made a pizza with dough Tom had made and brought with him from Toronto. The irony built exponentially with her blood alcohol level.

It was after Cassie opened a second bottle, this one of lesser vintage, she said to Karen, "I can't believe we're discussing our sex lives. But you know, I was just remembering the pregnancy test you did for me when you were a medical student. Boy, was I worried." Cassie laughed, then continued, "I wasn't thinking. I can't remember now whether that was Ben or Jerry. Just think I could have screwed my life up with one of them instead of Doug."

"Cass, let's not go there."

"It's okay. I'm not getting maudlin or anything. But that's when I got serious. After that scare. After that I've only been to bed with Doug. And now Tom."

"Let's eat something, Cass. We can have more wine later."

"You know, Tom is a much better lover than Doug. As for the ice-cream twins, they were just kids."

"Cass, don't say anything you'll regret telling me."

"When?"

"Tomorrow. In the morning."

"Oh, I'm not gonna bother with morning. I'm gonna sleep 'til afternoon."

"We'll see."

"And, kg…"

"Cass?"

"I wanna talk to Tommy."

"Well, as you said yourself, you could just pick up the fucking phone."

"I said that didn't I. The fucking phone. I don't think I've ever said fuck in my life."

"Okay, Cass. That's enough. Let's get something to eat."

"I won't do it, kg. I won't be the one to phone."


Later that night, Tom glanced at the time displayed on his clock radio before he grabbed his phone. Three-thirty-four. He shook his head as if to dislodge cobwebs and cleared his throat before he answered.

"Hello." No response so he tried again, "Hello."

"You called me."

"Hello, Cassie."

"Tommy."

"Yes, Cass."

"Tommy, I can't sleep."

"Are you okay?"

"No, Tommy. I had too much wine."

"Do you need help?"

"No, Karen's here. I got drunk after she went to bed. I've been awake all night."

"You're sure you're okay?" Tom asked.

"I'm glad you left me a message. I thought you might not call me again."

"I'm glad you phoned back."

"Would you have called me again, Tommy?"

"Of course I would. I've been awake most of the night myself."

"I told Karen I wouldn't be first to call."

"Are you okay, Cass?"

"I'm drunk. I need to sleep. I listened to your voice on the message."

"I'm glad you called back."

"I'm tired, Tommy. Will you call me again?"

"Of course, Cass. I'll call you tomorrow."

"Oh, maybe not tomorrow 'cause I'm doing things with Karen."

"Okay, I'm going to visit Keith for a day or so."

"I feel so good when I'm with you, Tommy."

"Cass, this is all my fault and I'm truly sorry."

"I'm so tired now. Will you call me soon and talk to me?"

"Of course I will, Cass." I'll call, he thought, but I'll have no better explanation.

two

# February 2002
## *Shkurt*

Several weeks later, they were at Tom's Toronto condo. They'd seen each other a few times in the preceding weeks and had talked almost every day on the phone.

"Tommy, when are you going back to Prishtinë?" Cassandra asked.

"Early April. In about six weeks."

"I'd really like to spend some time together before you go."

"Anything in mind?"

"Maybe my place..." she suggested, then hesitated. She reached across the table, rested her hand gently on the back of his. "My place hasn't been kind to us, has it?"

"You know Cass, we talked about going skiing."

"I'd love that."

"Okay, you're on!" Tom stood, pulled Cassie out of her chair into his arms and kissed the top of her head. Then he leaned back slightly until he could see her eyes. "We could probably get Keith's condo at *Tremblant*. If he hasn't rented it out."

"That'd be great." She hesitated then said, "I have the feeling I need to make up for lost time. I..."

"Then, why don't I come to your place and we can leave from there."

"I'm sorry the winter turned out the way it did..."

Tom kissed her deeply before she could say more. Then he spoke again, "I am curious about Doug."

"Oh, I'm finished with him. He can't come skiing."

"I'm serious. You'd mentioned joint custody."

"That's over. Jeremy's nineteen. Well, not completely over. There's still education costs to split. Doug hardly ever exercised his option to see Jeremy. But he fought like hell for custody."

"He doesn't see his own son?"

"He fully expects I'll get Kosova out of my blood and return to him. I'm sure he still expects Jeremy to miss him and pressure me to return."

"And, in those circumstances, would you?"

"Are you crazy? I want you. I love you. I'd never have kept Jeremy away from his father. But you know, if he'd wanted to live with Doug, it would've broken my heart, but I wouldn't have stood in his way. Anyway, Doug's not an issue. My family is. You met them and they like you. "

"He may take more interest in Jeremy if he thinks there's competition."

"And well he should."

"You're going to need to leave soon," Tom reminded Cassie.

"You're not coming?"

"I'm coming, but not today. I need to pack my ski stuff. And phone my brother about the condo."

"I'll wait."

"No, you get back home. Spend an evening with your son. Because when I'm there, I'll be very demanding of your time."

"*Oh la la!*"

"And Cass."

"Yes?"

"I love you, too."

# three

# March 2002
## *Pasnesër*

"I'm glad you could get the condo," Cassie said. "I'm thankful I've already met Keith and Amy. It'd be hard for me to stay at someone else's place if I didn't know them."

"They're there this weekend but by the time we arrive, they'll have cleared out. Working people, you know. They'll be back next Friday night."

"Tommy, should we drive separately? I'd like to come back at the end of the week."

Tom's smile disappeared. "I thought we'd planned two weeks together," he said.

"No, no. It's just the weekend. Jeremy'll be home. I'm away so much I hate to miss spending time with him when I can."

"He knows what we're doing this week?"

"Of course. I gave him the contact numbers and stuff."

"No sense both of us driving. Is it okay if I come back too?" Tom's voice expressed anxiety.

"I'd like that."

"Okay. We'll come back for the weekend." Tom grabbed Cassie in a hug. His smile returned. "Keith and Amy are staying with us at the condo next week so we'll have more than enough time with them."

"They seem like good people."

The following Thursday, Tom prepared one of his signature dishes for dinner. Cassie had tasted some of Tom's cooking in Prishtinë, but most of their shared meals had been at restaurants. Now Tom was making eggplant rolls, although, presumably because they were in Québec, he insisted they were *rouleaux d'aubergines*. She loved that about Tom. His silliness. She thought about the restaurant in the old village the one night they ate out.

"*Du café, monsieur?*" the server asked. Tom appeared to search for her meaning and answered yes in Albanian.

"*Po,*" he said, even though he had ordered their meals in better than passable French.

It's been a great week, she thought. Wonderful weather, good ski conditions, nice to be with Tommy again.

"I'm really enjoying our week, Cass," Tom said as though agreeing with her thoughts. "But my poor legs need a break," he said affecting a limp. He sat down and rubbed his knees. "If we don't go home, I'll need to ski the bunny hill until I recover."

Tom talked about heading back to Church Hill for the weekend as if it'd been his idea from the beginning. He tries so hard to make me comfortable, Cassie thought.

"I guess I could meander gently down the mountain on *La Crête* and the Nanson trails. But it's better to rest up. Keith's a black-diamond skier. We'll be spending next week on the McCulloch, Taschereau and Ryan and over on the north side."

"We did all that this week." Cassie wrinkled her forehead in puzzlement.

"I know but we won't tell Keith. He'll want to guide us with his superior knowledge of the place. We'll indulge him."

"Brothers! You guys are so competitive."

"*Moi*, I don't have a competitive bone in my body." Tom laughed.

Sunday evening, Tom and Cassandra returned to Mont Tremblant. Keith and Amy were back from the slopes and had a fire going in the fireplace.

"Welcome, *bienvenue*," Keith stretched his arms out to greet them. "Glad you didn't trash the joint. When I read your note I figured you'd broken all the wine glasses and decided to flee."

"Good to see you too, bro."

"Actually, you I've seen too much of the last fifty or sixty years. It's Cassie I'm going to pay attention to now." Keith grabbed Cassie in a bear hug.

"Don't worry about him. He's all bluster," Amy interjected. "Tommy, I'm glad to see you, even if your brother isn't. And Cassandra, of course." Turning to Cassie she said, "Hope you had a good week."

"Oh, for sure, Amy."

"How's your son doing?"

"Really well, thanks," Cassandra answered Amy's question. "He loves Ottawa, though his father had wanted him to move in with him and go to one of the Toronto universities."

"He's at U of O?"

"Yeah, he decided on the basis of graduate school opportunities. I'm proud of him for that. He's impressed U of O is intensely research oriented."

"Oh, it's that alright. I did my master's there."

"What field?"

"Biostatistics."

"So you're a math whiz."

"Maybe not whiz but I've always had an aptitude. And, well, it led to a good government job at StatsCan."

Cassandra offered to prepare dinner that night. She insisted she'd had a free ride to this point. She made one of her favourite baked pastas, full of broccoli and red peppers, shrimps and sea scallops, the big ones. She didn't have much liking for small bay scallops. She prepared a tomato sauce with just enough hot pepper to notice but not to overwhelm. And then whole wheat linguine. After she tossed the noodles with the other ingredients, ever so lightly sautéed, she topped the dish with a shredded Italian four cheese mix.

Once the pasta was in the oven, she joined the others around the fire sipping Keith's wine selection. Good choice, she thought, enough acidity and tannin structure to complement the seafood and stand up to the heat of the sauce. She looked at the label. *Le Clos Jordanne Pinot Noir.* She didn't know the winery but appreciated it was tough to produce a good *pinot noir* in Canada.

Keith followed her into the kitchen when she went back to check the oven and prepare a salad of mixed greens. They're so alike, she thought, but Keith's more outgoing.

"I'm glad you had a good week. Tom was so disappointed when you couldn't make it up in January," he said.

"Yes, I was quite frustrated myself." Cassie was unsure what excuse Tom had offered for the failure of their first planned ski trip. "But I'm really happy I had no commitments this time."

"I'm glad too. I'll go set the table."

# four

# April 2002
## *Më falni një moment*

Dirk O'Reilly had arranged to teleconference with Jordan Siemens and Greg Hanbruz. Before they started, he reminded them the conversation would be monitored. Just as with videoconferencing and electronic conferencing. A MIN requirement.

"That's the disclaimer," he said. "I have the signal our monitor's present so I'll start. Just a heads up. I haven't decided whether this is really a problem. I'd appreciate input. Tom Stephenson and Cassandra Borden met each other in Prishtinë in December. Subsequently they spent some time together over the winter."

Jordan Siemens suggested it might be an opportunity. "Do you really sense trouble? One thought though, Cassandra's such a straight shooter, it might be a problem if she discovered Tom's activities. She a stickler for honesty. Assuming they've become close."

"Close? Couple weeks together at Tremblant. That close enough?"

"She could inadvertently blow his cover."

"I've thought about that," Dirk replied. "I'm trying to assess the danger. At worst, he'd need to leave Kosova. Probably, though, he'd be useless for any other assignment."

"I could plant disinformation with Cassandra," Jordan offered.

"Good. I've already started a campaign with Tom. I know he's itching to establish lab capabilities for himself. Wants to follow leads without transporting specimens via diplomatic pouches. I told him the feds forbid the use of NGOs for intelligence gathering. I don't know whether we could drive a wedge between them. When the three of us worked together, they were very close. Anything from you Greg?"

"I've never met Tom Stephenson. I'm sure you agree, Jordan, Cassandra's good at delivering programs. If we're serious about rebuilding the public health system, we need her involvement. If you're thinking of pulling someone, Dirk, it can't be Cassandra. We can't lose a key delivery component and still expect CIDA support," Greg Hanbruz replied.

"Suggestions?"

"Can your architecture pull her into MIN? Even some minor role? She respects procedural confidentiality. She could become a good resource without anyone's knowledge."

"They're both strong microbiologists." Jordan explained he considered Tom's strength in virology and Cassie's in bacteriology and mycology to be complementary specialties. "I'm not suggesting we encourage or allow a union. But if we do nothing, just let events occur, it's possible we could achieve success in each of our programs."

"I can live with that. Do what we can to keep them apart including scheduling separate times in-country. Once things stabilize there, I'll need Tom to move on to one of the developing Asian theatres. I've already asked our contact at *The Magazine* to consider a new assignment. Unless there's anything else, that's all folks!"

"Dirk, it's Greg. Something you said earlier. The part about using NGOs for intelligence. Representing an NGO, should I know something about that? Is it true?"

"I have no idea. Canada doesn't have a foreign intelligence service. We only have domestic. Our arrangement's *ad hoc*. Seemed like a good comment at the time, though."

Date: Fri, 11 Apr 2002 18:26 EDT
From: Justine Tachereau
To: Dirk O'Reilly <doreilly@secure.gov.min.org>

Dirk, thanks for requesting my input. Let's not spook anybody. I don't know Thomas well. But I agree you should keep him away from Cassandra. We will need her later when Canada is not so involved. I'm going to phone you in the next five minutes. Justine

Dirk quickly answered his phone.

*"Bonjour, Dirk. Ici Justine."*

*"Merci bien, mon amie.* Thanks for being the monitor."

*"De rien.* No problem. I stop short of saying it was a pleasure."

"Seriously," Dirk continued. "I'm glad you were available. I really dislike having CSIS monitor. I don't trust them. They have their own agenda."

"I never understand the need for conversation monitoring. Your bunch is all on the same page. But I am happy to pick up the information about Cassandra and Thomas. I didn't know any of that."

"So, Justi, what are your plans for Cassandra?"

"Cassandra is not a field agent," Justine explained. "But I have asked her for some basic epidemiology data from Prishtinë region. She's given me some useful stats."

"Anything beyond that?"

"Dirk, you worked with her. You know she's a keen observer. Her eye for unusual detail is so good."

"Do we come clean with her? Will she react badly if she thinks she's being used?"

"Well, she can be an exceptional source. I could arrange for her to come to Montreal for minimal field ops training. But I have concerns with that. We need her to continue to be her usual self in the region. Above suspicion. I hope I can trust her to keep her mouth shut!"

"Tom's an old hand at concealment," Dirk said. "He wouldn't jeopardize your rookie agent! There's no need for them to work together though."

"Good. I will impress on Cassandra that no matter what seems to be happening she must not disclose her role to anyone. Thomas could rattle her if he identifies himself, though."

"Will she come on board?"

"Only reluctantly, I think. She must feel she is there to help, not to spy. To gather epidemiological data so we can design strategies the Kosovars can employ within their own system."

"I'm sure you've heard scuttlebutt that funding is about to be severely chopped?"

"What do you think is the plan?" Justine asked.

"Foreign Affairs and CIDA want to regionalize their approaches. Treat the whole Balkan area as one project."

"How would that work for Kosova?"

"I don't know. Imagine the logistical nightmare of running all operations out of Belgrade."

Neither spoke until Justine asked, "Isn't that like dealing with the enemy?"

"Well, let's hope they're pragmatic about it. I think they recognize the need to stabilize relations. They are neighbours."

"But not friendly neighbours."

"No. We need to maintain a presence in Kosova. We can't afford to lose track of developments in that part of the world. But, you know, so far, the change in focus and funding is only a rumour."

"Yeah, sounds like an Ottawa trial balloon."

"So, is that all, Justi?"

"Yes. But please Dirk, Siemens and Hanbruz have no need to know about Cassandra."

"Sure. Bye now. *À la prochaine.*"

"*Au revoir,* Dirk."

Tom intentionally arrived early at the Thai Palace restaurant in the Sunny Hill neighbourhood of Prishtinë. That provided him a brief opportunity to speak privately with Narong before Frank showed up.

"Hey Tom. Sorry I'm late. How'd you ever find this place? Taxi driver didn't know where it was. He drove around in circles before he stopped to ask directions."

"Glad you made it, Frank. Good to see you."

"Two young boys brought me through the alleyway. I gave them five euros. That appropriate?" Frank asked as he sat across from Tom.

He's really jazzed. Can't believe how talkative he is. Must've been concerned about walking through the narrow alleyways. He wouldn't realize how safe he actually was. No gang activity this far away from downtown. "They wouldn't have expected anything. But you've made friends for life. You're now responsible for their education, I think." Tom had come to enjoy ribbing Frank. Especially about local customs.

"What? No?"

"No. I jest. Cassie told me how to get here. She and her friends have been a couple times. They always seem to know the good restaurants."

Frank gazed around at Formica tables, folding chairs and bare walls with very few decorations. Not quite what he expected of a Thai restaurant. A poster of King Bhumibol, looking boyish belying his age, hung prominently, however. That redeemed the setting, he thought. Made it a real Thai restaurant.

Tom offered his opinion of Singha and Tiger beers both imported from Thailand. He characterized them as not a taste he liked, unsure whether they really stood up to hot food. "Best bet's Heineken or Efes. In Thailand, I usually stuck to the local version of Heineken. This is the real stuff here. What'd you drink over there?"

"Heineken's good with me."

"They'll make any dish mild or medium. Or as hot as you want."

"I'm good with hot."

"That's like Cassie. Way more into hot than me. I like the cooking style, crisp veggies, tasty noodles, coconut milk. A hint of hot's good but I don't want fire."

"How is Cassie? She back here?"

"She's well, thanks. She wanted to come tonight but had other things on her plate."

"That's too bad. Just you and me then, Tom?"

"Unless you've got something better to do on a Friday night." Tom ordered Pad Thai, medium hot with a Heineken pint.

Frank turned toward the waiter. "I don't see *Choo-Chee Plah Ga-Pong*. Can you make it?"

"Not on menu but chef make. How hot?"

"Make me cry!"

"Okay, sir. Usually dish for two."

"Can you do a half order with extra red curry sauce?"

"Excellent. And beer like your friend?"

"Yes."

"You let me ramble on about Thai food. Obviously, I shoulda known you were experienced," said Tom.


"More beer, Frank?" Sweat was pouring from Frank's face. Tears intermingled with sweat droplets. Looks like mission accomplished. They made him cry. Tom caught the waiter's eye. As Narong walked back toward their table, Tom was surprised to realize Frank hadn't recognized Narong. Although they knew of each other, he realized they may never have actually met.

Tom introduced Narong Amranand and Frank MacGregor. "Frank was the science contact at the embassy in Thailand. Has interesting stories to tell. You closing soon?"

"Soon as that other table leaves."

"You'll join us for a beer?"

"Of course, Tom."

They enjoyed a couple of beers with Narong until he decided he should resume his restaurant duties. "I need to clean up before I leave. But I'll meet you for coffee tomorrow, Tom. Will Agron and Cassie be there?"

Tom nodded affirmation then didn't wait until Narong was out of earshot before resuming conversation with Frank. "*The Magazine's* called me back to Canada for consultation."

"But you just returned."

"That's the nature of the beast. They're considering other projects. I wanna mention some of Cassandra's ideas for collaboration between the hospital lab and the forensic and agricultural labs. Maybe the Canadian Office would facilitate coordination since there're Canadians involved with each project... show support for a multidisciplinary approach."

"Sure, Tom. Partnerships between the hospital lab and the other labs would be good. Advancing a team approach is part of my mandate. Don't think that happens here naturally. Still powerful fiefdoms, if I can say that."

"Probably not the appropriate term, but I don't know the right one either." Tom laughed.

"With you making this request I get the feeling what we may discuss is classified?"

"Yes."

"I have security clearance. I keep Foreign Affairs secrets all the time." Frank paused for emphasis before continuing, "You seem to know Narong well."

"You already know we were in Thailand at the same time. But I met him in Vancouver some years ago. He was born there."

"Wondered. Lost his accent when he was sitting with us. Is he part of your team?"

"No, runs his own show. We keep in touch. Good man. Good virologist. But he's not involved with any lab here."

"Why's he working in a restaurant?"

"He spends a lot of time in eastern Europe. His brother owns this restaurant. When he's not busy he comes to Prishtinë to help out."

Frank scowled at Tom. "Odd place for a microbiologist to work."

"Hospital's nearby. Some Kosovar medical staff have acquired a taste for different foods. Prices are cheap, affordable. Lot of international clientele as well. Beer flows with hot food. Loosens tongues. Makes interesting listening for a person fluent in six languages."

Frank responded with his best *I don't understand* grimace. Tom decided not to offer any further explanation.

Date: Fri, 26 Apr 2002 06:04 EDT

Hi Tom. Just a follow up. I'm back in Vienna. I know you told me but I lost track whether you're still in Prishtina? Haven't forgotten about assisting Cassandra. Gradually getting things organized with the other people, but it takes time. Frank

Date: Sat, 27 Apr 2002 06:04 EDT

Frank, arrived back in Canada today. Passed your e-mail along to Cassandra. Maybe you can talk soon. Tom

# five

# May 2002
## *Gëzuar!*

Subject: REPORT ON THE THRAXITEST
Date: Wed, 01 May 2002 10:54 EDT

Dear Tommy, got off to a good start with sixty specimens. I attracted quite an audience, including most of the staff and several infectious diseases physicians. Amazing how word travels when something interesting is happening. I tried to have anthrax culture media ready to use today but ran into roadblocks.

Needed two duvets last night. To say I missed you is a significant understatement. Love, Cassie

"Gresa, do you have anthrax culture media?"

"No unnerstan, Dr Cassie. I get Dr Afërdita."

"No, wait," Cassie flipped through the index card box of culture media recipes. "This one." She handed Gresa the card.

"Oh no, Dr Cassie. No have."

"The floor's wet. Where's the water from?"

"*Nuk është ujë, Dr Cassie. Është ujëra të zeza.*"

"Now I don't understand. Black?"

"Black water, Cassie. Sewage, she say." Afërdita came into the room. She told Cassie she'd been phoned during the night by a frazzled security guard excited about a major catastrophe in the culture media preparation area. Water, reportedly sewage, coming up through the floor.

Cassie thanked Afërdita for interpreting and added, "That happens everywhere."

"Not in your beautiful labs in Canada."

"Oh yes, when they're located in the basement it can happen." Given the circumstances, Cassie thought, Gresa's worked through it with an amazing flurry of activity. She produced enough culture media and solutions for the whole week.

"Holiday is at noon."

"Holiday?"

"*Festë maj*. May first holiday. Gresa leave at noon."


Tom reached for the phone but on viewing his brother's office number on call display quickly enabled his scramble device before answering.

"Hey, bro."

"Hey Tommy," Keith replied. "I've got the Frank MacGregor info you wanted."

"Thanks, that was quick."

"At your service. He's a vet."

"What branch?"

"Sorry, vet as in veterinarian. Not military. Graduated Nova Scotia Agricultural College."

"Nova Scotia? Where's he from?"

"Halifax. Worked summers in the zoonoses lab at Dalhousie."

"At Dal? Holy shit, Keith. What's his employment history?"

"Not easy to discern. Seems to be a security blanket over his career.

Some gaps to fill in. Started with DFAIT about ten years ago as science officer in Bangkok. After that he was posted to Indonesia and the Philippines. Then pretty hazy until he shows up in Vienna as political staff. And, you already know, in charge of the Prishtinë office. Why'd you want to know?"

"Just like to know who I'm dealing with. Thanks for this Keith."

"Any time, Tommy. Talk to you later."

Well, thought Tom, let's see how this develops. Who's playing who... whom here?

Date: Thu, 02 May 2002 02:05 EDT

My dear sweet Tom. Good morning and thanks so much for the call last night. I miss you like crazy. Such a wonderful surprise since I wasn't expecting you to phone.

The Thraxitest looked good. In one specimen the strip detected *Bacillus anthracis* and traditional culture did not. So by definition false positive. But I'll do a confirmation. I suspect your test is more sensitive than culture. Otherwise every other result is comparable. The techs have already caught on to the method and tell me the Thraxitest is good.

I think your rapid anthrax test method will prove out. Nothing like having an answer in a few hours rather than waiting two days. I hope you have a good day. Love you, Cassie

Date: Thu, 02 May 2002 04:03 EDT
From: Cassandra Borden
To: Justine Tachereau

Justine, there are no good stats for sexually transmitted

diseases. Data are incomplete. There's very little laboratory expertise to support any numbers I can extract. Too much reliance on outmoded testing methods. Hard to know which figures to trust. The only available HIV testing is from the blood transfusion service. Their figures suggest thirteen people living with HIV/AIDS in the whole of Kosova. With a population of two and a half million that may be a reasonable estimate. I just have the sense of a Trojan horse.

On a positive note, Tom Stephenson's rapid anthrax detection method, the Thraxitest I told you about, works very well. It could easily be adapted as a field test. I'm quite certain it could be resensitized to work faster, about one hour start to finish. That would make it extremely valuable for investigators to diagnose presumptive anthrax in the field. Or if results are not meant to be shared. Regards, Cassandra

Olympia restaurant, Prishtinë *Centrum*, Thursday afternoon. Cassie arrived later than she'd anticipated. Catalina was already seated.

"Hello Cassandra."

"Hello Catalina! So nice to see you. I'm so glad you called me. How've you been?"

"I am fine, Cassandra. Do you have time for having coffee with me?"

"Of course."

"I am very upset. I need to talk. There are no Portuguese in Prishtinë right now."

"You're still working in Prizren?"

"Yes. Prizren is so pretty but I come to Prishtinë every weekend. There are more people here I know. I stay with my friends from Lisbon.

I have their apartment but they are gone home for month."

"*Kafe* or cappuccino?"

"Macchiato, I prefer. I maybe talk with some English friends. But I prefer talk to  you." Catalina tried a British accent. "Rachel would say, 'Oh, just leave him. Leave him high and dry'."

"Ah, it's Federico we're talking about?"

"Yes, Freddie. He send me e-mail. Simple e-mail. It say, *I live in Lisbon, you live in Prishtinë*. We plan to meet in Vienna for holiday, five days. But now he say he is not sure."

"Why Vienna? What's he not sure about?"

"Vienna is short flight from here and short flight from Lisbon. A beautiful city to get… I do not know the English."

"Get reacquainted?"

"Yes, that is good word. Start again."

"When was the last time you went home? Your town is near Lisbon, isn't it?"

"At Christmas. But then there was so many family and friends to visit, there was no time for us. How you do it?"

"I'm not married. So it's much easier. Long distance relationships are very difficult. Especially if one partner feels left behind. You know what I mean. Looking after the house, working at the same job. It's difficult here but someone at home could see it as an adventure. A carefree life. And being paid as well."

"Pay is so important for us. I am paid UN rate. A nutritionist in Portugal cannot make so much money. I have very little expenses here so I can pay for Freddie and me to go to Vienna and do other things. Still I save lot of money."

"I don't know Portuguese social norms. Is it a problem that you make more money?"

"But I share with Freddie. I do not say this is my money. This is our money."

"Can you telephone him?"

"I do that. He do not know how he feel about me. I ask if there is someone else and he say of course not."

"Can you stay in Prishtinë a few days? Stay with me? If you'd like company that is. Tonight, Sonja and Claire want to take me to dinner. You've met them. You could come too."

"Thank you, Cassandra. You are so kind. I would like if I stay with you."


Date: Thu, 02 May 2002 11:18 EDT

Good morning, my Tommy! *Mirëdite!* I'm having one of those uphill battle days. Just can't believe how much basic technique is still missing. No one seems to have a notion of working with pure cultures. Today I was waiting for Fisnik to join me to make up oxidase reagent so I could show him how to confirm a gonorrhoea culture and also to test some other specimens that looked suspicious to me. Wispy but heavy growth on Chocolate medium. Direct smear really impressive, loaded with pus cells with many intracellular diplococci. Male urethral specimen, of course. They seem reticent to obtain proper specimens from females. Thought it would give me a chance to demonstrate how to handle a suspect positive specimen. Alas, Zani was reading the cultures and he discarded them before I returned from lunch. I bet he didn't even recognize the growth because no one uses lights to examine cultures.

Later, in the stockroom tularaemia antiserum was stored at room temperature. They don't seem to value precious reagents. I don't believe any temperature monitoring has occurred since you left.

Tomorrow I'm meeting Frank MacGregor to discuss plans for me to present information to the agricultural lab about what the hospital lab could offer them and to explore what testing they could do for the hospital. I'm surprised he's so interested in my ideas. Bye for now, Cassie

Date: Fri, 03 May 2002 04:26 EDT

Good morning my sweetheart. Just a little message to say how much I'm thinking of you and looking forward to being with you.

Had a good evening with Claire and Sonja at Il Passatore. Catalina was going to join us but at the last minute she decided to book a flight to Lisbon. She'd been to Lake Batlava but she seemed distracted. Frankly I don't know how anyone expects to have a good marriage with long distance relationships and so much vacillating about life plans. At least we others had a good afternoon. A chance to be in the great outdoors is always a treat. The lake is one of the reservoirs for Prishtina's water supply. Quite a picturesque area. Lots of people out and about enjoying the day.

Cassie stopped writing and simply gazed at her screen. Sonja's become such a pleasure to be with, she thought. She and Claire spare no effort to entertain me. They're so kind. Funny, I assumed I'd have closer bonds with Claire. It's worked out quite differently.

I met Sonja and Connie Healy from the UK for lunch. Her husband's a medical microbiologist from Edinburgh so we're exploring the possibility he may be able to come here with her. Sonja's trying to hire her as a nurse trainer.

"You know Connie, I'd be very happy to have the Edinburgh group tender to supply the nursing training program. Especially if it's jointly with the University of Edinburgh. And happier still if you're the lead," Sonja said.

"U of Edinburgh won't be a problem. The Edinburgh group needs to decide if they want to be involved in something this intensive."

"But they've done other similar work."

"Only short term. This requires a year on the ground and at least six months in preparation," Connie replied.

"I can't promise you'll love it. But I think Cassie'd agree it's the experience of a lifetime."

Cassie quickly nodded agreement recognizing there was no opportunity to insert a word between these two.

"My husband retires next month. I'd be more willing to participate if there were a role for him," Connie said. "He's a medical microbiologist."

Wow, a UK microbiologist. What an opportunity for the medical microbiologists to have a model. Cassie didn't say anything immediately but with the sudden silence she realized the ball was in her court.

"I don't make program decisions," she said but knew that wasn't going to satisfy Sonja. "I'll speak with Jordan Siemens. He might be able to pull some strings. I can certainly relay the information."

Date: Fri, 03 May 2002 13:42 EDT

Dear Tom, just returned from the agriculture lab. I'm so full of

157

envy! Wow! Would I like to work with that facility; however, they have the challenge of setting up testing from scratch. Seems to me they'd be very good partners for the hospital lab. They're trying to achieve similar goals – testing for tularaemia, anthrax, brucellosis. Maybe that's where the public health lab should establish.

Interesting, Frank MacGregor came along for the lab tour. Asked some pretty insightful questions – for a diplomat. Love, Cassie

Date: Sat, 04 May 2002 05:34 EDT

Dearest Tom, I dreamed you were with me last night (not so much in the biblical sense) but that Odeta had put some alphabet confetti on our pillows. When I got up and then returned to bed it was gone. I asked you where it went and you uncovered yourself and showed me it was on your toes!! Wonder how this would be interpreted by a dream analyst. You could ask Albert. Remember, tell him alphabet confetti!! Not alphabet spaghetti! Probably a different psychological interpretation. I suspect the key to understanding this is you uncovered yourself. Lots of love for the weekend, Cassie

Interesting to almost feel part of this history. Especially with reports coming from the Hague. Had Tom and I not been here we would only be distant bystanders, perhaps only barely interested. I'd love to be with Tommy today. I'm missing him so much. Not feeling too perky. Must need exercise - maybe I can get Claire to go to Gërmia later. Dull headache. Gotta eat something.

Date: Thu, 09 May 2002 10:08 EDT

Hello sis. I'm flying home this weekend. Really looking forward to reuniting with Jeremy (and, of course, Tom). My one regret is I'll only be home a couple of weeks before I head back here.

Can't believe how fast things moved this winter with Tom. He gives me such a sense of peace. Tom's schedule does seem a little mysterious though, and I suspect he'll be sent back here soon. He writes some articles while he's at home but needs to come back here for more interviews and background material. Of course, I'm also pleased he's met all the lab people and helps at the lab when he's not busy.

Tom designed a rapid test for anthrax the lab's been trying. We can now confirm a diagnosis in about six hours instead of forty-eight. Data's so good I can see an important paper to publish. Tom seems a little reticent to have his name involved. Because he's been out of the lab field for so long, I guess. Actually, he had a great idea of asking the Kosovars to author the manuscript themselves. That would be a major morale booster. See you soon, Cassie

Date: Sun, 12 May 2002 11:32 EDT

My dearest Cassie, I know what you mean about your friend Catalina and her life style. But what a shame to receive such messages from home! It sounds so hit and miss, occasional e-mails and less frequent phone calls. Certainly being away from home for so long is tough on any relationship. You're much different from Catalina and thank goodness! If you accepted an assignment somewhere, I'd make sure I could accompany you, and vice versa, I presume. Much the way the Scottish Healeys are trying to play the situation, you'd find me right in there, playing for keeps.

I'm glad you're on your way home! We'll be together until Wednesday when I fly back. I'm sorry it won't be longer. But I notice on your calendar you're only home three weeks before you head back again too. Much love, Tom

I've the added benefit, although sometimes I think it's a curse, of being able to commit my thoughts to paper, thought Tom. A curse when those thoughts keep me awake but wonderfully satisfying when I'm able to compose a poem for Cass. I know she'll like it when she gets home.

## While I Was Walking

While I was walking Saturday, I saw a patch of blue
In the clouded morning sky, where the newly risen sun
Bathed a westward flying plane and its trail with golden hue.
I supposed with that clear sign your journey was begun,
While I was walking.

Where my two walking trails conjoin, where ridge and valley meet,
A circle of sun there formed, where I asked the Lord,
(Jehovah, Allah, Great Spirit, God – for I know not Whom)
To make your journey safe and sure, to comfort you as well,
While I was walking.

I faced the four directions, each to commune with you.
Facing firstly True North, anxious awaiting your return.
After that I faced far South, turning clockwise, ever so,
To receive your sunny smile and feel the warmth of you,
While I was walking.
Turning thirdly toward the West, turning clockwise, ever so,
The direction you are bound in your fast approaching plane.
And then also facing East, turning clockwise, ever so,
And opened my embrace to great and joyful union,
While I was walking.

I walked two extra miles to keep our thoughts together,
Communing over space and time my so strong love for you,
While I was walking.

If I was walking Sunday, I would do it all again,
While I was walking.

"Oh, Tommy, it's beautiful," Cassie smiled through her tears. "You wrote it for me? I had no idea you wrote poetry."

"I don't really, Cass. Just was inspired Friday... Saturday. I've never done it before."

"Never written a poem?"

"Never one I've shared with anyone."

"Oh, Tommy, now I'm really going to cry. I'm so happy... to see you... to read your poem... my poem."

"Did it seem strange to you? Coming home to me but at your own house?"

"No. But it's funny isn't it?"

"I think that's why I wrote the poem. I was feeling agitated, nervous I guess. Just kept walking, thinking about you. Just came to me. Rushed back here to write it down while I still remembered my thoughts."

"Thank you for that. Have you written other poems?"

"Like I said, I've never shared one. I've only written four or five."

"Now you've shared one. It means so much to me."

## six

# June 2002
### *Në befasi*

As soon as he returned to Prishtinë, Tom seized the first opportunity to meet privately with Andy Hamilton. For a long time, they'd talked of getting together for an interview, just the two of them discussing rich life experiences. But conflicting schedules always managed to intervene. Now, it was becoming urgent because Andy was returning to Arnprior, his three year assignment completed. So they planned to meet at the Canadian Cooperation Support Office before lunch. Everything felt good, a warm sunny spring day after a week of rain. When Tom arrived, Andy showed him into the backyard he'd transformed with grasses, flower beds, trees and shrubs, a picnic table and gas barbeque. Tom realized it was Andy's touch of home. Tulips from Ottawa still green but finished production and giving way to early summer flowers. Flowering shrubs in full display. Pear trees already bearing small fruit. One of the horticultural legacies of Andy's stay in Prishtinë, leaving the place better for his time here. He'd always hired good local staff, including a gardener whose passion for the property seemed personal.

Tom and Andy talked for about an hour before leaving to join Frank at the Baci Hotel, near the hospital, for a late lunch. After they'd ordered, Tom wanted to establish with Andy that lunch was his, Tom's, treat.

"Tom, that doesn't make any sense. We all receive food allowance."

"Well then, you just pocket that ten euros. I want to do this," Tom replied, then, to change the subject, turned to Frank. "Food's always good, Frank. I'm surprised you've never been here."

"Usually I just throw something together at the office unless I can swing a dinner meeting. I'm only in Prishtinë a few days at a time. Don't do much other than work when I'm here."

"You should've come to my place when you were in town," suggested Andy. "I can always scare up a few others for dinner."

"That's why I like those Canadian gatherings. Someone else cooks. Conversation in English," Frank replied.

"Of course, it won't happen now. I'm leaving on the weekend. But it would've been fun."

"You know, I've really only done things socially here since I've been with Cassie. Otherwise, I spent my whole time working as well," Tom offered.

"You've only been a short time with Cassie?" Frank expressed surprise.

"Six or seven months."

"You mean when we met at the Christmas reception?"

"Yeah, right about then."

"Now I remember you saying something like that. Looked like you knew each other forever, though."

"Oh, we've known each other awhile. This's a new phase."

"A Kosova only phase or are you together in Canada as well?"

Tom bristled at Frank's remark but before he could react, Andy jumped to his defence. "Cassie's no *femme du jour,*" he said then asked, "You married, Frank?"

"Not currently. Haven't met anyone serving here who is."

"Pretty thriving summer camp attitude is what I see amongst the internationals," Tom suggested.

"Well guys," said Andy. "I should get back. Still some packing to finish."

"Andy, I've enjoyed our association, however brief," said Frank.

"Cassie and I'd like to visit you and Anita in Arnprior when we're home," said Tom.

"I'd like that, Tom. You know Cassie's one of my favourite people."

They watched quietly while Andy left the restaurant. He turned, made a face and proffered a mock salute before he passed through the swinging doors into the hotel lobby.

Tom turned to Frank. "I'd like to interview you Frank. Thinking of a series profiling Canadians working here. I finished a session with Andy before we came to meet you. Don't have the format ironed out yet. Thought if I start interviewing eventually I could present a series. Okay with you?"

"Not sure, Tom."

"I was surprised to hear you're a veterinarian?"

"Yes, and my undergraduate degree is in microbiology."

"Thus your science officer assignment in Thailand?"

"There and other embassies as well. I need assurance our conversations are off-the-record."

"No problem. You know, I'm really gonna miss Andy. He was great for anything we needed. This may sound funny but he made sure we all had a supply of peanut butter. Brought it in by diplomatic pouch."

"I've heard of things like that. I may not be able to maintain that service from Vienna. Important service, though. I mean I understand completely. Necessities of life and all."

"Occasionally I'd have something to send back the other way."

"And Andy arranged that for you?"

"Yes."

"I have security clearance, Tom. No danger of me spilling secrets."

"Okay."

Frank changed the direction of the conversation. "Y'know, they watch too much CSI here. They love everything American. Especially movies and TV. They believe it. They want assistance in developing a forensic microbiology lab for zoonoses. Partly why I'm here, the embassy animal doc."

Zoonoses as a major forensics focus? "Wouldn't it make more sense to support zoonoses work in the health labs or the new agricultural lab," Tom said. "Country's trying to rebuild its devastated agricultural base. It was pretty much destroyed during the war."

"Sure, we could help there. But these other proposals make sense to me. They want the ability to investigate mass graves and other atrocities themselves, not relying on outsiders."

"Can't blame them. There's general distrust of UN and EU investigators. It's important to Kosovars."

Frank agreed, "Not just in this but every other facet I've talked with them about. They're keenly interested in entomology. Want to understand maggots and larvae in timing of deaths. That sort of thing. That's where they want assistance."

"You're able to do that?"

"We may not be the ones to actually provide the help but from the Embassy point of view, we want to know who is providing support. It's in Canada's interest to try to control that."

"What about biological warfare organisms?"

"Come again?"

"A number of the organisms are endemic here," Tom continued. Frank has security clearance for a reason. Good to know. May be able to use him as a resource. Need to figure out where the Embassy stands.

"Sure. I get your drift. How long's it been since you were a virologist, Tom?"

"Oh, a few years now, five, six." This could be interesting, Tom thought. "Another bottle of the red?"

"You wanna switch to cognac? There's a good selection behind the bar."

"I could do that." Ah, interrogation techniques, start soft, then onto the hard stuff. Local red wine, then onto *Courvoisier*.

Tom was pleased when Shpend asked if he'd accompany Avni to the airport to meet Cassie's flight from home. It was awhile since he'd been there waiting for arrivals. Usually Shpend, as local point man for CIPHA, met the Canadians attached to one of the public health programs. Today, he was required to be in Prizren. So, Tom was happy to accompany Avni who didn't know Cassie. Although Tom knew these hook-ups between drivers and arriving passengers usually were uneventful, he didn't want Cassie to have concerns about recognizing Avni either. He was also slightly amused that Shpend would think that he, Tom the foreigner, would be able to show Avni around.

With construction continuing on the new terminal, only ticketed passengers were allowed to enter the current building for reasons of security and congestion. Those awaiting arriving passengers, including whole Kosovar families, thronged outside in anticipation. Since Tom's last visit, a covered outdoor pavilion had been added to house a small coffee shop. Avni and Tom sat there drinking cappuccino. Ubiquitous cappuccino! This must be the cappuccino capital, Tom thought. Around noon Avni's mobile phone rang.

"One moment, Tom. I must answer. Call from Vienna. *Alo*... Oh, Cassandra, hello, it is Avni here. We wait for your airplane. Yes, Tom is with me. One moment."

"Hello there. What happened? Miss your flight?" Tom asked.

"I'm sorry, Tommy. We were late landing from Frankfurt because of fog. We circled for about half an hour before we landed. By then the flight to Prishtinë had already left."

"That's okay. You can get the next flight."

"That's not for twenty-four hours."

"We'll be here to pick you up. Not still here," he kidded. "I mean we'll come back again."

"Oh, Tommy, I was so looking forward to being with you this afternoon."

"That would've been nice. Your flight is landing as we speak."

"I spent the last three hours trying to phone. I had all the phone numbers with me. Tried to call Shpend but couldn't remember the country code. Austrian Airlines desk gave me the code for Kosova."

"That's not right for mobile phones."

"Yes, I know now but I'd forgotten. My mind doesn't work like yours. But, you know, a young woman, American I think, another passenger, overheard me and asked the desk to give me the code for Monaco for the cell phone. Then I remembered that was right. Shpend gave me Avni's number. How're you doing?"

"Great. Disappointed you're not arriving. But, it's a beautiful sunny afternoon. Avni and I are sitting on the patio drinking cappuccinos."

"There's a patio at the airport?"

"Brand new. Where're you going to stay?"

"The same young woman tried to convince me being stranded in Vienna is not a catastrophe. Treat it as an opportunity, she said. She gave me the name of a *pension* downtown. And she explained how the airport shuttle bus system works to get there."

"Sounds pretty lucky. I'm glad she was there."

"And she gave me her traveller's guide to Vienna. She's my guardian angel. You know, she wouldn't give me her name. Said it's better not to know."

"Strange. But, you know, her advice sounds good. Scope out Vienna, so we can plan a weekend."

"Okay. You know I coulda got a flight to Skopje but Shpend said there'd be no way to pick me up."

"That's right. Kosova registered vehicles cannot travel into Macedonia. Something about insurance, they say," Tom said. "I think there's more to it."

"I'm so tired. I'll phone later from the hotel. I have the apartment phone number."

"Alright. Bye for now my love."

"Tom, I am not hero. Mine is not big story. How to start?"

"Just start talking. We spoke of these events earlier. Tell me again as if I don't know any details. I'll start my recorder and we'll talk like we did when we were waiting for Cassandra," Tom pointed to Avni as he pressed the record button. "Introduce yourself to begin."

"Okay, name is Dr Avni Kurtishi. Thirty-six year old. Medical *doktor*. Right now I am family medicine resident, but I study for *mjeshtre shkallë*... I do not know how to say, Tom."

"Master's degree."

"Okay, yes. Master's degree in public health. Of course, I need to live and feed family. So, I work night shift at Health House, and work part time for CIPHA like driver, translator and errand person."

"How did you come to work for CIPHA?"

"I feel lucky because Shpend Veseli is good friend and give me job. I spend spare time with wife and two years old son. Spare time is joke! But life is good. Much best as before. You want me to tell my experience?"

Tom nodded for Avni to continue.

"In 1992, I leave Kosova to start again medical studies at Sarajevo. Everything Serbs do to us stop my studies at Prishtinë. Professional education and training end. I am teach science in parallel system.

Secondary school level. Later parallel system teach university and professional course. But not then. System was new. You know about parallel system?"

Tom nodded and said he knew.

"Teaching very much reward for me. I give to my people, such as be my contribution. But I need finish medical study. It is difficult decision. I do not receive full credit for completed study."

"No credit at all?"

"Part credit but not much. It is very strange that education in one part Yugoslavia not receive respect in same country. Especially I need only three examination more for medical degree. That how they make trouble for Kosova. We be poor step-child of Yugoslavia. Is correct in English? Step-child?"

"Yes," Tom replied. "But maybe step-children. Plural."

"Thank you, Tom. We be poor step-children of Yugoslavia. Unless they need from us something, something like military service. That is why never we give up new freedom. We fight again if necessary."

"Getting back to your education. You were able to go to Sarajevo, right?"

"That is correct. I complete bureaucracy requirement, then I get permission to studying at Sarajevo. But, almost immediate, Bosnia war start. Situation impossible. Yugoslavia pretend it is one country for Sarajevo Olympic. Better to get along than lose right for be Olympic host. For while we be proud Yugoslavs once more. Just like in Tito years. But Bosnia is problem area. I think you say powder keg in English."

"Yes, good description. A tense situation that could become violent. Boom! You know a powder keg was a container of gunpowder? Something that could explode?"

"No, Tom. It is good to learn more English. Thank you for teach me." Avni continued his story, "If we have peace in Yugoslavia, my medical education is outstanding. Hospital in Sarajevo all modern, new state-of-art facilities. For Olympic, you know. But, I think Bosnia war to be long and bitter. Neighbour fight neighbour. I think hardship back home be more easy for handle. I have many new friend at Sarajevo. They help me get away from Bosnia, to Montenegro and to Kosova."

"So, how did you get back to Kosova?"

"I walk and hitchhike ride in Bosnia. In Montenegro I use public bus. When I am back, I teach again in parallel education system. Is it strange to you, Tom, education be black market like we see on street today with CD and DVD?"

"I like your insight, education as a black market commodity."

"Then, I live with parent at Prishtinë. That very common, usual for unmarried son continue in family home. Same today. My fiancée, Maria, live with parent at Gjakovë, eighty kilometres distance. Of course, for Canadian, eighty kilometres nothing. But, for Albanian Kosovar, in nineteen-nineties, that be, would you say, epic journey. Our family did not own car. We use bus between cities before it was dangerous. Then Serb police take many Albanian from buses. Many we never see again."

"Tell me how you came to be in Macedonia."

"Not in Macedonia but at border on Kosova side. It is January 1999, Serb soldiers came to apartment, push my mother and father and shout at me to leave. Five minutes, they say, take nothing with you. There is bus waiting outside apartment building. All seats took from bus. They pack us three in bus with others, all standing. They take us all to Macedonia border to refugee camp still on Kosova side. In camp, I start work immediately with IMC. *Me falni*, Tom?"

"Just wondering. Tell me again. What's IMC?"

"Oh, sorry, International Medical Corp, IMC."

"Thanks."

"There is no way to tell anything to Maria."

"That must've concerned you."

"Very much that worry me, Tom. She not able understand for why I be silent to her."

"What happened with your parents?"

"In about two week they go in Macedonia. Because my mother have family there, it is allow. Later sometime, father of Maria visit Prishtinë to contact me or family. He return home and tell Maria Serb soldier live in our apartment. Maria watch foreign television on satellite every day, look for information. She hide satellite dish behind curtain in apartment window. Not like now, Tom, every balcony with one satellite dish, maybe two, three."

"I guess foreign television is still important?"

"We never again give up right to information from outside state. That time is finish. I think we be hard for govern, even for elected national assembly. You see how even driver not follow normal rule."

"But you were able to contact Maria eventually."

"Yes. After about eight week, Maria see me on BBC so she know I am alive. TV crew videotape me examine patient in refugee camp clinic. But I do not know Maria see that. Still I know nothing of Maria. I am glad now she see me because I was very worried. I do not want for her to worry sick for me thinking I maybe dead. And about three weeks more, *doktor* from Scotland, who work with IMC, come to get me. He work both side of border. He say my Maria in refugee camp at Macedonia. We and woman *doktor* jump in IMC truck. My comrade bandage his head and lay on stretcher like patient."

"That must have been dangerous?"

"No, not so dangerous, they are internationals."

"Perhaps not for them, for you?"

"I do not worry. They so great, those two. But I do not share names even with you, Tom, because I think there still be problem. You know us now. You are friend and do not use information to hurt us."

"We can talk about that later. It could be another good story if I could contact them. Really, though, I don't need their names."

"I think you do not understand Balkans still. Maybe it is not blood feud. Maybe it is dishonour for other reason. I do not know. Sometimes I think anything is excuse to fight or cause trouble. Safer be careful, shut my mouth with what I know."

"Okay, Avni. I respect your reasons."

"We allowed to cross border because evacuate injured international. My friends take me to Maria. I want her with me so we smuggle her back across border like injured Kosovar. Her parent remain on Macedonia side."

"They allowed her to leave with you."

"Yes, Tom. They believe she is safe with me. About two weeks more, war in Kosova is over. I and Maria return to Prishtinë. We marry immediate. To being refugee speed paperwork for some reason. We plan to  marry when I finish residency. Of course, we plan big celebration with both family and many friend from our towns. And it is to be in Gjakovë. In camp, I can protect Maria only if she live with me. So we be husband and wife. Because of circumstance. But we do not think that is right. Not Muslim family way. Tom, you know we not be religious at Kosova but family value is tradition. We do not want to shame two family. We do right thing. We marry. We are happy now."

"Thank you for telling your story, Avni."

"I like that you interview me, Tom, and let me say again mine is not big story. Many my friend have worse memory to tell. All my family and all family of Maria survive. Parent, children, uncle, cousin, all survive."

Date: Tue, 25 Jun 2002 08:09 EDT
From: Dirk O'Reilly
To: Thomas Stephenson

Tom, I found a Foreign Affairs five year environmental scan for Kosova. You couldn't access it because your security clearance needs to be updated. RCMP and CSIS will both need to interview you again. Your sordid past and all!! Let's meet Friday as planned.

You won't like what I'm going to share now. These are political decisions. Canada will not be involved in Kosova past 2004. I know we understood there'd be a ten year window. All Foreign Affairs and CIDA infrastructure including the consulate sub office and the support office will move to Belgrade with no presence remaining in Kosova. That means, my friend, neither CSIS nor MIN will agree to you remaining there without support and the ability to be extricated if necessary. We simply aren't able to maintain that architecture.

My appraisal is Canada cannot support independence for Kosova, a province of Serbia and Montenegro. Some think then they'd need to support self determination for Quebec. I'm sure you don't see that argument as having merit, but, as I said, it's political. Welcome home, and to reality. Best, Dirk

Date: Tue, 25 Jun 2002 17:56 EDT
My dear Cassie. Separation's not so bad but I preferred to be

with you twenty-four seven. Back to Thraxitest, sounds like a water quality problem. Love, Tom

Tom loved getting back to Canada, to Canadian roads. Nothing like a warm summer day with the sunroof open and Bon Jovi cranked up on the car stereo, rock anthems shouting to the sky. As he drove back home late Thursday afternoon after visiting his parents for lunch, he pulled over to make a phone call.

"Hello. Dr Tindall speaking."

"Hey there, Bert."

"Hey, Tommy. How's ya gettin' on b'y?"

"Good, Bert, good. *Ça va?*"

"*Très bien, moi.* Wazzup?"

"Went to visit my parents for lunch. Heading back home now."

"You driving?"

"No, pulled over. Can't do that Kosova thing, talk on cell phone, drive up, over and around sidewalks and potholes, all heading into oncoming traffic."

"No transferable skills?"

"Oh, I can handle the phone part. Just don't drive over there. Agron does most of it."

"What about the rest of the time?"

"Walk a lot. Taxis, sometimes the bus."

"How's Cassie?"

"She's good. She'll be back home for a few weeks in July. But we won't have much time together. I have enough material for maybe one more article. Then I need to go back to Vienna."

"Vienna?"

"Kosova. I said Kosova."

"Okay. Sure."

"Bert, did I say Vienna?"

"It's okay, Tom. Slip of the tongue." Bert quickly asked another question. "Honestly, how are you doing?"

"Okay, I'm okay with things now. Certainly sleeping better."

"Warn me before we slip into that doctor-patient confidentiality thing," Bert said.

"I spent most of the winter worrying they might be pushed into doing something with anthrax way beyond their capabilities."

"Anthrax, Tom?"

"Yeah, not really my business, but I envisaged disaster looming if they were forced into examining specimens they're not competent to test. Add to that no containment facilities in the lab." Don't know why I said that. Tom found it difficult to maintain a story line when he actually needed Bert's advice.

Bert hesitated then asked, "Can you come to Ottawa for the weekend? We can talk better then."

"I'd like to. Maybe just the day, though. I have to stay in Toronto for a meeting tomorrow. Then I'm going up to Cassie's because I promised her I'd visit Jeremy while I'm home. This is the weekend we arranged."

"Bring him with you."

"Don't really know him that well."

"Bring him anyway. If he wants to come. You probably need some bonding time."

"I guess."

"Seriously, Tom. Do something special with him. Show him he's important to you. You two have a relationship. Show him you're permanent, not just shacked up with his mother while it's convenient."

"Hey, you may not be as dumb as you look. You're on," Tom replied.

"Good. We may not have as much drinking time, but what the heck, it's supposed to be healthier to cut back."

"Hell, he's a student. We may be hard pressed to keep up with him."

"Okay. Interesting. See you later, Tom."

"Thanks, Bert. Bye for now. I'll call when we're on the way."

seven

# July 2002
## *Paralajmërim*

Date: Sun, 01 Jul 2002 10:26 EDT
From: Susan McElligott <mcelligott@staff.who.org>
To: Gregory Hanbruz <ghanbruz@cipha.ca>

Hello Greg, I need to discuss some loose ends from a WHO perspective. Specifically a three- to five-year outlook. Both the hospital infection control and public health infrastructure projects are progressing but we need to look at the public health education initiative which appears to be floundering. WHO cannot show a preference for one country's efforts over another's but we've been secretly pleased you Canadians took on this work. That way we can be confident in the results. WHO is criticized so often, unfairly I think, for lofty plans that cannot be accomplished.

Will you be in Prishtina this summer? I'm hoping you'll be back before I leave so we can discuss things in person. I'm reassigned to Kabul for October first. WHO is pulling out. Officially, downsizing, but really, there'll be little presence left here. We've had a great working relationship, you and I. I miss our late night debriefings. I hoped we'd be able to do that once more in Prishtina. Failing that, I'm taking R&R in Manchester before Afghanistan. We could meet there. Always, Sue

Date: Tue, 03 Jul 2002 14:57 EDT

Hi Sue. Sorry to take so long to respond. July first is a Canadian holiday... Canada Day. So my office was closed Monday to compensate for the holiday falling on Sunday. It's a colonial thing. Wouldn't expect you to understand. Suffice to say, bank holiday weekend.

Don't know if I can make it back to Prishtina this summer. Typically, we still haven't established our budget for this fiscal year. However, Manchester's manageable on personal time. Maybe we could go up to Scotland. I have fond memories of a twenty year old Aberfeldy single malt.

Heads up for you though before you make any public statements about Canadians getting the job done. Scuttlebutt has us reducing funding for specific Kosova projects in favour of a more regional approach probably based in Belgrade. I'm not certain we'll be able to complete our plans. All the best, Greg

Greg, I'm shocked. That's not consistent with your usual reliability. That's why you're respected in the world – you do what you say you'll do. Personally disappointing too. Is it official policy yet? I need to alert WHO. Let me know what's appropriate.

Sorry Sue. There's nothing I can give you officially. I

understand WHO's need to know. Perhaps unattributed rumour.

Thanks Greg. I'll keep your name out of this. Perhaps WHO can pressure CIDA to guarantee funding for projects already underway. We always think it folly for established nations to ignore the public health threats of less developed countries. It may be at their own peril. Cassandra is doing a great job with the lab. She could possibly stay involved. I know she has a UK passport in addition to her Canadian.

There is something else, Greg. I assume you know Tom Stephenson? He's lending a hand with some aspects of Cassandra's projects. Personally, the more competent hands, the better. But, I've encountered Tom elsewhere over the last half dozen years. There's a pattern. He comes into a post-conflict area as a writer. Before long, he inserts himself into the laboratory community and offers his assistance. He's very good and has certainly helped improve laboratory service wherever he's been involved. But in Tom's wake interesting things occur.

We can talk in person about specifics. Just a warning - there could be ramifications for CIPHA, CIDA and WHO. WHO must remain neutral. We can't afford to be finessed into being an intelligence conduit. All nations must feel safe to work with us.

Not to suggest Tom has status in the intelligence community. But, just after Tom left the Sinai three years ago, an Al Qaeda bioweapons lab was discovered and destroyed. This isn't the first time something like this has happened in countries where Tom's been writing stories. None of us can afford to be infiltrated. I have no proof, only suspicion. CIPHA should be careful.

Sue, thanks for this. I'm keen to know more. I'll pass this info to Jordan Siemens who works directly with Cassandra's project. I don't know Tom myself but I believe Jordan does. You are correct, we must remain squeaky clean. Until Manchester, Greg

Date: Mon, 09 Jul 2002 06:17 EDT

My dearest Tommy, thank you for taking the time to visit the lab. Next time you go there, please tell Elvira I'm looking forward to seeing her again.

I miss you on different levels like the way you take such good care of me one, as well as on the wonderfully romantic level. Many times through my days I'm reminded how much you do for me and how I appreciate you. I have no more clean underwear! Guess I need to do my own traditional Monday laundry. How does all that clean underwear get into my drawer while you're here? I think you spoil me.

I looked at Leonard Cohen's *Ten New Songs* hoping to send you some poetic thoughts of love – alas, too dark for our kind of love... Loving you always... and missing you, Cassie

Date: Tue, 10 Jul 2002 09:06 EDT
From: Cassandra Borden
To: Jordan Siemens

Dear Jordan, I think you realize Thomas Stephenson has been lending a hand at the hospital lab. Even after a few years out of the lab environment, he has a lot to offer. Elvira finds his expertise in anthrax very useful. He keeps up-to-date on biological threats. I suppose that helps him gain an edge over other journalists. Tom's back in Prishtina now so I'm attaching part of an e-mail he sent me that contains encouraging observations about the lab. Cheers, Cassandra

Date: Tue, 10 Jul 2002 09:09 EDT

Dear Tommy, I cut and pasted your observations about Elvira and the lab staff to provide Jordan Siemens an update. Left out the part about the underwear. But did explain you're offering your time to help out. Jordan and I have a very loose plan for the microbiology lab. A change in responsibilities is necessary to provide greater flexibility but that's something I choose to suggest and not impose. Though as they say "a new broom sweeps clean". Love, Cassie

Date: Thu, 12 Jul 2002 10:08 EDT

Hey kg. My boss, Jordan Siemens, is trying to spook me about Tom, I think. I'm sure he has no idea how close we've become. It feels like I've known Tom forever. He treats me so well and with respect. Jordan suggests maybe

Tom has not been away from the microbiology field at all. He wasn't expansive but asked if I knew Dirk O'Reilly. Dirk used to work for me. Now he's at the University Health Network providing disease surveillance data to health agencies across North America. Of course, I called Dirk. Played it as a courtesy call. Asked him to consider helping establish an infectious disease surveillance system in Kosova. He didn't seem very interested. Said he had his hands full with North America. Then I mentioned I'd met Tom in Prishtina. He said he'd heard we were close and asked to be remembered to Tom. You know how I worry. I haven't experienced self doubt since I've been with Tom.

Have I misjudged something? Maybe Jordan is jealous of Tom helping over there. After all, the work in Kosova is Jordan's responsibility.

I miss Tom a lot. He'll be back home for about three weeks soon. I'm hoping he can coordinate his return flight to Prishtina with Afërdita. Her training period here will be finished about the time Tom heads back. She has absolutely no travel experience. Love, Cassie

Date: Fri, 13 Jul 2002 10:08 EDT

Cass girl, sounds like men's games to me! Let them play. Maybe your boss is jealous, but of Tom's relationship with you, not his work habits. Try that one on. On the other hand, what harm if Tom has continued to dabble in microbiology. He's certainly a help to you in Kosova, after all. Love, Karen

# eight

# August 2002
## *Natën e mire*

"Flight's delayed again." Tom explained the loudspeaker announcement to Afërdita. At least we're in Toronto, he thought. We can go to the Maple Leaf Lounge. "Come with me," he continued. "I know a comfortable place we can wait."

Tom guided Afërdita around the long lines of passengers waiting in front of check-in counters and onto a small elevator. They emerged onto the second floor into a security check area and were quickly processed. After he'd signed in at the lounge reception desk, he offered his arm to escort her to a comfortable-looking leather couch in a private corner. He sighed as he dropped into an equally comfortable over-stuffed chair, pleased to have his airline loyalty points pay off with relative luxury while awaiting the call for their delayed flight. Tom thought Afërdita was suitably impressed.

"I can get you some wine, cheese and crackers, maybe a sandwich," he offered.

"Oh, I do not drink. Maybe some cheese," Afërdita replied.

"Okay, be right back."

Tom chose a variety of cheeses, cheddar, blue, edam along with a selection of crackers for Afërdita. For himself, he poured a generous glass of *Chateau des Charmes* Cabernet Sauvignon. So much better than waiting in the crowded departure lounge. The lounge attendant would let them know when the flight was ready for boarding.

"Thank you, Thomas." Afërdita accepted the plate of snacks from Tom. "I am so nervous," she continued. "I never fly before come to Canada. I never travel. Only when I go to Albania."

"You didn't attend conferences in Europe like Elvira?"

"I am fire from lab in year 1994. I go to Albania to work. I take children with me."

"And your husband?"

"Besnik is KLA commander. He stay at Prishtinë."

"When did you return home?"

"After war. *Tetor muaj.* Sorry, Thomas, I not know name for month."

"That's okay, Afërdita. October."

"Yes, yes, October."

"Nineteen ninety-nine?"

"Yes, Thomas. I come back in Prishtinë then."

"Did you return to work immediately?"

"Yes. All Serb *doktor* leave. Elvira is control of lab. She not be fire. She work whole time. Not as *doktor*, as technician."

"Was that a problem?"

"No. *S'ka problem.* Just..."

"Difficult?"

"Yes," Afërdita answered and then explained how many of the available jobs were given to men without any qualifications except they'd been guerrilla fighters with the KLA. "And other worker did not work for ten year. They do not know how work is done now, after long time away." She explained the chaos in the lab and in Kosovar civil society where most professionals had been removed from their jobs sometime in the ten years before NATO reacted. Because she had not been fired, Elvira was regarded by some staff as a collaborator, Afërdita explained. Some former fighters felt entitled to their jobs, swaggered about the lab and were openly rebellious toward Elvira's authority. Tom knew Elvira well enough to know she would brook no insubordination. Eventually she'd been able to remove most political appointees and staff the lab in her own fashion.

Afërdita no longer seemed relaxed discussing these memories and, Tom suspected, anticipating the twice-delayed long night-flight across the Atlantic.

"Thomas," she eventually said. "Please you get me some wine. Small, small, not like you. White wine, please."

"My pleasure. I'll be right back."


When the flight finally arrived in Vienna, three and a half hours late, the connecting flight to Prishtinë had long since departed. Tom checked their options at the Austrian Airlines desk but was reminded the next once-daily flight to Prishtinë was scheduled for twenty-three hours hence. They offered to switch them onto a flight leaving for Skopjë in the next hour but given Cassandra's earlier experience, he refused that suggestion and prepared himself to be stranded in Vienna. He was certain Afërdita would enjoy the opportunity to visit Vienna as well. I'll assure her all expenses will be covered, Tom thought. I'm sure she has no money. Maybe an assumption but I'm sure I'll be reimbursed what I spend. After all, she's been a guest of the Government of Canada while training in Kingston and Ottawa.


Tom didn't anticipate a problem but insisted Afërdita move ahead of him through the non-EU residents passport control line ensuring he could get the same agent. He tried to remember which airport shuttle bus would take them to the Hilton Hotel. He knew it was only a short walk from there to the *pension* where he and Cassie had stayed. Maybe too early to check-in but at least he could arrange rooms for the night then spend the afternoon showing Afërdita Stefandom and, later, the Bundestheatre, the Vienna State Opera. We'll enjoy lunch in the Tea Salon on the first floor of the opera house or one of the sidewalk cafés in the old city, he thought. He realized he was assuming a continuation of the same great weather they'd experienced at home the previous week.

Tom suddenly noticed Afërdita's exchange with the official in the immigration booth did not seem to be going well. He stepped forward to assist ignoring the agent's hand gestures insisting he wait his turn behind the red line.

"We are travelling together," Tom said proffering his Canadian passport. "Is there a problem with my friend?"

"Where is her visa?" asked the agent. "She cannot enter the European Union without a visa."

"Do we arrange visas at a different desk?"

"You do not need one, sir. Only her." The agent indicated Afërdita with a dismissive head gesture. "It will take more than one week to process a visa from Kosova. She does not have a passport even."

"She has official UN travel documents," Tom replied indignantly.

"It is no good without a visa."

"We're stuck here because our plane was late and we missed our connecting flight. We need overnight accommodations." Tom cautioned himself not to display his annoyance, not to offer a reason for the agent to summon the two security guards who seemed to be monitoring the encounter.

"No visa. No entry."

"So what do we do?"

"Wait for your flight in the airport." The agent shrugged, averting his eyes from Tom's withering stare.

Tom grabbed Afërdita's hand, assured her everything would be okay, and steered her back to the Austrian Airlines desk where he exchanged their tickets for the already boarding flight to Skopjë. He realized they would both need visas to enter Macedonia but knew old-fashioned greasing of the immigration agent's palm there would provide immediate positive results. Tom's parting question at the desk was about their luggage. The clerk assured him there would be no problem. Their luggage would be on the next flight to their original destination, Prishtinë.

Once outside the terminal building at Alexander the Great airport in Skopjë, Afërdita took charge. This was her home territory. She quickly identified an Albanian-speaking taxi driver, negotiated a fare to Prishtinë which she indicated Tom should pay in advance. Moments before Tom had thought to check the luggage carousel, just in case. Afërdita's two large bags had accompanied their flight but not Tom's.

From Skopjë, the driver proceeded along narrow mountain roads toward the border. About half an hour out of the city, the driver flagged down an approaching taxi whose driver, as the explanation went, would have credentials, insurance and other documents to allow him to cross the border and take them on to Prishtinë. The border crossing was easy requiring less than half an hour. Then the new driver was stopped on the Kosova side by a group of men, apparently taxi drivers themselves. A discussion ensued about Macedonian drivers taking jobs from Kosovar drivers. So Tom and Afërdita switched taxis again. Afërdita haggled with the Macedonian driver but it was immediately apparent no refund would be forthcoming. Tom paid the new fare, wanting nothing more than to have the journey finally end, twenty-four hours and six time zones since their flight began.

Date: Fri, 23 Aug 2002 12:26 EDT

Hello, my sweetheart. I'm alive and well but without luggage. My accommodation this time is your original apartment. I chose the room with two beds, realizing two can become one, pending your approval. Slept comfortably, knowing you'd lived here, feeling your essence.

Last night I walked to Ardi supermarket. That whole square was shoulder-to-shoulder young people. Looked like there might have been a concert earlier. Bought a few things but we'll need to stock almost everything. There's a package of tea here... looks like old stock chosen by non-tea drinkers but I'll check it out!

We now have internet available at the apartment, by the way. Shpend hooked it up. The cable runs through the window and into his friend's apartment on the next floor. Don't ask. All my love, Tom

Tom walked along Mother Theresa as far as Bill Clinton Boulevard, to the intersection he'd heard called Confusion Corners, because the traffic signals had not worked for at least a year after the war. Drivers then approached without any measure of caution. Pedestrians took their lives in hand each time they crossed the street and sometimes even when they walked on the sidewalk. Tom often observed impatient drivers mount the sidewalk to turn right rather than waiting. Later when traffic officers were stationed in the intersection to moderate the flow of traffic, he watched a policeman force a driver to reverse out of the intersection rather than allow him to continue before he'd been signalled to proceed. To Tom, it was anarchy although he accepted

Agron's explanation that Kosovars were oppressed by imposed laws and regulations so long they just wanted to live free until their own legislation was in place.

"What makes you think they'll follow new rules?" Tom asked.

"Because we want to be law abiding citizens of our own country. It is only a façade, this bravado, this frontier behaviour," Agron assured him. "We simply want our own rules from our own parliament."

Tom shrugged his shoulders, scowled in amusement and replied simply, "*Mbase.*" We'll see.

Today, Tom decided to head up the hill. Greater exercise value he told himself. He hadn't previously noticed the home appliance store in the corner building. Wasn't sure it was new but thought the economy must be improving if people were shopping for dishwashers and refrigerators. When he reached the World Food Program compound at the intersection with Agim Ramadani, he thought about turning south toward the university but instead decided to head north to check out some of the new boutiques, mostly women's wear he decided but definitely worth knowing about. Nice weather at first but when it started to sprinkle, Tom headed home hoping his electricity would be back on. He thought the rest of the day would bring reading, napping, maybe writing. He knew if Cassandra were here they'd find plenty to do on a Prishtinë Sunday.

The apartment was fine – clean, comfortable, good water pressure when water was available. Cassandra lived there on her first visits, but Tom wasn't familiar with it. About a forty minute walk to the hospital for Cassie.

Tom didn't find operation of the kitchen range patently obvious. In the previous house, cooking was often confounded by a stove that simply didn't work. These electric elements were large solid things that took forever to heat and a correspondingly long time to cool. He never found it self-evident which setting was the highest, one or three, but was confident he had it figured out this time.

In general, the city seemed to him cleaner, more vibrant, lots of people on the streets and in the sidewalk cafes.

Date: Mon, 26 Aug 2002 0:56 EDT

Hi Cass. *Miremngjes! Të dua!* Here, in this morning apartment, having water but no electricity evoked some childhood memories of summer at the cottage – showering in the half light, in the cool of the morning.

On balance, I slept quite well, tossing a bit at first until I turned the light back on and finished *No Great Mischief*. I think parts of me were various places in the night... but we're all together now, seated at the computer, having eaten muesli with jogourt and banana, and now enjoying a cup of tea.

I'm going into the lab this morning to talk with Afërdita but I need to pay more attention to writing. After all that's what pays my bills.

Looks like a great day – nice early morning blue sky, probably about twenty degrees. I know that from going onto the porch to retrieve today's underwear from the clothesline and then to hang tomorrow's there in its turn. Love, Tom

Date: Tue, 27 Aug 2002 15:34 EDT

Dear Cassie, I think this will get to you, my love, before you go to bed. Hmmm... bed! There's an idea!

Afërdita is chomping at the bit to get started with a Quality Assurance program. Obviously she found her time in Canada motivating. I printed your version of Quality Management procedure forms. She agrees to use those charts as a starting point. Let us not re-invent...

Can you check the microbiology conference program for eligibility criteria and deadlines for late breaker presentations? I fashioned an abstract from the completed Thraxitest material. Elvira would like to attend to present the paper if we can swing some travel dollars. She'd also like to do some of Willie's infection control program but is not interested in spending five weeks in Montreal. Love, Tom

"It's been more than a week. Any other way to find my luggage?" Tom asked Agron as if he should know the intricacies of airline travel. Washing underwear and socks every day was becoming tedious. Nothing was fully dry when he needed it.

"I don't know, Thomas. Maybe we should go to the airport instead of phoning the airline every day."

"Works for me. Do you have time?"

"Maybe in the morning. You can last? You need to borrow something?" laughed Agron.

"I can wait one more night." Tom knew Agron's offer of clothing was facetious, their sizes so radically different.

"Your luggage is not here. The computer says it is in Skopje."

That made some sense to Tom. Having arrived via Skopje even though he was ticketed to Prishtinë. In Vienna the airline assured him his delayed luggage would be sent to the final destination, Prishtinë.

"We could have it transferred here," the Prishtinë baggage manager continued. "But I would not recommend that."

"No?"

"It would need to fly back to Vienna. Then here."

"Why?"

"No Skopje–Prishtinë flights. But it'll take probably four days and let me emphasize, that's minimum."

Agron thanked the man for his help, turned to Tom and said, "We'll go to Skopje."

"I will phone a friend in Macedonia to meet us at the border," Agron explained. "He will take you across into Macedonia."

"Then *we're* not going to Skopje, *I* am?"

"Sorry, Thomas, it must be like this. Kosova vehicles are not allowed to cross the border. Insurance."

"More than that, Agron," chimed in Pjetër, another physician who'd accompanied them just for the adventure. Agron never went anywhere without company. "It is because we drive stolen BMWs and Mercedes."

Pjetër assessed Tom's look of doubt. "No, I am serious," he continued. "We treat it like joke but it is serious problem. Like black market. Cars come here that are stolen in Europe. Criminals do not care about nationality to do business. Just money."

"Okay, Thomas. We will walk to no man's land. Your guide is not yet

193

here. I will phone again. Hello, Rami... How far?... Okay. He should be just five minutes. He walks through checkpoint now. Look... there he is... red shirt."

Agron introduced them. "Rami here is money for expenses."

"No, is not necessary, Agron."

"I insist. Not my money. It is euros from Canada." Agron shoved some bills into Rami's pocket. "We will wait here. How long, Rami?"

"About two hours."

"And, Thomas, I asked Rami to show you a building at the airport. Just look, see if it could fit what we talked about. Do not go in. You will be under surveillance when you pick up your luggage."

Tom was passed off to the Macedonian handler. They walked through the border – Kosova exit booth for a passport check, then Macedonia entrance passport check. Tom thought the border guards ignored Rami but looked him over well, comparing his passport photo to the real thing. Then they walked about a kilometre to his new friend's car, a Turkish model based on a Fiat design.

"This not my car. I borrow from friend. That why I be late. My Renault is in shop. You know Renault in Canada?"

"Yes, not very popular though."

This was craggy mountain terrain. The journey uneventful except for oncoming vehicles passing on curves into the face of traffic. Tom felt lucky to be able to rely on skilful drivers like Agron and now Rami.

"I am family with Agron. My wife is cousin to Agron's mother. I work at airport. We have no trouble." Connections worked wonders. They avoided any red tape. Tom collected his luggage from a secure luggage storage area without passing through Macedonian customs.

"Thomas, that is building over there. Look like every airport building, maybe for repairs or small aeroplane hanger. I tell Agron Russian use building for many years. Agron very interested. Russian all gone now. Why you wish see?"

"Not sure. Agron's idea."

"Okay, we go back now."

Two hours later, it seemed important for Rami to fly under the radar. "I cannot cross border with you. Police very interested if I cross both ways, two times on one day."

There were probably two hundred trucks lined up for customs inspection. Rami bypassed them. Tom thought about how much he was at the mercy of his guides and handlers travelling in the Balkans.

Rami and Tom shook hands. Tom started wheeling two heavy suitcases the one kilometre to the checkpoint. A Macedonian driver stopped and suggested it would be easier if he threw his bags into his car and rode with him. So the stranger handled all the immigration dealings and customs expressed no interest in them. He realized his new friend was angling to be paid to drive him to Prishtinë, but Agron was waiting on the other side.

Date: Wed, 28 Aug 2002 17:21 EDT

Hi Cass, I have luggage! Underwear! I also found and will cherish your hidden note. Good night, my love! *Noten amir!* All my love, Tom

# nine

# September 2002
## *Telefonatë*

Date: Sun, 01 Sep 2002 15:42 EDT
To: Keith <keith.stephenson@symplicity.com>

Hey bro, thanks for your message. Weather's been good here. Still reaching temperatures in the thirties. Probably the same at home. Cassie's coming back middle of the month. That'll be good.

Not as many Canadians around as funding dries up. I sure miss the Saturday night get togethers we used to have with people from various projects. Strange, I'm not at all sure we'd be friends at home but we all enjoy each other's company here.

Glad things are good with you, Tom

"Today is UN holiday. Weekend work only in lab," Elvira explained as she approached Tom in the laboratory corridor.

"What holiday is this, Elvira?" teased Tom.

"Not know name, just UN holiday."

"In Canada, this is Labour Day. We have a holiday to celebrate achievements of workers." Wonderful system, Tom thought. UN celebrates all the ethnic or statutory holidays from around the world, and the Kosovars celebrate them also. Actually, only the Kosovars with a direct working relationship with the UN administration. But that means government services. When asked which holiday, they usually don't know, but regarded a holiday as a holiday!

"Like May Day? We still celebrate. Communist government always have big parade celebrate workers. Is like that?"

"We have parades, sure."

"You speak with Cassandra, tell her hello for me. Can you stay for talk ? I have much things for discuss."

"Sure. I'll say hello to Cassie and no problem, I can stay awhile. You know, things look good, the floors, lab work stations. Labs areas look more organized."

"Yes, Thomas, clean is good but I want more change. Last week, one day, I look at $CO_2$ incubator and it say zero percent. I say to Pashko 'Do you notice this?' I say to microbiology resident, 'What is meaning this?' They make excuse. So I say 'Do you want person from epidemiology or administration come and read gauge?' They say they would not expect. I tell them I find again they both are fired. What to do?"

"You must continue to state your expectations – that quality is the number one aspect of laboratory analysis." Tom continued to explain that without quality measurements, like reading and recording $CO_2$ content, any test results based on that equipment is invalid. Insist they perform all testing again, he suggested. And again, until they comply with her stated expectations. And those expectations must be written and become part of the lab policy and procedure manual.

"Yes, that will work."

"Your demands for quality must be consistent. Monitoring the $CO_2$ atmosphere of incubators is basic quality assurance. Tomorrow you must visit the same work area in the morning and ask to see the results.

And the next day as well. This should not be up to you alone. Delegate to the medical microbiologist working in each area."

"Okay, I do."

"But check on the microbiologists also. They are key individuals. They need to understand accountability for lab results includes even basic equipment monitoring."

"You come tomorrow meet with medical microbiologists? I tell them what is to be."

"Sure, I'll come."

"Okay, Thomas, thank you. Must go home now spend time with family."

"But, one last thing, Elvira. Please don't fire anyone."

Date: Tue, 3 Sep 2002 4:44 EDT

Dear Cass, I must be in charge of the place as everyone's gone off to visit someone with Elvira as driver. As you can imagine, I received a warm welcome but with a difference. They still ask about you but it's not the first thought out of their mouths. First, they inquire about my well-being, not yours. I must have arrived!! But everyone is glad you will be coming soon... *moi aussi!!*

Zani is going to Cleveland at the end of the month. He's hoping to negotiate to be allowed to have his family join him, especially since his youngest has been ill, hospitalized for the last ten days. Apparently both respiratory and digestive tract problems. No definitive diagnosis, but thoughts range from lactose intolerance to cystic fibrosis. The child's home now and much better, now he's been rehydrated. I asked Zani to stay in touch while he's in the US and said we'd visit him in Cleveland. He'll be joining a program geared to people from developing countries who plan to return home with their new knowledge and experience. Zani has assured everyone that there's no way he won't return home!

Pashko's a new father. A son. I picked up a little gift from both of us at that new baby shop across from Renaissance restaurant. Pashko was very pleased, almost emotional, that we'd do such a thing.

I think Afërdita is doing much as we'd like everyone to do. Even Elvira commented to me yesterday that Afërdita gets it, notices increases in *Shigella* isolates, for example, and initiates steps to determine why. This morning, Afërdita was telling me most of the winter passed without any *Salmonella* but with quite a pile of *Shigella*. She has accumulated a collection of stock cultures, so she set out to determine whether the culture media was adequate. Now that's progress! You'll be proud!

By the way, today's Elvira's forty-eighth birthday. She got a kick out of an e-card I sent. Would've been better if she had a sound-card on her computer. But what the heck.

If it's possible could you "borrow" some more Owen Piggy reagent. Sorry! ONPG! I suppose I should refrain from mocking local pronunciation, especially when my Albanian vocabulary is so limited. Embarrassing, to speak only one language. I'll get back to work now. Love, Tom

Rami had escorted Tom across the Macedonian border once again. When they arrived at Alexander the Great Airport in Skopje, Agron was waiting. He'd made his way separately. Tom knew better than to ask. He assumed Agron was concerned about them being seen together at a border crossing. Indeed there were many observers, official and unofficial. In addition to customs and immigration personnel, there were soldiers and police, then another layer of hangers-on each side of the border, but far more on the Kosova side. Ostensibly, many would be taxi drivers or family members waiting for someone specific to cross. But Tom thought immediately of the bridge watchers in the divided city of Mitrovicë. Quite certain names were being recorded and photographs taken.

"There is the building." Agron pointed toward the nondescript low structure amongst a row of repair sheds. The same one Rami had indicated to Tom on the previous trip. Tom noticed a lone man in a hooded sweatshirt watching them from the parking lot in front of the terminal building. Tom caught Agron's attention and with a head movement indicated the man. Agron glanced quickly then looked at Tom. A shrug of Agron's shoulders told Tom he was aware of the observer. They continued to walk toward the building, moving in for closer inspection.

Rudimentary barricades but nothing to seriously impede their entrance into the structure. Inside, all equipment had been removed but the interior still had a lab look, feel and smell. Some garbage was left behind.

"If I piece this broken glass together, it looks suspiciously like tissue culture flask fragments," Tom said. "And this was an air-handling system. Primitive though."

"What do you think was here?" Agron asked.

"Looks to me like maybe chemical fume hoods or rudimentary old style safety cabinets. Look at the patched holes in the roof. Looks like they'd be for shotgun exhaust pipes."

Exhausting straight to the environment, unfiltered, Tom thought. This wiring's not heavy enough for incineration in the air handler. Yeah, microorganisms dumped straight into the atmosphere.

"You said shotgun pipes?"

"Yeah, air from a safety cabinet is expelled with force through a tall pipe. Any pathogens would be immediately diluted in air and pose no problem."

"Does that work?"

"Theoretically. We did the same in North America at one time."

Microbiology was outside Rami's experience but he proved to be a keen observer of people. "When I work at airport there was Russians around this building. They would come in restaurant at terminal building. They stay to themselves."

"Any idea what they did?" Tom asked.

"No, not know. When you are interested in building, I ask friend about it. I have many friend at airport. Some remember Russian but don't know what for building used. Some think storehouse. One old man say maybe rest stop for Russian worker who go home from Africa. What you think they do here, Thomas?"

"I'd guess a virus lab of some sort. It's very, very primitive. And unsafe. These fragments of tissue culture flasks support a lab theory. Bizarre as it seems, looks like they grew their own tissue culture cells here. Maybe did virus culture. But why?" Tom turned to Agron and continued. "Maybe what Rami said about an Africa connection should be an important clue. What were Soviet workers doing in Africa? You know, I'm thinking about a possible quarantine facility for returning workers rather than a rest stop."

"You know that fits," Agron offered. "Use Yugoslavia as a stopover so no infection would be released in the Soviet Union. Keep it here. The Soviets did not much like the Yugoslavs. We were expendable."

"It would make me think the returnees would be health-care workers or scientists. But we may be jumping the gun. Putting the cart before the horse."

"Rami, don't you like when Thomas speaks this way? We have some sayings, too. Just as funny."

When they moved back outside, Tom noticed the observer had moved toward them. Doesn't look to be armed, he thought. No camera apparent. But the man continued to approach, moving straight toward Tom.

"I'll deal with him," Agron said but the man walked up to Tom.

"You want see more building?" the man asked. "I show you."

Before Tom could reply, Agron explained in Serbian that they were looking for an aircraft repair hanger for this American businessman, motioning toward Tom.

"Look at other building, Mr Jones?" Agron asked Tom.

Tom understood Agron wanted him to agree. Then Agron signalled Tom he should pay the man five euros.

Agron and Tom gave a cursory once over to the interior of an adjacent building, determining it had indeed been an aircraft hanger now fallen into irretrievable disrepair. Rami awaited them by the cars.

"What was that about?" Tom asked Agron when they were ready to leave.

Rami quickly answered, "He work at airport long time. No job now. He wait in parking lot, help passenger with luggage, job like that. Just for some money."

"Always wise to stay on good terms with the locals," Agron added.

Date: Tue, 03 Sep 2002 14:35 EDT
From: Thomas Stephenson
To: Dirk O'Reilly

Dirk, our Macedonian contact remembers that a few Russians seemed to be stationed at the Skopje airport until the late eighties. Apparently, no local knowledge of the abandoned building we're examining. Conveniently forgotten or truly unknown.

I swabbed some surfaces, stained areas and heavily soiled areas. Actually swabbed some of the air handling duct material. Watch for the swabs to arrive via diplomatic pouch. Little hope any virus would be cultivable. Not much hope for undeteriorated nucleic acid but get your molecular diagnostics people to have a look anyway. Sorry I can't provide testing guidance. Any DNA or RNA of probable viral origin would be useful.

Please also examine for some of the usual bacterial suspects. I know molecular hates that sort of request – test for everything. Sounds like a TV show. I'm sure you can work up a yarn to explain our interest in this.

I'll have a rudimentary diagnostic virology lab running in the hospital next week. Pretty basic, but I'm training some good people to staff this new unit. Tom


Date: Sun, 08 Sep 2002 16:01 EDT

Hey Tommy, glad to hear things are going well. Also glad Cassie's joining you soon. With winter coming, a man should not need to face those long cold nights sleeping alone. Just not good for the metabolism to be forced to provide all the heat when a significant portion could be provided by another body. I suggested to Suzanne that another woman or two would be ideal, probably could heat the whole house. Anyway, the offshoot is, Suzanne says if I'm truly interested in a three dog night, she'd make arrangements with the local kennel club. Women have no sense of humour! Take care, Bert

Date: Sun,  08 Sep 2002 16:26 EDT

Hi Cass, I walked to the old place today but nobody home. I'll try again another day. I took the path down from the upper road past the Serbian church. The church is intact but boarded up. Two UN guards secure the area. The original crimes are horrendous but evidence of retribution is still appalling.

I expect this will be a good week especially looking forward to your arrival next week. In loving anticipation, Tom

Tom had invited a group of Kosovar friends to his Prishtinë apartment Sunday afternoon. If he wondered before, he now knew he should have cut off the supply of beer earlier to avoid becoming an object of their humour once again.

"Thomas, we want your Albanian poem before we go out."

"No, Agron. I'd feel foolish."

"I will ask. *Mbaj vesh*! Listen, guys…"

"This is crazy," Tom protested to the others. "I don't speak much Albanian. I can buy bread. One loaf only. *Një bukë*. To buy a dozen eggs, I ask for *gjashtë ve e gjashtë ve,* six eggs and then another six eggs. So don't do this, I beg."

Agron regarded him quizzically. He knew Tom's language abilities. "Thomas, come on, we all are friends. They will enjoy it. *Mbaj vesh*, listen everyone, our friend Thomas has wrote poem in *Shqip*. He should read it?"

"*Po, po!* Read, Thomas!" the other five shouted almost in unison. They'd gathered at Tom's apartment before heading out for pizza and more beer.

"The poem is called *S'ka,"* Tom began tentatively, still reticent to show off his Albanian language skills. He was usually careful to engage only in simple good morning type conversations before switching to English.

"No, Thomas, wait. You must stand on stage. Most famous poet from Canada. Like Mr. Leonard Cohen."

Agron supported Tom as the others grabbed his arms, lifting him, manhandling him onto the back of the couch until he complained. They reluctantly relented, allowing him to stand on the seat cushions.

"The poem is called *S'ka*," he started again.

"Yes, yes, we know," the audience responded. "You told us already."


*S'ka ujë*
*S'ka rrymë*
*Asgjë nuk punon*
*S'ka problem, falemnderit*
*Ngase ne jemi të lirë*
*Të dua*

"Ah, nice," Alëks interposed. "No water, but lots of love. This is how you speak to Cassandra?"

"Just wait. There's a second verse."

"Quiet everybody, there is more. More love, Thomas?"

*Mirëpo, nesër*
*Do të ketë*
*Ujë*
*Rrymë*
*Gjithçka do të punon*
*Ngase në e kemi lirinë*
*Të dua shumë*

"Thomas, that is wonderful. You are such good friend for Kosova," said Skender. "Now, let's go drink."

Date: Sun, 08 Sep 2002 21:26 EDT
Hi Cassie, sent you a copy of my Albanian poem, but forgot to include the translation. Love you, Tom

No water
No power
Nothing works
Not a problem, thank you
Because we are free
I love you

However, tomorrow,

There will be

Water

Power

Everything will work

Because we have freedom

I love you very much

Date: Tue, 10 Sep 2002 10:07 EDT
From: Thomas Stephenson
To: Dirk O'Reilly

Dirk, what's up with molecular? It's been more than a week. We need a status report. Have any nucleic acid fragments been detected? Agron and I are working on a concept of possible association with the cave situation. Skopje may not be the right connection. But we need info. Tom

Date: Tue, 10 Sep 2002 10:43 EDT

Tom, be patient. Molecular's detected a nucleic acid mixture. Some human of course. We know with certainty your Skopje facility handled anthrax, plague, botulism. There's also uncharacterized viral and bacterial DNA and RNA. A dirty mess. One large fragment of RNA viral genome appears to be a segment from a single virus rather than a recombinant. Amplifies rapidly in a minimum number of cycles. Conclusion from that, very biologically active segment if not a whole virus. But no match with any primer in our pathogen library. Either it's not been seen before or there's been little interest in sequencing because of low pathogenicity in humans.

Tell me about your caves. Dirk

Appears to be nine bodies. No local memory of nine people missing in the last fifty years. Before that some local men were killed during WWII but those bodies are in known gravesites. Conclusion so far, not locals. Nor from surrounding villages. Don't know if you realize how tightly information is held within a village when it serves the community purpose. Folks we talked with are genuinely concerned and surprised. They believe strongly bodies of locals must be recovered and laid to rest at home. Discrete inquiries have been made of surrounding municipalities. Existence of the caves has been cloaked in secrecy since their discovery. Some elders were visibly shaken with the suggestion someone else not only knew of the caves but used them for covert purposes. And, indeed, everyone believes this was covert. Tom

So, the bones aren't likely from bodies of locals. What else?

We're trying to piece the facts together. Visited the hill over the cave mound and although overgrown we found suggestion of a structure. Perhaps an opening into the cave. Please keep after molecular for definitive results. Thanks, Tom

Date: Mon, 16 Sep 2002 09:17 EDT

Dear Mom, I arrived safely Saturday afternoon. Tom says I brought him beautiful weather after a summer of rain. Today's a Muslim holiday so no one's working. Love, Cassie

Date: Tue, 17 Sep 2002 15:12 EDT
From: Dirk O'Reilly
To: Thomas Stephenson

Tom, molecular cannot shed any more light on the viral RNA. We've reached the end.

What happened to academic interest? Can someone continue investigating as a project? Tom

You know the real problem is funding. We've simply exhausted our ability to follow obtuse leads to conclusion. If you can provide more specimens to tie this to something, I could have nucleic acid comparisons done, comparing sequences and searching for an entire genome. However, that doesn't mean we'll ever be able to identify the virus unless we can grow it in culture. Dirk

Date: Wed, 25 Sep 2002 14:25 EDT

Hi Marianne. Such a short trip this time it almost seems useless. Except of course I really appreciate spending time here with Tommy. We have trouble coordinating our schedules so we can be here at the same time. For instance, last month when I was set to join Tom, Jordan Siemens suddenly decided I needed to attend some high level meetings in Winnipeg. Well, the meetings were hardly high level, only dealing with mundane lab issues.

I am making progress in the lab, however, and Tom helps me when he can. Before I came back, he set up a virus lab, trained a few handpicked staff so we now offer a diagnostic virology service. The docs love it. They appreciate Tom's work at the lab so much they're willing to interview for his magazine articles. I think they provide a lot more information than he would normally get. Tommy guards this information tightly. He only tells me a few things. I know he thinks he's protecting me. We'll have late dinner tonight at *Il Passatore Restaurante*. Just a chance to be together alone. I'll be leaving for home Friday noon. See you soon, Mom

"I should really be writing a story about you," Tom told Cassandra.

"*Pourquoi?*"

"Well firstly, because you're here. I've been listening to your friends. They're amazed at the changes you've made in lab practice. That's an accomplishment."

"Well, I've had willing collaboration. Haven't done anything on my own."

"You know, you can get stories out of people faster than I can," Tom continued.

"Who've you been listening to?"

"Everybody. This place is a Cassandra love fest."

"C'mon Tommy, don't be crazy."

"Oh no. I'm a trained observer. I see it. And I'm part of it. I love you too."

"I'm sorry I have to leave. It's been nice just us in the apartment without Greg or somebody else here."

"Yeah, we caught a break."

"Not that I don't like Greg..."

"You know, since you keep coming back, people feel comfortable with you. They trust you. So they're sharing something like a traditional oral history."

"It's like that isn't it? Thirty weeks here must count for something."

"Elvira was telling me some things. I could tell how anxious she is for you to continue to be here. Hey, I'm thinking, I'm here helping out too. What's so special about Cassandra? I mean other than me wanting you here, also."

"And so?"

"Well, it appears you're the only one who's ever assessed and understood day-to-day lab functions and problems. Now, there's a résumé statement, if I've ever seen one."

"C'mon, lots of people have been here helping. They just haven't stayed long enough to be effective."

"Yeah. Elvira told me about microbiologists from Germany, Denmark, Italy, Japan. Even Cuba. All coming to aid the hospital microbiology laboratory."

"She mentioned the Cuban? Did she tell you he was here six months? Walked in the first day, looked at the equipment and facilities. Immediately declared it wasn't modern enough for him and refused to actually do anything. He spent his time in Elvira's office using her computer or sleeping."

"Yeah, she said all that. That's why I should write a story about you."

"No, Tommy, please."

"It's okay Cass. I'm teasing. I wouldn't do it while you're travelling back and forth. I'd be uneasy drawing attention to your activities. Wouldn't want you to be a target for anything."

"We should get to bed. I'm leaving early in the morning. Shpend's picking me up."

"Why don't I tag along and see you off at the airport?"

"Oh Tommy, I'd like that."

ten

# October 2002
## *Mjet komunikimi*

"Thomas, she is Roza." Elvira motioned toward the woman she led into the microbiology office.

"Dr Elvira, I am not Roza," the young woman protested.

"You are Roza for Thomas. Thomas do not need real name," Elvira continued.

"I... no, it's okay...," Tom stammered.

"Roza is easy name for him. He have trouble with *Shqipe* name. Thomas, Roza is new *doktor*. Roza have woman story."

"Pleased to meet you Roza. I'm Thomas Stephenson. I'm a writer. Do you want Dr Elvira to translate?"

"No, Mr Thomas, I don't need translation. I study medicine in Switzerland. My English is good."

"Please call me Thomas or Tom. Elvira tells me you have a story. I'm certain it's not your medical training."

"I will go in lab now," Elvira interjected. Tom was relieved. The last thing he wanted was Elvira directing story flow.

"You are right. Medical training is not the story. But because of my story, I'm studying gynaecology so I can help with women's health. Most gynaecologists here are men. I believe women should be in charge of their own health."

"Are you in residency here?"

"No. I've returned to Prishtinë for two months only. It is *praktikë mjekësi*, a practicum. After that, and Christmas break, I return to Geneva. Many doctors here are women but women's medicine is still dominated by men."

"You said you're studying gynaecology because of your story?"

"Yes. Mine is a woman's story as casualty of war. I was treated in a way no woman should be. No person should be. Civilians should not be deliberate victims."

"You're right about your English. It *is* good. You speak like it's your mother tongue."

"Thank you. My father was professor of English language before our Kosova troubles. Then he was a secondary school principal. Later demoted to classroom teacher to teach Serbian literature. Finally assigned a caretaker's job. My father believed in public education."

"Your father must have felt degraded."

"Serb police interviewed him every week asking him about the parallel system. My mother is Serbian. From a well-known family. I know my father's continued employment was because of my mother."

"Was your father an Albanian nationalist?"

"No, not at first. My father believed in Yugoslavia. When Slovenia and Macedonia were able to secede without much bloodshed and the Croatian and Bosnian wars were over, he still hoped cooler heads would prevail, the politics would change, there would be recognition of the noble experiment that was Yugoslavia."

"I see."

"Like many, he hoped the remnants of Yugoslavia would continue as a country. He hoped the central government was not involved in Bosnia. He didn't trust Slobodan Milosevic but believed him when he saw him on BBC. Milosevic said he would intervene in Bosnia. We didn't know he planned the genocides. My mother's name is Milosevic. Only a third or fourth cousin. But Serbs killed my father."

"Roza, I'm sorry …"

"Thank you. Thomas, I'm not Roza. I'm Shpresa. Translates as Hope in English. Dr Elvira wanted to protect me. That is not necessary."

"Your father …"

"Serbs didn't shoot my father. They gave him a slow death. They harassed him and they raped me."

"Roza … Shpresa …"

"I want you to hear my story. It is what happens to women in many wars. It was punishment for my father because I was half Albanian. Because he contaminated the Serb race. Because I had the audacity to leave Yugoslavia to study at international schools as if I was worthy. I was studying to become a doctor when everyone knows Albanians are lazy and stupid."

"You were told this?" Tom asked incredulously.

"Listen to me, Thomas. I know the reasons. Five Serb policemen grabbed me near the corner of Mother Teresa where Hotel Baci is now. They carried me across the roadway to the centre of the traffic circle. You know the place, very open, clearly visible to all sides of the intersection. I didn't think anything bad would happen."

Tom pressed his record switch.

"The two young policemen were from our neighbourhood," Shpresa began. "I knew them. This was intended to be public. They called me bitch, Albanian bastard. They screamed at me, started to touch me. They groped me. The older ones. Then the leader ripped open the front of my blouse. The young ones looked humiliated and scared. I appealed to them for protection.

The leader turned to them and said, 'You will be part of this. It is your right and your duty. She is a bitch and a snob, this Albanian whore.'

He shoved Nikola toward me, 'You will do her.'

Nikola said he would not.

'Yes, you will. It is your duty,' the leader said. Then he hit Nikola's chest with his, I think, truncheon?"

"Truncheon, yes, good word. Night-stick, club." Tom was surprised his voice sounded normal missing the tone of anxiety he felt. He was relieved to be able to focus on language, to break the tension, the tightness building in his chest.

Shpresa, the physician, recognized his difficulties. "Thomas, it is more than five years now. I am okay."

"Shpresa, I'm so sorry." She's so composed, so calm, so... so beautiful. She's tall. Lithe. Long dark hair, classic Kosovar beauty. He couldn't focus.

"Don't be sorry, Thomas. You were not there. It is not your fault. I was calm until Jovovic hit Nikola. I realized they wanted a public spectacle, a circus. I refused to participate. I was quiet, not screaming or sobbing. I was determined not to give them any satisfaction. We were in the middle of this traffic circle. I felt humiliated but I thought passers-by might intervene. A crowd gathered on one corner. Traffic kept moving slowly. No one tried to intervene, to move against the hated Serb police. The leader wanted more action, more response from me. I know his name now, Jovovic. He's in The Hague but for other matters, not this.

Jovovic shouted to the onlookers across the street, 'This whore will pay. Her father is Albanian pig. Her mother is Serbian slut.'

The two older officers held my arms while Jovovic beat me with his night-stick. Hit me across my forehead." Shpresa pushed her hair back to show Tom the scars on her scalp. "Then, he used the stick to beat my breasts. They held my arms behind me. With the stick, he pulled and twisted my brassiere until it tore and my breasts were exposed. I realized then this wasn't just harassment. Then with the night-stick, he ripped the rest of my clothing off. I remember thinking it was funny, no, not funny, strange. He wouldn't touch me with his hands. As if I were grotesque. It's stupid but I think I felt offended. Amazing isn't it, what can flash through your mind. Then, he lifted my breasts with his stick.

'Your turn,' Jovovic says to one of the others as he took one of my arms. The man unzipped himself. 'Albanian pig,' he says. 'Bend her over, boys.' He fumbles around trying to penetrate me from behind. With difficulty. He can't enter my vagina so he settles for anal penetration. The pain is excruciating. I start to scream. But my mind plays tricks. I remember thinking at least I am still a virgin."

I'm not sure I really want to hear more, Tom thought. He stood, moved to the credenza, tore some paper towel from the roll sitting there and wiped the sweat from his brow. Then sat again, seemingly frozen, forced to hear her words. He asked Shpresa to carry on.

"Then it was the other's turn. He was even more brutal. He slapped my head again and again. When he realizes his partner has settled for anal intercourse, he is incensed. 'That is for pretty boys. Not for me. I am real man,' he shouted. 'This pig still virgin for me.' He then grabs the night-stick from Jovovic and reaches around me. He rubs the stick against my vulva. Jovovic grabs the stick back. He orders the younger two to hold my arms. They force me to hunch over even more and he rams the stick at me, against me, then beats me on the head. Then he forces the stick into my vagina. I scream again and again as I feel myself tear.

'There, try that, he says. 'She is ready for you now. Ready and waiting.'

I am screaming uncontrollably now, writhing, shaking. So much pain, so angry, so torn. Jovovic shoves his partner back at me. He gives a half-hearted effort, shoving against me. He inserts his penis between my labia but doesn't penetrate any further. Then Jovovic grabs Nikola. 'Your turn. For your country.'

Nikola tries to pull away from him. 'I can't do it,' he says.

'Do this! Or I will shoot you.' Jovovic lays his pistol against Nikola's face. 'Now!' The others hold me on the ground, face up this time. Nikola is white like a ghost, shaking and agitated. Just like me. He lays his flaccid penis against me. He will pretend. He leans his lips against my ear and whispers, 'I am sorry, Shpresa. So sorry.'

I think, 'This boy will be shot. This is not enough entertainment for Jovovic.' Suddenly I realize my arms are free but I don't struggle to get away. Suddenly I am concerned about Nikola. With one hand I started to encourage his penis. I don't know why. He responded and penetrated my vagina.

I whisper, 'Please, Nikola, do not finish in me. It is wrong time of month.'

Elvira burst through the office door, back from the lab.

Shpresa, at first startled, turned to Tom, "I need to stop awhile now."

Tom was ready for a break also, so when Elvira suggested they walk downtown for *kafe*, he was relieved. But he felt trapped by Elvira's suggestion. He wanted to get away from the confining situation, away from Shpresa and, even, Elvira. He felt drained of adrenaline. But did crave fresh air. A quick beer more to his liking than cappuccino.

The two women decided on pizza rather than coffee so the three of them headed for Vullkano restaurant.

"Dr Elvira knows my story, Thomas." Shpresa picked up her narrative once they were seated at a table. Tom didn't know what to say. He hadn't expected Shpresa to continue. In fact, he hoped she wouldn't. That he'd have the time he needed to calm down. He didn't like his continuing feeling of apprehension. She's in denial, she's not okay, she's still more affected than she admits, he thought.

"She helped me get to Geneva to a good gynaecologist and a good psychiatrist. That's why I decided to continue my medical studies in Switzerland. I know you are concerned but I am fine. I am okay. I needed much internal repair, downstairs and upstairs. Don't be shocked, Thomas. It's medical humour. You call it black humour. But my body and mind are okay now. I was pregnant from the rape. So, in Switzerland, I had an abortion. Dr Elvira does not know that. See how surprised she looks. Will we have a Vullkano special pizza?"

Tom and Elvira looked bewildered by Shpresa's change of focus but nodded their silent agreement, the three of them sitting there, sipping cappuccino. Brightly coloured tablecloths failed to lighten the mood of the conversation. Please, can we do this another time? Tom thought but remained silent.

"If I didn't have an abortion, I would want to have my baby in Prishtinë with my family around me. My parents know everything that happened. They were so supportive. My father's dead now. He could put up with harassment from Serbs. That was a problem only to himself. He could not survive his daughter suffering brutality and indignities. He died from a broken heart. That may not be a medical diagnosis, but it's my diagnosis."

"I'm sorry," Tom said.

Shpresa shook her head. "My mother lives in Prishtinë still. If people realize she's Serbian, it doesn't seem to be an issue. She speaks good Albanian. But, Thomas, there is a Roza. Similar things happened to her. She was not so lucky as me."

"Please don't diminish what happened by saying it's nothing," Tom said. "That others had it worse. Everyone here minimizes their own hardships. They point to others who had even greater trouble. You're so calm, Shpresa. This happened to you."

"I see a psychologist and a mental health team. All in Geneva. I cannot live here right now. I need too much support."

"We can talk about other things, the three of us. You can tell me Roza's story another day. We can have lunch nearer the hospital one day when you have time."

"There is more about Nikola. 'I am virgin too,' Nikola whispered in my ear. 'I am so sorry, Shpresa. Sorry that it is this way for you.'

'I am sorry for you as well,' I whispered back.

'Don't talk to her,' Jovovic shouted. I started to sob and Nikola was sobbing when they pulled him off me. Then they grabbed my ankles and held me upside down to prevent Nikola's semen from seeping out. They wanted me pregnant. I screamed but went silent when I heard Jovovic reproaching Nikola. 'What are you sobbing about?'

'We did not need to be so brutal.'

'She is just an Albanian pig. She is a whore. This your first experience with a whore?' Jovovic laughed derisively, then he said, 'It doesn't get better than this. You need to show these whores who's boss. Then they will be submissive. Next time, this bitch will just lie down for all of us.'

'She was my neighbour.'

Jovovic drew his gun and shot Nikola in the head. I screamed and screamed and screamed. Then they beat me unconscious. They wanted me pregnant but they would not be concerned if I died from my injuries. They knew an abortion would not happen in Kosova."

Tom couldn't remember coming back to the apartment. Probably one beer too many, he thought. But he continued to be alert, Shpresa's story coursing through his head. Contemplating writing this story seemed so hard. He doubted his ability. Needed Cassie's input to keep a female perspective. It's too easy to inadvertently trivialize the experiences of others, he thought. He needed someone to talk with. He e-mailed Cassie. Asked her to phone him. When the phone rang he grabbed it quickly.

"Hello Cass. Thank you so much for calling. I need to talk badly.

I'm agitated. Hands shaking, heart's racing. Need to calm down."

"Tommy, tell me."

Tom told Cassie Shpresa's story exactly as she'd related it. They talked for an hour. He was relieved to have someone to share with, even troubles.

"Cass, does this whole story ring true with you?" he eventually asked.

"There's one problem. I don't really understand what she told you at the restaurant about Nikola. Portraying him as a victim, too. Showing compassion toward him."

"That part bothers me too. I would think the last thing a woman wants is to facilitate her own rape. Am I wrong?"

"No, no you're not wrong."

"Yet, she told that so calmly. So composed. She is still in therapy and five years have passed, but..."

"You say she was so beaten up, so damaged. What do you think?"

"I don't know. It hits me almost as someone else's story. Maybe an amalgam of experiences. She's a physician but so unemotional and clinical in the telling, I don't know."

"She didn't appear upset but you were?"

"For sure, I was upset. She described distress but showed little. Such senseless brutality. Bullying, control, subjugation. Humiliation. Yet she described parts of her experience almost dispassionately. Maybe she needs to distance herself from being the victim."

"That doesn't make it less true."

"No, no doubt. It's not fabricated."

"Maybe she and Elvira want the story told. You've been selected as conduit," Cassie said.

"The story should be told. I'm just not certain I'm the one to tell it." I'm not certain I can be objective.

Date: Sat, 12 Oct 2002 6:41 EDT

Hello again, my sweetheart. Thank you so much for talking me down last night. I feel better this morning but hardly slept, tossed physically and mentally most of the night. In some ways I feel almost giddy, flippant. Must be trying desperately to compensate. This interview has affected me more than any other so far. But enough of that. I hope you'll go to your family reunion. I know staying connected means a lot to you. And you've not had as much opportunity as you'd like. Whatever you decide, I wish you a nice day and a good Thanksgiving weekend. All my love, Tom

The taxi dropped Claire and Tom outside the UNMIK checkpoint. Russian soldiers protecting the village had waved the driver off, reinforcing that he wasn't permitted to enter the enclave. Once Claire and Tom identified themselves to the guards, they were allowed to walk the last two hundred metres to the restaurant.

"Let's meet my Romanian friends for Sunday brunch," Claire had said. Tom jumped at the opportunity to distance himself from his thoughts about Shpresa. "They wanna go to a pork restaurant," she continued.

"That means Serb." Tom's internal alarm bells triggered. He'd visited Serbian enclaves but never socially. He didn't express his misgivings but instead asked, "Where?"

"Not far from the hospital grounds. Y'know the highway to Macedonia? There's a Serb village at the top of the first hill. Caglavica it's called."

"How'll we get there?" he asked, knowing he wouldn't ask Agron to drive them. May not be a really good idea, going to a Serbian restaurant.

"We'll take a taxi," replied Claire matter-of-factly as if she were speaking of downtown Regina. "Then, the Romanians will bring us back to Prishtinë."

"How do you know these people?"

"I met them when I was stranded in Vienna."

"Pardon me? Stranded in Vienna?"

"Didn't you know? That's why I wasn't around last week. Fog. I took the shuttle to the airport each day. And each day the flight to Prishtinë was cancelled. Five days in a row. I got to know Dorinel and Mikhail because they showed up for the same flight as me every day. After a few days they showed me around Vienna."

"Hello, Claire. Nice see you again."

"It is nice, Dorinel. This's my good friend, Tom." Introductions made, Dorinel and Mikhail. Dorinel's English passable, Mikhail's non-existent.

"Please sit at table. I order flask of slivovitz for start. It is on table. We start already, Mikhail and me, with small toast. Perhaps we toast again?"

"Good for me," Claire said. "You, Tom?"

"Sure. *Santé*." Tom decided not to use the Albanian *gezhuar* to propose a toast. He was sure the Serbian staff wouldn't appreciate Albanian being spoken.

"*Noroc, sânâtate.* Good luck, your health." Dorinel toasted in Romanian.

"*Şi moarte Ţiganilor*," added Mikhail, laughing.

Dorinel joined Mikhail in laughter but added, "Naughty, Mikhail. We do not say that no more. It is our toast from older day. Good luck, your health, and death to gypsies."

Tom immediately disliked these guys. So far, he didn't appreciate their humour. He wondered what Claire saw in them, but decided he should give it a chance. He didn't know why he should feel suddenly protective of the small community of Roma in Kosova.

"I order already. I speak Serbian. Tell waiter pork steaks for three. That be enough for us. There be very much food." Dorinel signalled the waiter to proceed with the order. "We drink *Jelen pivo*, most famous Serbian beer. Order it too."

"There is Joseph," Dorinel continued. "He join us."

More introductions. Joseph worked with the other two. More slivovitz, more toasts, without reference to gypsies.

"We work for Teletechnika. We coming back from Paris when we meet beautiful Claire." Dorinel answered and expanded on Tom's question. "Teletechnika is giant French telecom company. You know them? Company operate all of Europe."

"Why is Teletechnika in Kosova?" Tom asked.

"We say Kosovo. Especially in Serbian village."

Okay, correct me on that. That seals it. No more chances, I definitely don't like these guys.

"We here to fix telephone service. PTK need new land line and improve mobile service. Tom, mobile phone service have one hundred twenty employee. So much profit it subsidize four thousand more employee for land phone and mail. You know PTK is phone company and post office?"

The food arrived, platters overflowing with grilled pork steaks still sizzling, two huge salads, mounds of boiled potatoes. And three large pitchers of beer. Even with Joseph added to the table, there'd be food left over. Hope there'll be beer left over as well, Tom thought. Especially if these guys represent our transportation back into the city. He felt a guilty pleasure enjoying food not available in the rest of

Muslim Kosova. He hoped Agron won't ask about his weekend.

"We work here because Teletechnika pay good. I hate work with Albanian. They so lazy. And so stupid. PTK is disaster. Four thousand employee do nothing."

"Things are better in Bucharest?" Tom asked, trying to disguise his growing annoyance. So typical in the Balkans to maintain old prejudices. Strike three. Dorinel's struck out.

"Oh, yes. Much better. Ever since Ceauşescu."

"He was executed in eighty-nine. Romania's had thirteen years to get their act together. That's quite a head start over Kosova." Tom emphasized Kosova.

"This should be still Yugoslavia. Romania and Serbia, we are neighbour. We know each other, we are friend. We eat same thing. In Belgrade and Bucharest we know each language, we celebrate together. We not be Muslim."

"So you don't care what happens in Kosova?"

Dorinel gave him a startled look. "I care about Teletechnika. I care I get paid."

"So, you're a mercenary."

There was silence at the table. Then Dorinel said carefully, "Not understand you, Tom. Pay better here than at home. Of course, I come here. You think that be wrong, look after myself and my family? We suffer, too."

"No. No problem. Just wondering. I see how you feel." Tom forced himself to back away from his antagonistic stance.

"Albanian hate Serb. Here, there is back road between many village so no Serb must use highway. Everyone afraid. Afraid of Albanian. They born here in Kosovo province. Is their home. They not from Serbia."

I'm ready to leave. Claire isn't looking very comfortable either. I hope my behaviour hasn't ruined her Sunday. As they left the restaurant, Tom looked around. The village was a collection of huts with a few decent looking houses interspersed. Each car bore old Yugoslav license plates, because the inhabitants continued to see themselves as part of Yugoslavia. Everyone on the dusty streets looked unhappy. The whole area was under very obvious UN protection, a tank and a guard posted at the entrance to the village. Chain link fencing and rolls of razor wire around the perimeter.

"Tom, will you sit beside me going back, please." Claire approached him quietly.

"Is there a problem?"

"Not really."

They returned to Prishtinë. Claire asked to be dropped at the Baci Hotel. She politely asked the others to stop for cappuccino. They declined graciously.

"You know, Tom. We could've walked back. Only three kilometres."

"I thought you were enjoying their company?"

"They were hitting on me. Proposing something with the three of them."

"What?"

"Tom, you're so naïve. I don't know why Cassandra puts up with you. I told them you're my lover."

"Oh."

"Don't worry. It's not important. But I'm glad you came with me. I might've had trouble otherwise. Thank you, my friend."

"Hello, Thomas, *mirëmëngjes*." Shpresa joined Tom at his table in the coffee shop.

*"Mirëmëngjes, Shpresa. Si jeni? Si u zgjuat?"* Tom replied.

"Thomas, this is Roza, who I told you about."

"Hello, Roza. *Gëzohem që u takuam."*

Roza didn't carry herself with Shpresa's confidence. Tom wasn't sure how he should respond to a victim of men's violence.

"Roza does not speak English, but I want you to know Roza is real," Shpresa said.

"Okay. Thank you."

"Roza's story is like mine. Brutal public rape by three Serb soldiers, each one participating. Cowardly Serbs running away from NATO taking time to loot and plunder. And rape. They tried to destroy what was left of Kosova. It is a pattern. The same throughout Kosova. I will tell you Roza's story. I can ask her about parts I don't know and translate."

"Let me ask. I assume you're telling me because you'd like this story published?"

"Yes, of course, that's why we're telling you," Shpresa said.

"And who is we?"

"Me and Roza. And Dr Elvira."

"I'm not sure I'm the person to write this."

"Dr Elvira says you are. You're sympathetic to us but you're objective in your writing. You tell credible stories."

"You seem to know Elvira well. Are you related?"

"Well… yes, she's my father's cousin."

"Ah, I see." Tom looked at Roza then back to Shpresa. "Please tell Roza what we're talking about. She looks ill at ease."

"I'll tell her story now." Roza nodded in agreement.

"Sorry to interrupt. Please ask her if I can record what we talk about." Tom gestured to Roza with his recorder.

"Yes, she understands. I asked her earlier. Her rape was similar to mine. Much brutality, but by three men. After they raped her, they continued to violate her with other objects. Sticks and rifle barrels. They left her to die. Some other Serb soldiers found her and rushed her to University Hospital."

"Oh, really."

"Yes. Not all Serbs are monsters. Most doctors and nurses were leaving Kosova as quickly as they could. NATO was coming. But a nurse triaged her and asked one of the doctors to treat her. They did only basic first aid."

"Why?" Tom asked.

"There were no supplies. Retreating soldiers and medical staff stole equipment and destroyed anything they couldn't easily move. One of the doctors took Roza in his car to a Health House."

"So, the Serbs knew about the Health Houses?"

"Some, yes." Shpresa glanced around, then continued in a low voice. "Some would steal hospital supplies and pass them to their friends in the Albanian medical community. You must understand, Thomas, Kosova was in transition. No Albanian doctors at the hospital yet, no sophistication in the Health Houses. They stabilized her. They saved her life."

Shpresa continued to describe how the preceding year she'd taken Roza to Geneva for surgical correction of much of the damage. Physical damage. Three years after the attack. Tom pressed the record button.

"She was a virgin. She's had no lovers. She may never have. She's spoiled, contaminated. Because she was raped, you understand, not because it was by Serbs. I know you want to ask, so yes, she is a cousin also. We look after family in Kosova. Because she was in so much pain and was so sick, nobody realized Roza was pregnant. Her nutrition was very poor so it was only apparent to the doctor at the Health House at about seven months. Pregnancy out of marriage is not tolerated in rural Kosova, still. Even as result of rape. Her father had barely accepted Roza since she was violated. Now she was pregnant, he threw her out of their home."

"So her family wanted nothing to do with her? Even though she'd been raped?" Tom shook his head.

"Her mother would be sympathetic but it was her father's orders. And, Thomas, especially because she was raped. My mother brought her to our apartment. I was in Switzerland so my bed was available for her. You understand, Thomas, our apartments are small. We don't have a bedroom for every family member. But we have a bed. My mother's a kind, compassionate woman. And a great cook. She looked after Roza's nutrition and gave her tender care. When her time was near, my mother took her to the maternity hospital. Albanian doctors had moved into the hospital. Roza was in a ward with fourteen other women. In Switzerland, the room would be for... well, in Switzerland, we don't have such rooms. In former Yugoslavia, the room would be for six patients. No glass in the windows, no heat, dirty. This isn't like the maternity hospital you Canadians have reconstructed, the one the obstetricians now call the palace."

"Would her outcome have been different in the palace?" Tom asked.

"I don't know. Roza's birth canal was torn still, with many adhesions, so a botched Caesarean was attempted. The baby died, Roza survived. I'm glad Roza doesn't understand English. I think it was the best outcome. One doctor attempted some repairs but that was bungled also."

"You seem unsure whether the result would be better today?"

"Frankly, Thomas, I really don't know. Facilities are better. It's just that doctors still need training. And, this level of brutality is not routinely encountered in an obstetrical practice. The outcome may not be different even somewhere else."

"Yeah, I understand. I can see that."

"Also, if the baby survived, there would be another problem,' Shpresa said. "For all rape mothers and babies, really for any mother and baby, it is for the family of the father to decide whether the family will accept the baby. And whether they will accept the woman. Until this happens, mother and child remain in hospital. If the father's family does not want one or either, it's the turn of the mother's family to decide."

"You mean either family can decide to accept the woman, the baby, both or neither?"

"Yes, I mean that. A woman has no means of support otherwise. Of course, it is much different for urban people. But the hospitals include orphanages still full three years post-conflict. I see that every day. And many mothers are in hospital still, unaccepted. Our society will change. But, Thomas, when I finish my residency, I'm not certain I can practice here. I've become too European. Next year, I'll be eligible for Swiss citizenship."

"Was Roza accepted back by her family?"

"No, she lives still with my mother."

Date: Mon, 14 Oct 2002 9:47 EDT

*Bonjour mon amoureuse! Comment ça va, ce matin?* Had lunch with Zani today at Shark restaurant. It's a small place on the second storey in the new shops across from Pepto-Bismol. Just various sandwiches, salads, pizzas and things like that. Zani sends his regards. He wants to help Elvira develop a new microbiology residency program. They presented a request for funding in Paris but now need to formalize something. I told him residents would be better able to guide technical staff performance if they had a good handle on practical bacteriology including culturing and classical identification methods.

On my early morning walkabout in the lab, I noticed the readout on one incubator showed an eleven percent $CO_2$ atmosphere. Did nothing. Expected result would be recorded and, hopefully, would ring alarm bells or raise the red flag or whatever the next metaphor would be. Especially after Elvira threatened to fire everyone for ignoring quality indicators.

"Ishmael, is this your writing on this form?" Tom asked.

"What is wrong, Thomas?"

"Would you please tell me what this gauge reads?"

*"Njëmbëdhjetë për qind."*

"But you wrote six percent."

"That is what is correct."

"No. That's not what the gauge read. The $CO_2$ atmosphere has not changed all morning. I've been looking at the gauge since seven-thirty."

"You trick me." Ishmael fixed Tom with an accusatory stare, then shrugged his shoulders when Tom wasn't intimidated by his belligerence. "We are all the time too busy. Too busy for forms. It is what we expect – six percent."

Although Tom challenged Ishmael quietly, two residents and four student technologists who apparently assumed something worthy of their notice was taking place watched the two men.

"Come join the discussion." Tom beckoned to them and the other technologists in the room. "Ishmael and I are talking about the importance of quality assurance to the crucial work we do in the lab. We're discussing what could cause $CO_2$ levels to vary from day to day.

Can someone get me a screwdriver?"

Pashko searched the desk drawer and produced several screwdrivers and a hammer. Tom selected the Philips screwdriver and opened the small panel on the side of the incubator. He pulled out a twenty-five millimetre in-line air filter capsule.

"This should be white," he said. "*Borëbardhë.* Not black like this. This filter is clogged. Is there a replacement filter?"

The assembled group looked at each other and at Tom as though they didn't understand.

"All right, I'll ask Zani to order filters," Tom said. "For now, it will work better without a filter."

I allowed Ishmael to save face, but reiterated to all assembled the importance of quality assurance. I know this mystifies you, too. Not a great effort's needed to measure the $CO_2$ level. The lab misses you being there. But I miss you on a whole different level. I really see what you've been up against. Hope you have a fine day. Love, Tom

*"Mirëdita,* Thomas. Hello."

"Hello, Shpresa."

"Thomas, I want to change my story." Shpresa smiled shyly at Tom. "Have you published it yet?"

"No, I'm having trouble writing it."

"Good. Not good you're having trouble but good you haven't finished."

"Your story isn't true?"

"Oh, yes, it's true, mine and Roza's. Some details are different, especially about helping Nikola... I don't know why I said that. Nikola is dead. Jovovic is in prison for other atrocities."

"Okay..."

"I hope you'll not think less of me. This is the same story I told my first psychiatrist:

'This is what you believe?' the psychiatrist asked.

'This is what happened,' I answered.

'No,' she replied. 'The ending is not true. Was Nikola kind to you? Did you help him? Was he shot like that?' She did not ask those questions all at once but, over time, she encouraged me to question my own story."

"What do you want to change?"

Shpresa explained Nikola was a neighbour, living in the same apartment building. Older than she was. But as children they played together, walked to school together. "I idolized him. I don't know why I didn't tell you the whole story. I didn't go to the parallel schools. I continued to attend the regular elementary school and secondary school.

For university preparation, my parents sent me to an international boarding school in Villars, Switzerland, near Geneva. American school for the children of diplomats. Later I studied at the American University. That's why I speak English fluently. Now I study medicine in French at *l'Université de Genève*.

I always came back to Prishtinë for school breaks. Nikola barely acknowledged me when I was around. He told my friends I was a snob, little rich girl who lives at a ski resort, just because things are hard in Kosova. I was there always on scholarship. We are not a rich family.

My parents told me Nikola asked about me from time to time. I'm sure he didn't and they thought I'd be devastated with his disinterest.

Now the truth, Thomas. Nikola did seem reluctant with the rape.

Maybe because he knew me, or maybe he didn't wish to harm anyone. Sorry, Thomas, I'm attributing motives to him. Really, I have no idea. I'm still working on that with my mental health team. But he participated. And brutally. He said to his officer, 'Hope this bitch gets pregnant and is forced to raise my bastard. Serve her right.' Then addressing me he continued, 'You always thought you were better than me. Not too good for me now, Shpresa, this is for you.'

He entered me from behind. I was a medical student so I had enough information to alter the story I told the psychiatrist. And you. I desperately wanted him to be my friend. Maybe even my lover, if things had been different."

"My God, Shpresa."

"Is something wrong?"

"He was your neighbour. He knew you." Tom folded his arms protectively across his chest.

"Are you cold?" Shpresa asked.

"I don't know what to say… "

"This time it is true, Thomas. You're the first man I've talked to about this. Women understand what happens with rape. They often know the perpetrator. But there's more… I told you I had an abortion. I don't know I was pregnant but that detail seemed to add a romantic ending for me. I know that's crazy. Cousin Elvira had good connections with IMC, International Medical Corps. She arranged an immediate medical evacuation for me. She told them I was American, a student living in Switzerland. IMC took me right to Geneva. When I arrived, as a rape victim, as a precaution, I was given RU-486, you know, the French abortion drug. My medical treatment was so much different from Roza's. And yet, Roza's treatment, because of my mother, was so different from many other women. And yes, Thomas, that is why I'm studying gynaecology."

"I don't understand. Did Jovovic shoot Nikola?"

"No, he wasn't shot by his officer and he did not die during the NATO bombing. He was executed. Part of an old-fashioned blood feud. For what he did to a daughter."

Tom broke in, "I still don't follow."

"It was my father. So, Nikola knew why he was about to die. Then, my father died within a few weeks. Broken-hearted as I said. Devastated because the country he loved fell apart, devastated by continuing harassment from his own countrymen, heartbroken about the rape of his daughter. And, I think, not insignificantly, against his beliefs and moral code, he took the life of another human being, his neighbour's son."

Tom tried consciously to ease the tightness in his chest by slowing and deepening his breathing. He repositioned himself in his chair hoping to hide his discomfort from Shpresa. Gotta say something, he thought.

"Shpresa, I'm sorry. That's so... so devastating. I'm sorry. I'm..."


Date: Tue, 15 Oct 2002 6:09 EDT

Cassie, please phone when you're able. More about Shpresa. Don't want to do it by e-mail. You were right. There's more to the story. I wanted to write the truth about the conflict. Now it's staring me in the face and I wonder what I'm doing here. Love, Tom


"She told me I'm the only man she's shared her story with. I feel strangely privileged and devastated," Tom began.

"Shpresa trusts you. It is a privilege."

"Cass, it's a burden. I'm not naïve. I know abuse happens

everywhere. During war, during peace."

"Tommy, it's okay to be upset."

"I shouldn't be troubling you with this. I should contact Bert."

"It's not a trouble to me. I love you."

"Thank you for listening. I need to talk. I'm blocked, Cass."

"You can't write?"

"Can't even get this one started. I feel like I need to protect the story."

"What do you mean?" Cassandra's anxiety came through clearly.

"I don't know what I mean. That's the problem. I'm puzzled about my feelings. The word that comes to mind is proprietary but don't know how that fits."

Cassandra didn't answer. Tom recognized her apprehension.

"No, no, Cass. It's not like that."

"I know, I know, Tommy."

"But there is something, Cass. Shpresa could be any one of the young physicians we worked with at home. Intelligent, good looking, self-confident but so brutalized. She's Marianne's age. She could so easily be one of her friends."

"Yeah, I understand, Tommy. What about Roza?"

"I'm struggling not to be elitist but Roza's story doesn't hit me the same way."

"But Roza's story is even worse. No, sorry, that sounds like a qualitative comparison."

"I know. That's what I'm trying not to do, either."

"Maybe Bert could help, Tommy. Do you want me to ask him to call you?"

"No Cass, thanks. I need to look after this myself."

"Shall I call you again tomorrow?"

"That'd be great."

Date: Fri, 19 Oct 2002 19:37 EDT
From: Agron Shalla
To: Thomas Stephenson

Hello Thomas. I am at Health House in Lipjan. I worked here today for one of my friends whose son is being married. Dr Ahmed asked my consult on four young patients with arthritis/arthralgia signs. One has enough fluid on her right knee for successful aspiration. Aspirate is still in the syringe because there are no sterile containers. Hope syringe is sterile. I will bring specimen with me when I return to Prishtina tonight. I do not know how many cases total from Lipjan region. All these four live outside city. We took careful history and examined total skin area of each patient thinking about tick bites. Each one has pain in all major joints. Two have finger joint involvement as well. All four report fever but no temperatures recorded. Still no thermometers. Each mentioned nausea and one vomiting with fever. One has late stage petechial rash. Can you ask Elvira to open lab for us tonight? Maybe time to test your new virus lab. It is better we work alone. Agron

Date: Tue, 23 Oct 2002 14:37 EDT
To: Dirk O'Reilly

Dirk, we've grown a virus from a knee aspirate obtained from a young female arthritis patient. Rapid grower. Too early to have any idea of type. Patient part of cluster, young rural people probably from farms, all presenting with arthralgia or arthritis. No handle on real numbers but Agron estimates about one hundred. The virus lab is now operational! Along with this finding several herpesvirus isolates from routine clinical

237

specimens. The two staff are feeling comfortable, successful and not just a little proud. Best, Tom

"Frank... over here." Tom signalled Frank MacGregor from the corner table he'd chosen in the Grand Hotel coffee shop.

"Hey Tom. How've you been?" Frank smiled as he extended his hand.

"I'm well, thanks. You?"

"Ah, you know, life in Prishtinë..."

"I'm glad you could get away. Coffee? Or a beer?"

"I'm not going back to work. What's that local beer you like?"

"*Birrë e Pejës*." Frank nodded so Tom asked the waiter to bring two. Coffee shop was clean but devoid of decoration.

"How's Cassie?" Frank asked.

"She's well. Enjoying time at home with her son."

"What's his name?"

"Jeremy. Great kid," Tom said.

"Not surprised. She's a great person."

"Yeah. For sure. Actually, Jeremy's not really a kid. He's a student at University of Ottawa."

"I assume you didn't ask me here for small talk?" Frank looked around the café.

"I need your advice." Tom made sure he had Frank's attention. "The virology lab at the hospital's functioning now. We've... they've successfully isolated a few viruses. Herpesvirus mainly but one unusual organism. I think chikungunya virus."

"Chikungunya? That's an animal virus. From Africa. Doesn't sound right. How'd they come to that conclusion?"

"Growth parameters on cell culture. Clinical picture typical. Including severe arthritis. Cluster in young people, so likely infectious not autoimmune."

"How're you involved?"

"Just helping Cassie in my spare time."

Frank arched an eyebrow. "Well sure, but that doesn't explain your role. Do you know anything of chikungunya?"

"Not much. Checked on the web."

"So, whadda you want from me?"

"There's a veterinarian at Dalhousie. Iain Cameron. He's involved with *l'Institute Pasteur* studying African outbreaks in non-human primates."

"Yeah, we were classmates. Why do I think you knew that?"

"There've been human outbreaks in southern Africa and the Indian subcontinent. "

"Sure, but Prishtinë?"

"Cluster of rural young people from Lipjan. South of Prishtinë. Maybe a hundred in the cluster."

"How're you involved in this investigation?"

"Agron works some shifts at Health Houses. Asked for help."

"But you're a writer, Tom. Agron's a forensic epidemiologist."

"Agron asked for my help."

"Sounds like Thailand all over again. Thought you hadn't worked in virology for years."

"You know I'm helping set up a virus lab for the hospital."

"Bare-bones lab. Simple procedures. C'mon, Tom, they can't have isolated something this unusual with just minimal training."

"I need your help, Frank."

"Yeah… yeah, I'll help. I'll get hold of Iain Cameron. He owes me. But you're being evasive, you bugger."

Date: Thu, 25 Oct 2002 14:51 EDT
To: Dirk O'Reilly

Dirk, further on the knee aspirate. Bacteriological and fungal workup negative, this virus the only finding. Chikungunya virus. Could fit the pattern of a biowarfare organism. Not well known. Importance likely to be downplayed. I know something of the organism but no practical experience. Studied the virus as one of my early graduate school projects. May have simply liked the name. Didn't proceed further - too obscure a virus and I decided to focus on human pathogens, not animal viruses.

I've enlisted the help of Frank MacGregor, chef de mission at the Canadian Office here. Has a friend at Dalhousie who may be able to help with biotyping. I want to compare this isolate to the RNA fragments I sent you from Skopje.

Agron has proof the deserted lab building at the Skopje airport was a Soviet establishment. Apparently used since the early fifties. Skopje was refuelling stop for Soviet scientists returning from Africa. Perhaps crude quarantine facility for personnel investigating African outbreaks and, we're guessing, involved in early polio immunization trials. Quarantine may be too strong a descriptor but at least a medical check station before returning home. Soviets had a healthy fear of introducing exotic wild-type microorganisms into the homeland. Tom

Date: Fri, 26 Oct 2002 08:51 EDT

Dirk, I can't believe molecular didn't keep the RNA. They keep everything. Surely they recorded the pattern? Added it to their library of unknowns? Please don't let this be about budgetary considerations. Does Terry Abbott still run molecular diagnostics? Let him know what we're about. Why this's important. Tom

Date: Fri, 26 Oct 2002 14:32 EDT

What do you mean Terry can't get security clearance? Terry's a straight shooter, model citizen and top molecular scientist. They still pissed he helped China develop a viral diagnostic lab in the seventies? Why do we care? We've been friends of China since the Trudeau era. Must be US pressure. Dammit, Dirk, I'm exhausted starting all my messages with what do you mean ...

Renaissance Restaurant, Prishtinë, Wednesday evening

"Food here's really good. More traditional Albanian," Tom explained to Frank. "No menus. If we ask for mixed grill, they'll prepare us something special. Kind of an Albanian sampler."

"Take it on faith?"

"Sure. Or else, look around at other tables. If something looks good just point it out to the waiter."

The young waiter brought appetizers to the table. Plates of olives and cheeses and a basket of freshly grilled pitas.

"Always this busy?" Frank asked Tom.

"Always. But then there's only eight tables. I had quite the experience here one time. See the first table by the door? One step up from the entrance?"

"That one?"

"Yeah. Well I was here with Cassie waiting to meet Agron and Flora. As usual, we're early and Agron phones to say he's running late. Don't know why he even bothers. I tease him a lot. Call him the late Agron Shalla. Anyhow, he and Flora arrive and I move around to the other side of the table. The door side, eh? So Flora can sit beside Cassie. So I pull the chair out to slide in. Not much space, you see? It's a small room. Well, I don't realize the back legs aren't resting on the floor. And I'd only had one glass of wine. But it's dark when I sit. And, kaboom! Arse over teakettle. Me and the chair upside down on the floor blocking the door. Provided some mirth for our table but you could hear a pin drop in the rest of the room. And those two guys, over there behind the grill? They dropped everything, rushed over, picked me up. They've treated me special anytime I've been here since."

"Were you hurt?" Frank asked.

"Nah! Not even my pride. One of the owners brought over a nice bottle of Vranac red."

"Roasted peppers are great. And these dips, hummus, tzatziki, what's this one?"

"Roasted eggplant," Tom said. "By the way, fair warning, you keep eating the pitas, they'll keep bringing more. They're making them on the grill. Unless you want more, don't finish what's here."

"D'ya know these meats?"

"Not really. Recognize chicken pieces. Assume the other chunks are beef. I don't eat much meat over here, but this is good."

"Still astounds me, quality of the restaurants. Like the Thai restaurant."

"You wanna do Thai again? We could do that one night. Cassie'd come for that."

"I was just thinking about Thailand. I spent some time lining up assistance for the forensics lab. Central Institute. They work closely with the Aussies and the Kiwis. You'd already been in Thailand filing stories. But since you had forensics lab experience, you offered help with the virology programs."

"Yeah, of course."

"Some time after you were reassigned by *The Magazine* to another interesting and exotic spot, the lab discovered their stock of Chinese biowarfare viruses had been tampered with. Security records from the two days prior to your departure were missing. Samples of avian flu and human influenza viruses were missing." Frank paused, surprised to see just a slightly interested expression on Tom's face as if he had been describing an encounter at a diplomatic function. *I know it was you,* he thought before continuing. "They were left with adequate stocks to carry on with their research. But it was such a major security breach that heads rolled – in security and in the lab. Narong left his job shortly after. It's only later I find out he's Canadian. Decided to check the records. He was never registered with the embassy. Then his trail leads to Toronto and Jordan Siemens. Strange coincidence, eh? Jordan's Cassandra's boss on this project."

"Interesting. Strange story." Tom spoke calmly. *I need to be more careful around Frank but I need his help.*

"Really. And now he's here. I'm sure there's more. Nothing personal, Tom. I enjoy socializing with you. You and Cassandra've been great, making sure I'm entertained when I'm here. Introducing me to people I'd never meet through embassy work. Don't get me wrong, Tom. I'm excited to help with this virus. I still don't understand your involvement."

"Actually, Frank, my involvement's simple. I had some experience with chikungunya as a grad student. When they found it here, naturally I was interested. Could be a good story – unusual virus, unusual location."

"Have you written anything about it?"

"Not yet. I need to think about it." Frank's not going to lay off. "Let's have another beer," Tom continued. "There's things I don't want to talk about yet, but I need your help."

"You don't need to recruit me, Tom. I'd spend more time at the Prishtinë office if you'd let me get my hands dirty in this. I'd love to do some microbiology."

"Maybe some veterinary field work first," Tom suggested.

Tom declined Frank's invitation for a ride back into the *Centrum* area. As much as he appreciated Frank's company, he wanted to be alone. He needed time to think, to strategize. He felt like the proverbial juggler with too many balls in the air. I'm used to the nitty-gritty, but I'm not sure I trust Frank. Just a feeling. No reason. He knew when he was agitated his best strategy was to walk. And walk. Letting his thoughts swirl like snow.

Besides he had plans. He and Cassie were going to meet Agron and Flora for dinner and Tom didn't really want Frank tagging along. Frank would monopolize the conversation with Cassie, he thought. He loves it when he thinks I feel uneasy.

He was glad Agron had pressed him to meet with the President again. He knew of their close friendship but was surprised when the President asked him about chikungunya.

He walked along Mother Teresa Boulevard, very close now to the fuchsia-coloured stucco building the Canadians called Pepto-Bismol. Agron hadn't understood the joke until Tom had produced a bottle from his backpack. Now Agron used it as a reference point when giving Tom directions. Even when it shouldn't be in play as part of the route.

"Picture yourself at the Pepto-Bismol corner, Thomas," Agron would say. "Got it, yes? Well, that is not where you should be..." And he would laugh.

Funny how we nickname everything. Tom was now approaching Confusion Corners. His thoughts returned to his conversation with the President the previous Sunday.

They'd talked about chikungunya virus. Even though the President had no scientific background, he seemed to have a good understanding of the problem the virus posed, questioning Tom's evidence. Tom was taken aback by the amount of information Agron had passed on. But thinking about it, he realized Agron was a patriot. As much as he was helping the West, Kosova was his first concern.

When the President had expressed reticence about identifying the countries involved in the transmission of the virus, Tom said, "Let me be sure I understand. You don't want to jeopardize relations with Russia and Serbia by revealing activities of previous governments – the old Communist regimes. You need support from the current governments to achieve independence."

"You're exactly right, Tom. It's a problem for me," the President said. "I've been an activist my whole life. I've fought against misinformation, disinformation and outright lies. Now I'm in power, I've become pragmatic, a very practical politician. I want independence for Kosova."

"When do you expect to achieve independence?" Tom asked.

"In the next four years. Certainly this decade. I believe a negotiated settlement is the preferred route."

"Your main opposition would like to simply declare independence."

"Yes, but that, I am certain, would lead to renewed war with Serbia. And this time the international community may not support us."

By now, Tom was approaching the Grand Hotel where he intended to sit in the bar until it was time to meet Agron and Flora.

He offered me a job. Spokesman for the Kosova government.

"We need someone who speaks the language," the President had said.

"But, I'm not Kosovar," Tom replied.

The President suggested that could be an advantage as Kosova moved toward independence. But Tom told him he was expecting to be reassigned shortly to Afghanistan and Iraq and suggested the President, with his excellent command of the English language, assume the role as his own spokesperson to the world. That's when the President confided he'd been diagnosed with a terminal illness.

He brushed away Tom's condolences saying, "Don't be sorry. I've led a remarkable life and I've been able to profoundly influence my country. To shepherd Kosova toward peace and independence for the first time in its history is my legacy. I'm too young to die by your standards. Here a man in his sixties has lived a full and long life."

And all I need to do is juggle a few balls. He decided to reverse his route and walked back along Mother Teresa, planning to catch Cassie before she left the hospital. That'll be better. We'll come back to the Grand and share a nice Montenegrin red. I'd rather not drink alone.

# Part 4

# January – December 2003

one

# January 2003
## *Nuk të kuptoj*

Sunday afternoon, Cassandra walked to the Canadian Support Office to send e-mails. She was surprised to meet Claire and Sonja there. Claire hadn't said anything to suggest they'd be there today.

"Hey Sonja. Good to see you. It's been awhile." They gave each other a quick hug. Cassie thought Sonja felt stiff so she offered what she thought what might be a conversation starter, "You here to see Shpend?"

"Yeah, needed to sort some things out. Not sure we got anywhere," Sonja replied tersely, then seemed to relax a bit. "Good to see you, Cassie. How's Tom?"

"Tom's well. I'm looking forward to him being back in a few weeks."

"Really! CIPHA's paying him?"

"No, not really. He's writing for *The Magazine*."

"But CIPHA pays something, right."

"Yeah, his airfare. In exchange for helping me in the lab."

"That's just not right. Claire and I can't continue our vaccine project because CIPHA has no budget left. How come they fund Tom?" Sonja asked.

"It's Shpend," interjected Claire. "Damn him. He's not giving us support. He's in contact with Greg Hanbruz every week. If Shpend wanted our project to continue, it would. Greg relies on him for the local view."

"Look," Cassie replied. "I know nothing of the financing or the politics. But, I do know Tom's airfare expense wouldn't cover you guys. CIPHA pays the flight, health and emergency evacuation insurance. Less than three thousand dollars. That wouldn't go far for vaccines."

"But why?" Sonja was tenacious.

"Just a trade-off. CIPHA gets Tom's expertise for almost nothing." What's this crap? Cassie thought. "Underfunding's a serious matter for all of us. It's not Tom's doing," she continued, her voice a little more high-pitched than she would prefer.

"But he's a journalist. Don't get me wrong, Cass. Tom's saved my butt more than once. I think you know that," Claire said. "He's a good friend. But if his magazine covered those expenses, there'd be more CIPHA project money."

"I know you guys are unhappy." Shpend had come down the hall. "It is not in my control."

"What about the money for Tom?" Sonja continued.

"Tom is not part of my funding," Shpend replied. "That is direct from Ottawa. In addition to my program spending."

"Why?"

"I don't know, Claire." Shpend rubbed his forehead as if to get rid of tension. "It is not my concern. It is something worked out with CIPHA."

"Then what about Cassie? Is her funding cut?"

"Your funding is not cut. Your request for additional funding is not approved. By CIPHA. And, don't you worry about Cassandra. She is well looked after here."

"She and her boyfriend..."

"What? Boyfriend..." Cassie started to respond but drew back. Whoa. Stay calm. I don't like that put-down. But stay calm. That's just Sonja lashing out, venting. Haven't seen that in a while. But that's her character, her *modus operandi*.

"Look, vaccine distribution is a WHO responsibility. They've built a depot with a sophisticated refrigeration system. It is not a CIPHA obligation," Shpend continued.

"But Shpend, we can do it better."

"No. Canadians do not always know how to do things better than everyone else. You just want to do it differently. Don't talk to me about it. Take it up with the Minister of Health." Shpend raised his voice. He was close to losing his usual cool.

"Hey guys, I'm sorry you're upset. I just got back." Cassie recognized her response as weak. But she didn't know what else to say. We've been good friends, she thought. I don't like the way they go after Shpend. I've seen them gang up on him before. But Shpend's right. I'm taken care of in Prishtinë. They know Tom volunteers his time.


Microbiology laboratory, University of Prishtinë Health Centre, Monday.

"*Mirëdite, Cassandra. Si jeni?*"

"I'm well, thanks, Afërdita. *Shume mirë.*"

"How is Thomas? Did he go home okay?"

"He's fine, thanks. He's home. No flight delays." Tom's definitely achieved status now. They're asking about him.

Elvira charged down the corridor toward her. "Cassandra, welcome. I like see you. Happy you be back. We do good thing this time. How is Thomas? I need he help get supply for new reference lab."

"Don't worry, he's already working on a supply list."

"I leave now. You come to my lab later, Cassandra?" Afërdita gently pushed loose strands of her long black hair from her face.

"Sure, Afërdita, before lunch." Cassie watched her walk the narrow corridor toward her lab.

"We talk about reference lab?" Elvira continued, anxious to bring Cassie back to her conversation. "I be so happy when Thomas come back."

"He'll return in about three weeks or a month."

"Oh, is good."

"How was your trip to Atlanta?"

"Oh, is good. Get lost in Atlanta. We walk for shopping at mall. On morning we go Emory Hospital. Fisnik and me leave Ervin for training at hospital. We have map. Mall is close on map. We walk. Then we walk more. We find mall. So much things for shopping. For buying. We buy presents for family, present for staff. So much things. Then we walk back to CDC. But I lose map. I not know address for ask. I think I know way. We walk for hour and hour. Rich houses so not afraid. We ask man at one house where is CDC. He not understand accent at first. Then say look over there. See over there. I say thank you. He say no you not walk, I drive you."

"Really! You could've put yourself in danger."

"Cassandra! Was nice man. From nice house."

"All the same…"

"We two old Albanian woman!"

"Not so old, but okay, it was good of him. So how was the rest of your time? How was the training at CDC?"

"Oh, so good. I know how make reference lab. So good training. American so good people. So friendly. They take us to their home for party and for dinner. We lonely without family. No one speak Albanian."

"Culture shock."

"Yes. This how you feel when you come in Prishtinë?"

"Very much. But you take good care of me."

"You very good to us, Cassandra. And Thomas very good to us."

Later, Cassandra examined a microscope in Afërdita's lab. She turned and called across the small room, "Afërdita, look at this sticky substance on the oil immersion objective lens. Can you get me a bottle of the immersion oil you use?" She waited for Afërdita to return. Such a gluey mess. The techs can't possibly see anything in their smear preparations.

"Here is, Cassandra. Bottles from storeroom."

"Okay. That's Cargille oil. Top quality, non-drying. Something else must have been used. Is there any other oil?"

"That is from storeroom," Afërdita asserted. But they both knew what's in the storeroom was not necessarily what was in use. This reminded Cassie of a *MASH* episode where the quarter-master told Hawkeye, "If I let you have that incubator, I won't have one." The sole rationale for stock keeping was to keep stock, not distribute it.

Afërdita left the room but was back quickly, brandishing a bottle of a yellowish oily liquid. "This we use."

"This smells like cedar oil to me. Very pure cedar oil can be used for oil immersion microscopy but it's not yellow like this. This looks like what's used to make paint. Afërdita, please confiscate... sorry, please find every bottle of this oil and bring it here. I don't know how

I'll clean the lens."


Early Thursday morning in the microbiology laboratory, Elvira was already agitatedly charging about.

"Cassandra, do you e-mail Thomas? He is fine, yes? Come to staff meeting."

Dr Genc Krasniqi chaired the meeting. He acknowledged Cassandra in English but quickly switched to Albanian. Staff applauded his announcement. Elvira took over the meeting and Genc left. Cassie realized she'd need to wait for a translation but amused herself watching interactions. Afërdita seems quietly emotional, she thought. Not very happy. When Afërdita left the room, Cassie hurried to catch up with her, seeing little purpose in continuing to attend a meeting in Albanian.

"Afërdita. Would you tell me about the meeting?"

"Elvira will be in charge at new public health lab."

"That's why the staff applauded?"

"Yes, but she still be in charge in hospital microbiology lab."

"Oh, I thought you would take over."

"I think also. Staff happy now but maybe not long. Elvira say technician will make forty euro more than hospital lab. Elvira say she pick technician herself."


Back in the *Piokultura* lab, Cassie had demonstrated proper culture methodology to four technicians. This was the laboratory area for such critically important specimens as blood cultures and cerebrospinal fluids. Such a *miscellaneous* area required superior technical skill to recognize dangerous pathogenic bacteria. Cassie felt she was doing well to contain her frustration. I've explained these same techniques at least three times, she thought.

"Pashko, where are the lights?" she asked.

"No unnerstan."

"The lights. Over the work area." Cassie used hand gestures to illustrate.

"Gone."

"Now I don't understand. How gone?"

"Zani take."

"To the stockroom? Why?"

"No unnerstan." Pashko shrugged. Cassie interpreted a what's the big deal glance.


Monday morning.

"Dr Spartak, I want you to show me how miscellaneous specimens are handled. Do you have time today?"

"No, Dr Cassandra. Today is training by internationals. Today, Tuesday and Thursday."

"What kind of training?"

Spartak shrugged. "It is training by internationals."

"Okay. Then Wednesday?"

"Wednesday is holiday."

"Really? What holiday?"

"UN holiday," was his explanation. Better I find out now than on Wednesday when nobody's at work, Cassie supposed.


"Cassandra," Elvira shouted down the hallway. "Cassandra. There you is. You in charge. I go with Spartak and Zani and other resident for training now."

Afërdita was close to tears, neither invited nor left in charge. Nice timing! Cassandra thought. Obviously the first she's heard of this training, whatever it is. She's their most competent microbiologist. Certainly, the hardest working. Maybe that poses a threat.

"Look, Cassandra. Look how Spartak follow my work from weekend. We think we have *Haemophilus influenzae*. Spartak report *Streptococcus pneumoniae*. See." Afërdita continued to be disturbed.

"Did he record any testing results? What's the lab number? Do we still have the petri dishes?" Cassandra donned latex gloves and worked her way through the piles of petri dishes awaiting autoclaving in the discard trays. The culture media had growth on it that could only be *Haemophilus*, the only question the species, *Haemophilus influenzae* or *parainfluenzae*.

Afërdita spoke emotionally, "You see, Cassandra. We work so hard but residents not know their job. Not listen. Maybe not listen to woman. Young doctors, they not want to work so hard. They think life should be easy. They think they spend all day on internet and talk to friends. They know stories from past. They went to parallel schools. They should know life is hard. They think we are free, not need work so hard."

"I agree totally. They need to realize freedom and independence cannot be sustained without hard work. Let me handle Spartak."

That Friday morning, Cassie skipped early morning coffee with the microbiologists and epidemiologists and waited in the lab for Spartak.

"Dr Spartak, hello. *Mirëmëngjes*."

"*Mirëmëngjes* Dr Cassandra. *Si jeni?*"

"I'm well thank you, Spartak. How was the international training?"

"Not so good. You teach better. They have many suggestion don't work here."

"Ah, I see." Cassie recognized an opening. "You know, I'm very disappointed when I need to show the same technique over and over. Yesterday, I helped Mirlinda culture swabs. She didn't streak them at all. Just swabbed the entire agar surface. So, I demonstrated culturing AGAIN. She was trying to say she's too busy to do it my way."

"I speak with Mirlinda."

"Don't stop at Mirlinda. Everybody needs to know it's not *my* way. This is the internationally accepted way to culture medical specimens."

"Okay, I tell Cassandra say this."

"And, I need to discuss your work from the weekend. You must subculture blood cultures to more than just a blood agar plate. Then you'll be able to isolate *Neisseria meningitidis* and *Haemophilus influenzae*. You know *Haemophilus?*"

"Yes, of course." Spartak replied with obvious annoyance.

Don't get huffy with me, she thought but said, "I don't like the way you followed-up the work Afërdita and I started. We worked very hard to isolate *Haemophilus.*"

"It is *Streptococcus pneumoniae.*"

"It was not. You didn't record any of the work you did to identify the organism."

"I am medical microbiologist. This is Dr Elvira lab not your lab."

"Actually, you're just a resident. I'm wasting my time teaching proper technique when it's blatantly ignored."

"But I…"

"I told you a month ago proper susceptibility testing methods were not being followed." Cassie pointed her index finger at his head. "I told you antibiotic disks were being stored at room temperature. I mentioned that as well to Zani and Lekë last week – still no change. We brought experts from Canada to teach. You're wasting their time too. I'm quite exhausted trying to be patient but….."

"Sorry Dr Cassandra. Sorry," Spartak replied insincerely, glancing over his shoulder to be sure this conversation was indeed private and he would not lose face with his co-workers.

two

# March 2003
## *Çfarë një surprize*

"Hey Cass, I'm home." Tom, just back from Canada, had taken a reorientation walk-about through downtown Prishtinë after meeting with Agron for a quick strategy update.

"I'm in the laundry room, Tommy."

"Ran into Claire at Ardi. She wants us to go for dinner at Dora restaurant. Peter and Michael'll be there. She's not sure about Sonja. Depends how late she's working."

"I thought we were going to catch *Erin Brockovich*."

"We can do both. I'll check the times."

"How?"

"I'll just run up the street until I can read the marquee."

"Okay, sure. Where is Dora?"

"You know. On the corner, upstairs. Near the OSCE building."

"Yeah. Restaurant and movie in our own neighbourhood. That'd be good. Don't feel up to wrestling taxis tonight. I'll need to do that tomorrow. Shpend's not available to take me to the airport."

"Sorry you're going home when I just got here. Whatever you want's good with me."

"Peter and Michael are Financial Services?"

"Right."

"Okay, let's go then."

"I guess this's meant to be the vegetarian alternative," Peter pointed to the *varios vegetables* plate on the Restaurante Dora menu.

"Yeah, including *pommes frites,*" laughed Claire.

"You want fries with that?" Peter retorted. "Guess we don't own that franchise. Universal suffrage."

"Peter, you sexist! Don't get me started! The word is suffering, universal suffering." Claire was in good form too.

"Pay no attention to Peter," Michael interjected. "We were here the other night. That dish is excellent. Fries, fresh-cut shoestrings. Mushrooms sautéed just right. Served with a crisp stir fry. Liked it a lot."

"What's the border closing going to mean this time, Michael?" Tom changed the direction of the conversation.

"Well, food prices are already up. That affects most people. Peter and I eat out mainly, so I'm not sure. But all of you shop and prepare food, right?" Four nodded in assent as Michael continued. "You won't even notice. D'ya even know the price of bread? Twenty-five euro cents? It may go to forty. Sixty percent price hike but to us it's still cheap. UN's rationing fuel for its staff, though. That'll cut back the weekend jaunts."

"Why'd you call them jaunts?" Cassie sounded annoyed. "Those UN people are here two years at a time. They're only allowed to fly home every three or four months. It's great they can use UN vehicles for a long weekend in Macedonia or Greece."

"It's not the lower ranks doing it! They make good money but they send it back to Africa or southeast Asia to their families. It's the middle class people like us, Europeans and North Americans, who can commandeer a vehicle for the weekend."

"But..." sputtered Cassie.

Tom interrupted, "Are we all going to the movie?"

"If it's *Erin Brockovich*, seen it. No desire to see it again." Michael, the wet blanket.

"I thought you finance guys enjoy repetitive action. Same thing over and over again."

"Leave Michael alone, Tom. Let him be dull if he wants," Peter said.

Sonja hadn't said much all meal. "I'm not going either. Have you been to the UNMIK theatre? English language with Albanian subtitles. Two euros admission and popcorn's twenty-five cents."

"Well come with us. Sounds like fun."

"No, I'm tired. Need some sleep."

Claire nudged Cassie, "You think Sonja and Michael have something going?"

"I heard that." Sonja laughed. "And the answer is no. Michael's wife is joining him tomorrow."

Michael offered a laugh but was clearly not amused.

"Albanian subtitles, you say," said Tom ever the peacemaker. "Gotta see that. I've seen the movie but I want the total experience. Gotta see how they handle the language. Maybe I could add some colourful phrases to my Albanian vocabulary."


Date: Thu, 22 Mar 2003 10:33 EST
To: Dirk O'Reilly
Cc: Agron Shalla

Dirk, this chikungunya virus occurrence could have resulted from a biowarfare event or experiment. Here's what we know. First the sexy name amongst researchers is CHIKV, pronounced chick vee. Frank MacGregor obtained strain specific antisera from *l'Institut Pasteur*. He was also able to interest friends at Dalhousie University to study the genome.

Although the reservoir for CHIKV is non-human primates, Frank stumbled onto similar findings amongst cattle in the Lipjan municipal region. Because this area was previously famous for horse breeding, Frank at first thought they were dealing with equine encephalitis. Aren't many horses there these days. Cattle not numerous either. Each farm is a small cow/calf operation with a few animals. Just like fresh produce post war, most meat is still imported. Frank could prove useful to us.

Our human isolates have him interested in a closer look at both animal and human disease. The hospital virus lab did all the culture work. All human and animal isolates so far identify as CHIKV strain Ross.

Iain Cameron at Dalhousie found a mutation in ten isolates in a normally highly conserved region of the genome. In culture he finds very rapid multiplication and postulates the mutation may confer increased virulence at least in culture. He suggests this heightened virulence leads to very high virus numbers. This high titre could be the key to cross-species infection. Interesting also, this mutation itself is now highly conserved through multiple culture passages Iain's performed. Finding CHIKV in the Northern Hemisphere, in Europe, is dangerous. In reality, only a short plane ride from home.

Since the molecular lab discarded samples and, quite frankly, because of MIN's disinterest, we've lost an opportunity to tie the Soviets to this current outbreak. I know we're all friends now. Except we still don't communicate well. We all need to acknowledge our roles in these biological disasters, however motivated. Tom

Date: Fri, 23 Mar 2003 09:29 EST

Hello, my sweetheart. Hope you got home okay. I'm just back from meeting with Shpend. After some phone calls he found supplies can be delivered by air into Prishtina regularly from Ljubljana. So, we ordered blood culture bottles. Shpend offered to take cash to Austria to buy some if all else fails. His only concern is Customs has greater interest in returning Albanians at the airport than in internationals. Perhaps I should be the one to go if necessary. I'll let you know what happens. Love, Tom

Date: Mon, 26 Mar 2003 10:13 EST

Hey Cass. Saw Andy this morning. He's back here to follow up on one of his projects. But he's fit to be tied. He'd expected funding from Ottawa for projects already approved. Some CIDA big wigs, here assessing the progress of big projects, spent half an hour with him at the end of the day, on their way out of town. Funding for a small three thousand dollar agriculture project approved previously by Ottawa is now being withheld because they're suddenly concerned with the environmental impact of the fertilizers, insecticides and fungicides he proposed. Imagine, worried about environmental impact. Obviously, their eyes could not have been open while they visited here.

On the other hand, I'm impressed with Elvira's growing sense of the environmental footprint of the lab with its reliance on single-use plastics.

Right now, I'm off to check on the virology lab. They've grown another suspicious virus that I think may be another chikungunya isolate. I'm anxious to see the subculture.

R-E-S-P-E-C-T is blaring from the translation office. Love, Tom

Tom searched out Dita at the Canadian Office to say goodbye and congratulations. She'd been recruited by Frank as Canada-Kosova liaison officer at the embassy in Vienna. She'll do a great job, he thought. They chatted awhile over glasses of Russian tea. Dita was always amused that Tom took only lemon slices in his tea rather than lacing it with sugar in the Kosovar style. They had always talked comfortably.

Out of the blue Dita exclaimed, "Canadians have everything, but still they complain!" Then she told Tom about her neighbour in Moncton when she'd been a refugee there. The neighbour's baby was born just before Dita and her husband returned to Kosova.

"He complained to me about hospital air conditioning and other things. How uncomfortable it was for his wife."

Dita said she listened awhile then said, "Jerry, when you are hospitalized as I was, in a room with all the windows broken, surrounded by Serbian doctors and nurses whose verbal abuse is non-stop. When there is no heat in January. When there is no food provided because I am Albanian. When there is no care given for three days after the birth of my child. When you experience all this, then you may complain!"

Date: Mon, 26 Mar 2003 13:10

Hey bro. Hope all is well is Kosova. I'm headed to Edmonton

tomorrow for a federal-provincial conference. And the fun doesn't end there. The week after, it's another conference in Berlin with my boss. After that I'm taking time off. Amy and I may come visiting when you're home. I'm particularly interested in talking to you about the story of the family who'd been in Moncton. We need to know more about whether some refugees, in their homesickness and urgency to get back home, don't later regret leaving Canada, and more importantly giving up that one and only chance for refugee status here. Keith

Date: Mon, 26 Mar 2003 13:06 EST
To: Dirk O'Reilly

Dirk, another attempt at this funding plea! Soviet virologists probably isolated CHIKV from a patient's blood in 1953 in what was then Tanganyika, now Tanzania. Pretty sophisticated for time and location. Not much information available except we know the Soviets were heavily involved in vaccine trials. Tissue culture techniques were new. Some poliovirus vaccine teams were experimenting with primate tissue culture to allow vaccine to be made in situ. That way, they could avoid shipping large quantities of heat-sensitive material overseas.

Since CHIKV causes disease in primates, easy to speculate accidental transmission to humans. Agron has evidence the Soviets used Kosova as a biological weapons testing ground. Unusually virulent strains of microorganisms have emerged post-conflict in Kosova. We're not claiming the Soviets were able to accomplish gene insertion in the fifties or the seventies. Genetic modification is relatively new, but genetic selection of strains is not. Too many loose ends to simply walk away. Tom

Date: Wed, 28 Mar 2003 14:50 EST

Tommy, I wonder whether lasting Balkans peace is achievable. How will things look ten years from now? It's so personal when we have friends there. I read the newspaper each morning but have a hard time concentrating on Toronto-centred stuff that seems so trite, like medical backlogs. At least when we get into the system we can trust what goes on. Hope you're feeling better. I'm so sorry you're still having problems with the Shpresa and Roza stories. You can't shoulder responsibility for women's issues any more than you can responsibility for any of the combat issues. I miss you a lot. See you soon, Cassie three

# April 2003
## *Është ditë e bukur*

Date: Mon, 2 Apr 2003 05:00 EST

Dear Cassandra, really nice work with both you. Here are so empty now you leave. I hope we be together soon. Now I hope also you are happy because you are together all family. Thomas will tell you about us. Here are without nothing new. Best regards, Elvira

Date: Mon, 2 Apr 2003 10:03 EST

My dear Elvira, I am so pleased to hear from you. I missed being able to say goodbye. I did miss Tom but I know he was in good hands there. He will be home tomorrow. My trip home was fine. It's a long way and there is not much to do while travelling. The movie during the flight was quite funny so that passed some time. I also had a good book to read.

I was glad to see my son. My daughter will come home next weekend. Some day I hope our children can meet. That would be fun! I loved meeting your daughter. I know you are as proud of her as I am of my daughter. Please thank your husband for taking time from his job to come home to meet us.

I know I will always remember this trip to Prishtina. I feel we made progress. Unfortunately, funding for this project will not be continued. I have talked with Greg Hanbruz about returning. I am not sure how I'll arrange it but I will be back. I'm working on it. Very best regards, Cassie

Date: Tue, 3 Apr 2003 04:44 EST

Dear Cassandra. I am worry about Thomas. He not funny man no more. Maybe he be depress. Do not tell Thomas I say. Elvira four

# May 2003
*S'ka persë*

Date: Thu, 15 May 2003 2:30 EDT

Hi sis. Well, it took me a month to organize funding but, as you know, Tom and I are back in Kosova. Some residual money from CIPHA for me. *The Magazine* wants wrap-up stories from Tom before they send him elsewhere. It's such a pleasure to travel with Tommy. Not an opportunity I've often had.

I'm home from work for the third day this week. Started with Montezuma's revenge but now battling Montezuma with added sore throat and cold symptoms. Whole spectrum. Tried to return to work this morning, walked part way but every step was such an effort. Not a good spot to feel unwell. Returned home. Told myself didn't want to share the bug with anyone. Good justification so I didn't feel I'd simply wimped out. It's frustrating to be here such a short time and not able to work. At least I'm feeling more functional than Tuesday.

We had a great time at home together but I'm concerned about Tom. He seemed to withdraw from me the moment we landed back here. Maybe just my imagination cause it seems better now. Cassie

Tom looked round the patio as he and Cassie awaited their macchiato and baklava. Nice warm afternoon after a cool start that morning. They'd left work early to enjoy the day, walked to the apartment for lunch but decided instead to drop their heavy back packs and head to the outdoor café at the Grand Hotel. Now after lunch they intended to relax over dessert and coffee.

"Have you had baklava here, Cass?" Tom had asked.

"No, not at the Grand."

"Even thinking about it makes me salivate. Remember when we bought some at the corner bakery?"

"Of course, I remember that fateful night."

"Well, it's just as good here."

"You remember the rest of that evening?"

Tom simply grabbed her hand and smiled. "*Mais oui, je me souviens.*"

"There's Sonja." Cassie pulled her hand away and gestured toward a tall, blond woman walking through the patio.

Tom got up, hurried over to Sonja, embraced her and motioned to Cassie still seated at their table.

"Are you meeting someone or can you join us?" Tom asked.

Sonja chuckled as they walked toward Cassie. "I'm not doing anything. This is my new shortcut. Across the patio. Cuts the corner on the street."


"Hey Sonja. Glad to see you."

"Hey Cassie. Me too."

"Oh, I can't," Sonja replied when Cassie suggested they get an extra piece of baklava. "But I could handle a cappuccino."

After a while, Sonja asked which people were in town. Turned out, she was back on a three-month contract.

"For the EU," she explained. "Canadian money's dried up. I won't get into that." Looking at Cassie she continued, "You already know what I think of Shpend and Greg Hanbruz."

Later the three of them walked the short distance to a large outdoor market where vendors sold all kinds of produce usually in large twenty kilo mesh bags. Entrepreneurial men and boys with wheelbarrows offered *taxi* to transport their purchases outside the market area. Of course they didn't need a *taxi* for the few yellow beans, cucumbers and eggplants they intended to buy but they were approached several times. This was the first time for Tom and Cassie at that market. Usually they shopped at a much smaller one.

"Does anybody sell normal quantities?" Cassie asked Sonja who shopped there regularly when she was in Prishtinë.

"Sure, but mainly the stalls at the back. They don't get as much business so I think they'll sell you what you want."

"What about these vendors here?"

"No, they're bulk only. Sell to restaurants and families."

"Families?"

"Well, yeah. Most Kosovar women buy huge quantities to preserve. You should see when red peppers are in season. Everybody leaves with wagon loads."

"Reminds me," Tom said. "Skender teased me that he thought our *paprika*, our peppers, were crap when he was in Canada. No flavour he said. I told him in the winter they come from Mexico. But he said theirs come from quite a distance too, Turkey or Greece."

"Yeah, Tom, but here they prefer hot peppers."

They examined products they definitely wouldn't buy like fresh ricotta scooped from large, uncovered plastic garbage cans sitting in the full sun, ripening, buzzing with houseflies. No words necessary, they were on the same page recognizing potential public health problems.

They also wandered on to find vendors who would satisfy their requirements, through many booths of clothing, this and that, like any flea market. Huge and permanent, it covered most of a city block. Mostly men doing the buying and selling, Tom noticed. I'd rather simply pay the stated price. I'm uncomfortable haggling. Tom appreciated that about shopping in Prishtinë, set pricing normally. Watching the heated negotiations was causing him to feel unsettled, jittery, like too much caffeine.

"Wanna look at eggplants?" Cassie asked.

Tom gazed around, shook his head quickly and, no longer interested in being there, said abruptly, "Get what you want."

Sonja caught Cassie's eye, saw the distress Tom's uncharacteristic insensitivity caused, knowing how particular Tom always was about food purchases since he did the bulk of the cooking. Sonja inquired with a gesture of her eyes and hands but Cassie dismissed her concern with an almost imperceptible shake of her head.

"It's okay," Cassie whispered but Sonja was unconvinced.

Date: Tue, 20 May 2003 8:00 EDT
From: Dirk O'Reilly

Sorry Tom. I'm only able to allow you about six months, until the end of November, to wrap things up. But beyond that your mission will not be extended. That means you'll no longer have permission to be in Kosova, *The Magazine* operating cover notwithstanding.

Our experts suggest your findings add nothing to understanding current biological threat potential. All agree Kosova has an interesting and debilitating chikungunya virus outbreak. Let WHO look after outbreak management strategies. These are normal farm diseases. You seem to think there's been pressure from governments, ours and others. Your continued contention about such interference makes you look paranoid. Simply put, it's time to stop examining the past and pull out of Kosova.

*The Magazine* will reassign you so your exit looks normal, end of current assignment. Everyone understands Kosova is no longer newsworthy. Even the UN's having difficulty maintaining the attention of donor countries now with new conflicts to address. We need you to produce environmental scans in Afghanistan and Iraq. Maybe Somalia as well. Our assessment is that's where real threats are posed. Dirk

Date: Tue, 20 May 2003 9:23 EDT

Dear Mom, yesterday I went with some of the women from the lab to see a colleague's new home. Eleven of us went by taxi after work. A house in a nice area of Prishtina where it begins to become quite hilly. It's situated with others to give a kind of terraced effect. We had wonderful traditional food – served one course after another. Everything was so delicious but the amount served was a little overwhelming for my recovering digestive system. It was great to be one of the gang.

You would envy these women as their daughters, teenaged or early twenties, help with food preparation and serving – and beautifully I must add! Tonight we had beef tenderloin, pickled peppers, two wonderful salad plates with tomatoes, cucumber, cheese, potato, cabbage and more.

This family's never had a house but now have something we'd value at half a million dollars minimum. Afërdita's husband's an engineer. Although he'd been unemployed many years, he works for the American division of the Kosova police/security force. He works about eighteen hours six days a week at American wages. That's how he could build a beautiful new home.

When I got back to the apartment, I'd invited Sonja to join us to celebrate Tom's birthday. I was just hostess – couldn't even look at more food.

I'm so glad Marianne has spent some time with you – it's nice for you to see her as an adult without the jumble of family or a holiday celebration. She's a fine young woman, isn't she? Love, Cassandra

Cassie and Tom arrived at Olympia Restaurant before the rest of the group. They chose an umbrella table on the patio thinking of both solar protection and privacy. Other customers seemed happy to bake in the sun. Cassie noticed what she perceived as the usual pattern of men in twos and threes filling about half the dozen or so outdoor tables. Little interaction between tables piqued her curiosity. They must know each other, Prishtinë's not that big a city. They look Mafia-like, short-cropped hair, leather jackets. Very few women in restaurants mid-day. Not their habit, I guess.

They watched Frank stroll confidently toward them. Cassie remarked how she thought he fit in here, dark hair, slightly swarthy complexion, no excess weight, medium height. Handsome, Cassie suggested. Tom didn't agree but saw no point in voicing an opinion.

Frank greeted them both, then requested, "Can we stick with coffee today, Tom?"

"Sure, Frank, at least until Agron joins us. He missed out on last night's fun." Tom pointed to the street. "There comes Agron now with Narong," he said.

Cappuccino and macchiato eventually gave way to *birrë e Pejës.*

"How're your stories received at home, Tom? Do you get feedback?" Frank asked.

"Sustained readership, supportive letters to the editor. That sort of thing." Tom replied matter-of-factly then paused and stared at his beer mug before shaking his head as if to clear cobwebs before he added, "And then, some, shall we say, constructive criticism."

"Tom's stories are appreciated here," Agron said. "Though, I am certain the Serbs may not like them. His stories are true."

Cassie watched Tom for reaction as she added her perspective, "Tom's reporting Kosova stories not Serbian or Croatian stories. Guess I shouldn't be surprised by the amount of vitriol. Not expressed in very nice language."

Everyone laughed so Tom smiled nervously and added, "I'd prefer my readers to discontinue trying to enlighten me with complicated suggestions for shoving my stories into various anatomical orifices. I'm just not up for implausible physical gyrations." That line elicited a few snickers but didn't really contribute much to the mirth. "But seriously, I'm thankful to be Canadian, writing for a Canadian magazine. Criticism always encouraged and expected."

Narong had been quiet. Like Tom, Narong was selective with information he imparted. "So Tom, now that you're leaving, there must be stories you wish you'd written?"

"Yeah, some. Like slamming the Milosevic government for neglect. They allowed the re-emergence of diphtheria, polio and whooping cough because they deliberately discontinued immunization programs. They endangered all of Europe."

"Yugoslav immunization programs were thorough and inclusive," Agron explained for Frank's benefit. "Immunization in Kosova was allowed to lapse since 1989. Direct interference from Belgrade."

"Hardly benign neglect, then. The withdrawn gift that keeps on giving," said Frank.

"Post-war life includes anthrax, tularaemia, tuberculosis, haemorrhagic fever. In the West you have little regard for these diseases. To you they are foreign curiosities. But we have them here, endemic in Kosova, part of the microbiology landscape just waiting for breakdowns in social services or community and personal hygiene."

Agron's just getting started, Tom thought. He had heard his rants before.

"Not good," responded Frank.

"Also, most of these organisms could be candidate agents for bioterrorism," Agron continued.

"So, Cassie, what would you do if you were a bioterrorist?" Narong had a mischievous sparkle in his eyes. "Have you ever thought about it?"

"Sounds like men's games to me. The what ifs. What do you think?" Cassie passed the subject back to Narong.

Narong talked about the futility of outright attack, suggesting strategies like anthrax by snail mail had not proven effective, so quickly contained by US authorities in the autumn of 2001. "Anthrax is a deadly disease," he agreed. "But, to me, better to use agents causing chronic illness. Create confusion with a poly-microbic attack, a variety of organisms. Terrorists seem to want to claim immediate responsibility for something. Concerned with the news cycle, I guess."

He continued, suggesting it'd be smarter and more effective to bring the enemy to their collective knees, use up their resources, inflict populations with maladies neither easily recognized nor easily cured. Guerrilla warfare by changing the microbial geography.

"Use tularaemia bacteria, use hepatitis viruses, Epstein-Barr virus, maybe polio viruses," Narong suggested. "Watch the enemy blame their own people for lifestyle contributions to poor health outcomes. You know the list: obesity, lack of exercise, decline in personal hygiene, poor adherence to immunization schedules."

The others listened attentively. Target populations could be relied on to continue with divisive blame games, to impugn the motives of the greens or religious groups for refusing immunization, thereby allowing already defeated diseases to re-establish.

"The goal," he concluded, "would be to bankrupt health care budgets, exhaust medical personnel, overwhelm hospitals and chronic care facilities. To the point where a country's ability to respond to any emergency is totally incapacitated."

Dead silence. Frank weighed Narong's words then said, "Biological disasters are different from physical disasters or infrastructure damage. Difficult to control. You can't limit it to the original target population."

"Yeah, but that's not their concern," Narong snapped.

"I agree," continued Frank. "No microorganism is ever truly defeated. Hit them with the horror of tuberculosis and leprosy, genetically modified. Multi-drug resistant. Not easily treated. But that's easy conjecture. It'd be so time consuming. Begs the question how you would recognize victory."

Tom decided to accept the bait. "What're the logistics? Simple methods like spraying suspensions of organisms onto fruits and vegetables? Rely on the microbiology twenty/sixty/twenty rule?"

"Is that a real rule?" Cassie laughed.

"C'mon, you're not supposed to trip me up like that." Tom realized his comment sounded like a rebuke. He tried to lighten his tone with an example as he explained his theory that a high percentage of people always wash raw foods before eating but an equally high number don't. "Twenty percent always follow good practice, twenty percent never do and the sixty percent in the middle shift with the wind."

"Is spraying a good method?" asked Narong.

"Don't know. I'm not a terrorist. Haven't worked out any delivery systems."

"Well, what about models? Consider West Nile Virus and the money spent there." Frank explained how the sudden appearance of the virus in people rather than just birds and animals led to panic. Programs were introduced to eliminate mosquito larvae. New tests developed to screen blood donors.

"You really buy the theory of infected mosquitoes from an endemic region coming on an aircraft surface?" asked Cassie.

"More likely in luggage or on air freight."

"But, Frank, would mosquitoes actually survive sub-zero temperatures during flight?"

"Well, you know, they do over-winter. That's why we have them every spring."

"Don't I know it. Specially round my new property. Billions of them. Only thing I really miss about living in the city."

"What about infected birds blown off course during migration?" Narong asked. "After all, that's how the virus spread in North America, through birds."

"Makes sense to me," Cassie said. "Not that I'm there a lot but the numbers of crows and bluejays around my place is way down. I could go with the bird theory."

"Bottom line, though, millions of dollars were taken from other health-care programs, animal and human, to fight West Nile Virus," Frank concluded.

Tom was surprised by Frank's depth of knowledge. I like his approach. He'll work with us just fine.

Cassie wanted to take the discussion in another direction. She asked the others to consider HIV/AIDS as a biological weapon. She started to explain her current knowledge of HIV statistics. "We're losing the battle to contain HIV's spread. It's cost us a pile of money. It's impoverished anyone living with HIV/AIDS."

But before Cassie had the opportunity to clarify her points, Agron excused himself. "I am sorry Cassandra, I must go home. Flora's brother is coming for dinner. Only do as I do tonight." He directed his comment to the whole table.

"Maybe you mean don't do anything I wouldn't do?" Cassandra suggested.

"Yes, of course, that's the saying. But I mean you terrorists go straight home." Agron laughed as he stood to leave.

Narong also excused himself saying he was working in the restaurant that evening. He shook hands with Tom and Frank and kissed Cassandra on both cheeks. That left three. Cassie solved that quickly, "C'mon back to the apartment, Frank. We'll whip up something simple to eat unless you'd rather move on to Ballantine's Restaurant."

"Honestly, I'm restauranted out. Is this all people do here?"

"The internationals. Locals go out for coffee or dessert only infrequently."

"Can I take a raincheck, Cassie?" Turning to Tom he added, "I know you want to discuss chikungunya in cattle. How about tomorrow or Monday? I'm dead tired now."

"Tomorrow's good for me. We could hike into the hills at Gërmia."

"Sure but I don't know how to get there."

"Meet me at eleven in front of the Grand Hotel. We'll take a minibus."

Tom and Frank squeezed onto the number five bus, an oversized van with space to carry eight or nine passengers. A teenaged boy had stepped out of the vehicle, offering his seat, saying he'd wait for the next bus. Tom thanked him knowing his wait would be short. He'd noticed another number five bus was already on its way from the stop at Bill Clinton Boulevard.

About twenty minutes later they were dropped at the end of the line, the turn-around point just south of Gërmia Park. Tom suggested to Frank they would plan their route through the hills to end with an easy walk back into the city. "It'll be an ideal cool down. Easy walk. Downhill all the way," he quipped. "Besides, some great shops along the route."

"Good idea. Could always use more exercise. Especially after hiking." Frank laughed then gestured toward a group of kids wrestling on the grass. "Didn't realize there was so much green space close to the city. Regular weekend spot for families?"

"For sure," Tom replied.

"Parents watch their kids closely."

"Family's important here. They live for their kids. But they worry about unexploded ordinance."

"In this park?"

"It was heavily land-mined. There's still danger."

"Really? Still?"

"Definitely. Parents are justifiably wary. For us, there's only one hiking rule – stay on the path. Let's head this way." Tom led the way up the sloping trail. "Tell me about the cattle disease. Anything different happening?"

"First thing I noticed was swollen joints. Animals in obvious pain. Movement restricted. Now you've told me it's chikungunya, it's like viewing a disease on the internet. You know, when you recognize every sign and symptom in yourself. Course, it helps to know what I'm looking for."

"So should these animals be put down? I mean are they that debilitated?" Tom asked Frank.

"In Canada, for sure we'd put those animals down. Keep them out of the food supply. Here, a farmer has only a few cattle. Maybe just two or three. Can't afford to lose livestock. So he'll await the outcome. Maybe recovery, maybe death. He wouldn't allow an animal to die, though. If he thought it seemed terminal, he'd slaughter it for meat."

"For his own consumption or for sale?"

Frank shrugged his shoulders. "Who knows?" he said. "That's life, Tom! I wouldn't trade our system for anything, but reality happens."

"Have you examined any animals yourself, Frank?" They talked as they hiked the treed path, heading uphill through a mixed forest of mature hardwoods and conifers.

Frank halted to catch his breath. "Yeah, I've looked at a couple. Had a chance to observe the natural progression of the disease. Seems very painful for the animals. Mildly symptomatic ones we'd save in Canada. Minor cases seem to be symptom free in ten or twelve days. Interesting coordinating with the infectious diseases docs and the hospital virology lab. They've been great."

"Yeah, I thought they'd help. From the human side, Agron saw patients at a Health House in Lipjan," Tom said. "All experienced high fever, gastric symptoms, severe arthralgia and joint pain. Particularly knees and fingers. Severely debilitating. These were rural people. Young ones, usually farm labourers. Too affected to work."

"I'm still curious why you suspected chikungunya in the first place?"

He's questioning my ability. No, stop it. It's a legitimate question. Jeez, I'm paranoid. Tom stopping walking, bought a little calming time by focussing intently on taking deep breaths while he stretched the calf muscles in both his legs. Then in an easy voice he described what he and Agron discovered at the Skopjë airport. He connected the dots for Frank. "In the early fifties, Soviet scientists helped manage some of the first recognized chikungunya outbreaks in southern Africa. Then, the virus all but disappeared. Which is interesting when the natural host for the virus is monkeys and apes. First cases were in hunters."

"So what happened? Change in hunting practices?"

"That'd seem unlikely. Best answer is I don't know. Maybe the susceptible primate population died out. Replaced by resistant individuals."

"Interesting."

"Yeah, very speculative. However, chikungunya now being found in India as well as Africa and south-east Asia. It's the age old virology conundrum, one virus, many diseases; one disease, many viruses." Tom rubbed his beard before continuing. "You know, when you look at the initial reports, the list of signs and symptoms are the same for any number of viral diseases, typically 'flu-like symptoms."

"Yeah, reminds me of side-effects disclaimers of TV ads for prescription drugs – nausea, vomiting, head ache, diarrhoea."

"But one difference, chikungunya has a characteristically high fever, then chills, severe joint pain and rash."

"Quite the challenge." Frank stopped walking and stared toward an upright metal tower in the bush. "Is that a ski lift over there?" he asked.

"Yeah. You can tell by the undergrowth it's awhile since it was operational."

"Would've been great this close to the city."

"Mild winters probably killed it. Along with the presence of Serb security headquarters on the other side there."

"That'd be a downer."

Tom pointed through the trees. "I'll show you the ruins when we get around to that side. Great example of NATO pinpoint bombing. Took out a heavily fortified bunker with inconsequential damage to the surrounding area."

Frank headed the conversation back to the topic of the day, "You guys were talking pretty freely last night. Everyone have security clearance?"

"You didn't hear anything classified. Normal conjecture amongst microbiologists." Tom spoke sharply.

"So Cassandra has clearance too?"

Tom paused. He was well prepared to share information but Frank's questions were beginning to feel like an interrogation. He knew his face was showing his stress, his rising sense of panic. He had become adept at hiding his increasingly emotional responses but he also knew he couldn't avoid an answer, "Well, actually no. She doesn't have clearance but we need her on-side for her lab access. Cassie's not a risk."

"As I said before, I'd like to be more involved." Frank used both hands to emphasize his request. "So, is this mosquito-borne?"

"Could be other vectors but most likely *Aedes aegyptii*. They're the most common mosquito species in Kosova and, and this is a problem, in eastern Canada. If it can establish here, it could be our next West Nile at home."

"Arbovirus family?"

"Yeah, but reclassified. Chikungunya's an alphavirus, part of the togavirus family."

"I'm rusty on nomenclature."

"Difficult isn't it, renaming, reclassifying? Blame genetics for that. Ability to map genomes redefines relationships every day." Tom was more at ease discussing the science. He did two quick shoulder rolls and felt the tension drain.

"Your index case? What was the story there?"

"Agron introduced me to Dr Ahmet Belushi. Belushi estimated a cluster of about a hundred cases seen by physicians at the Health

House. Agron saw one of Belushi's patients, female with a knee so swollen they were able to drain about fifty millilitres. Gave us enough specimen for virus culture and to rule out other causes. We got our virus from the aspirate. Belushi told me having an accessible virus lab was key."

"Did he realize who set up the lab?"

"For sure. He was thankful we helped establish virology service. He said lab diagnosis was valuable because patients could use over-the-counter anti-inflammatories and pain-killers instead of expensive antibiotics."

"That's the real benefit of us being here isn't it? Don't know how you feel, Tom. You're coming at this from another direction. Know what burns my butt most about foreign aid? We never seem to finish anything. Can't bureaucrats, guess I gotta count myself as one, can't they ensure taxpayers' money buys a lasting benefit? This lab is barely operational and already it's contributing to understanding this outbreak."

"But the money's finished, Frank."

Frank was taken aback by the vehemence of Tom's statement as if he held Frank personally responsible for the failure of donor countries to establish a better funding mechanism. He didn't comment but listened as Tom continued, "There's no one to hand off to except the local government. It's frustrating. They're already financially stressed."

"To me, exit strategies are as important in foreign aid as in military conflicts. Pour good money after good for a change – fund experts for as long as it takes," Frank said.

"Bureaucratic mindset is strange. I once suggested to one of my CIDA contacts Kosovars were experiencing freedom for probably the first time in their history. He told me it's not freedom when someone else foots the bill."

"That's an astonishing view of foreign assistance!"

"Right on, Frank. Glad to hear that coming from a diplomat's mouth." Tom chuckled.

"Ah, Tom. Don't bait me."

"At the least, we should regard foreign aid as self-interest. This outbreak scares the hell out of me. If chikungunya can establish in Kosova, it could establish in Canada. Prishtinë and Toronto are about the same latitude, forty-three degrees north, give or take. *Aedes aegyptii* mosquitoes are abundant both places. Arthralgia and arthritis are as debilitating in North America as in the Balkans or southern Africa."

"What about vaccines or anti-viral treatment?" Frank asked.

"There's nothing. And nothing on the horizon."

"So, speaking of terrorism, d'ya think chikungunya could be distributed unknowingly through blood donors and IV drug users."

"Theoretically," Tom replied.

"Wow, a perfect candidate to paralyse an economy! Think West Nile, bovine spongiform encephalopathy and HIV/AIDS. Jeez, Tom, forget whether the cows are mad, we may all be flaming idiots."

# five

# September 2003
*Tung*

"Can we cross the border here? Just to say we've been in Slovenia?" Cassie asked.

"Don't think so. Guidebook calls it a local convenience crossing, for local residents only," Tom replied.

"Let's ask at the guardhouse. They're probably bored out of their skulls. Even if we could just step across and come right back."

"I'm not so sure, Cass…"

"Aw, c'mon Tommy. Nothing ventured, nothing gained."

"Let's make sure they notice us before we move in. They probably don't get anybody approaching on foot. Let's not surprise them."

"Tommy, you're so nervous…"

"I have a lot of respect for boundaries…"

"Oh, sure you have…" Cassie laughed.

"I mean borders, international boundaries."

The *they* turned out to be one stern-looking customs official. He was sceptical of the *mélange* of spoken English, hand, arm and body language Cassandra used to convey their request to cross the border. Turned out it must have been a slow day as Cassie suggested. He finally smiled and chuckled, then lifted the gate and motioned them through. But it was not free passage. The guard accompanied Tom and Cassie as they proceeded about a hundred metres across the border, his hand pointedly resting on the hilt of his holstered handgun their whole brief incursion into Slovenia.

Back into Hungary and out of view of the customs hut, Cassie animatedly pumped the air with her fist. "Yes, yes, yes. Today Slovenia, tomorrow the world."

Tom didn't seem to share Cassandra's enthusiasm. She carried on with her suggestion anyway. "Tommy, look in your guidebook... find us a locals-only crossing into Croatia."

"Cass, there's something I need to tell you," Tom began. "There's a reason I'd rather not attract attention in Eastern Europe."

"Tommy, we're on vacation for heaven's sake. Those weren't high shenanigans. We didn't cause trouble."

"Cass, please listen." Tom paused before continuing. "I pass information back to Canada in my articles and... well, other ways."

"What do you mean pass information?" Cassie was suddenly serious.

"You remember Dirk O'Reilly, of course." Tom felt his way.

"You mean from when we worked together?"

"You know what he's doing now? Microbiology Intelligence Network?"

"Sure. I used to contribute epidemiology data from the forensics lab. Most labs did."

"It goes further."

"This isn't just American and European data, is it?" Cassandra apprehended Tom's concern.

"No..."

"And not only epidemiology?"

"No..."

"Is this something you should be telling me?" Cassie was suddenly aware of her own avowed secrecy, deciding then she wouldn't disclose her role, even to Tom. Justine Tachereau told her to tell no one. "Is this what all the terrorism discussion was last week? With Agron and Frank?"

"I need your help, Cass. But I won't put you in danger."

"Is this why you help with the virus lab?"

Tom ignored her direct question but answered obtusely. "Chikungunya virus could be used as a biological weapon."

"Jeez, Tom. We can't even get away from these things on vacation."

"Sorry, Cass, guess I didn't expect this to come up."

Ironic, I stepped across the border for two minutes and discovered what Tom's been doing these last years. He tried to protect me by leaving Toronto without saying anything.

"Sure can pick vacation spots, eh Cass? Nothing but corn and squash fields." Tom tried to change the subject. "Just add some bean crops and we'd have the Three Sisters."

"I don't know that reference."

"The Three Sisters?"

"Run it by me. Is it First Nations?"

"Yeah. Companion planting. The crops benefit each other. Squash spreads along the ground, the leaves act as mulch to prevent weeds. Bean plants climb the cornstalks and are classic nitrogen fixers, contributing to soil nutrition."

"These are just big fields here, though."

"Maybe they use crop rotation to achieve similar results."

They continued in silence, headed back to the resort hand-in-hand, each contemplating what had just happened. A warm autumn afternoon highlighted the maturity of the crops in the field, the greens having given way to yellow and brown against a backdrop of reds, oranges and golds of the surrounding deciduous forest.

Their accommodation was fine once they'd upgraded from a studio unit to a one bedroom for comfort and privacy. Even though the resort restaurant was lousy and there was no place nearby to eat or buy bread, milk or breakfast stuff, they were able to laugh off those circumstances and their naïve choices.

All of Europe had been colder and rainier than usual that summer and fall, so they spent time reading and generally enjoying being together. It was the first real vacation either of them had taken in years.

"The other day, I thought you were going to talk about HIV in a terrorism context," Tom said one afternoon.

"Only to offer some stats the others probably wouldn't know."

"Like what?"

"Are Agron, Narong and Frank all part of your... in your... other profession? Is that why we were talking terrorism?"

"So what were you going to say?" Tom ignored her question. Cassie didn't pursue it further.

"Nothing really, Tommy. I was kinda jazzed up at the time. But we're on vacation. Let's not talk about HIV."

He thought about their plans for their final afternoon together before he continued his journey to Toronto and Cassandra returned to Prishtinë. Now that the relentless rain had ceased Cassie suggested they check out the stables, maybe arrange a trail ride. He'd rather continue to contemplate and discuss microbiology but was more than willing to follow Cassie's lead. It's vacation after all. I'm glad I finally told Cassie everything. I feel better than I have for months.

### six

# October 2003
## *S'ka punoj*

"Dammit! Dammit! Dammit!" Tom shouted when he understood the implications of the message he'd called up on Cassandra's computer screen. He was alone at Cassie's, having driven up from Toronto to check on the house in her absence. He'd booted the computer just to ensure he hadn't left any traceable evidence of encrypted messages he'd sent from there. But the message he found wasn't his.

He paced around the house then went out into the backyard, normally a place of tranquility and contentment for him, ten acres to wander and explore. But he couldn't shake his disquiet and finally decided to confront his concerns and went back inside to e-mail.

> Date: Sat, 4 Oct 2003 14:35 EDT
> From: stephenson@secure.gov.min.org
> To: borden@secure.gov.min.org
>
> Cassandra, please acknowledge. I know this address is yours. I'll get an automatic receipt when the message is delivered to your account and another to confirm you've opened it.

Cassie was jolted by Tom's secure communication. Disquieted when she saw his name as e-mail originator. I'm sure I could explain better by telephone. Offer something plausible. Maybe I'll walk to the PTK international phone kiosk near the hospital. Don't know when it's open. Or how the service works. Don't even know the international phone codes.

She returned to Tom's message recognizing an aggressive tone she couldn't interpret. She didn't see any immediate option than to simply acknowledge the message:

> Tommy, this is my address. We need to talk.

Tom's reply came back almost immediately:

> I need to know things now. We can't talk. There isn't a secure phone line in that whole country. When were you recruited? Get whatever clearances you need to answer.

Should've known he'd find out. Should've told him.

> Tommy, I don't need clearances to talk with you. What do you want to know?

> How long have you been at this? How does your role relate to mine? Why didn't you tell me? Why didn't Dirk tell me?

At this? I don't even have a role. I'm sure I was approached only because I have a UK passport. So MIN can maintain a presence when Canadian projects are finished and EU takes over. I thought when you disclosed your status to me, I could protect you and your work. I'm sure I don't have your security clearance.

That bit about protecting me. Did you scuttle my chikungunya project?

MIN thinks you've lost objectivity, are focused on past grievances, that you've taken sides. They don't accept your chikungunya virus hypothesis. I'm squarely with you. I support your chikungunya work. You know that. You know I love you.

How long?

I was recruited awhile back. Backup status only. They told me one of their high powered agents would be working in the field. Didn't know it was you. Your cover worked with me.

May not have been referring to me. So, recruited and trained right under my nose? Since we've been together?

Tom, hold on. Before you rip me further, you weren't in any hurry to clarify your MIN status with me. I was instructed to tell no one. My role's to provide continuity. So far, my only contact with MIN has been to provide hospital based epidemiology data. Data that should be readily available from any hospital. Let's not fight on-line. Please phone me. Trust me. Call and we'll talk.

I'm seething, frankly. I will phone. It'll be about six hours until we can count on getting a line. What do you think of our little spy business now? You work for both an NGO and MIN. Not kosher.

Cassie sensed Tom would not relent. In their time together as a couple and previously as colleagues she'd never seen him angry. He'd always exhibited an elegance in expressing a dissenting opinion or dissatisfaction with a decision.

Tommy, I'm truly sorry. Last thing I'd ever do is hurt you. You're too important to me. But does volunteering with the lab give you special status?

One thing more. When you send or receive a secure message,

it's not secure on your computer. When you delete, you must also empty the recycle bin. I was looking for a message I'd prematurely deleted. I opened your message because the SECURITY ENCRYPTED MESSAGE tag was there. Assumed it was one of mine. MIN should've trained you better. You've got to keep your operation safe so you don't out your contacts. Do not save these messages.


Tommy, please don't go after Dirk. He may not know anything. Justine Tachereau at Montreal General is my handler. Her only interest is normal infectious disease epidemiology. We're not in your biowarfare league.

seven

# November 2003
## *Në të vërtetë*

Subject: ARRIVED SAFE
Date: Thu, 6 Nov 2003 10:08 EST

Hello sis, I'm safely back in Prishtina. Long flight but not bad. Didn't tell you before I left that Tom's not here. *The Magazine* reassigned him. You'd know soon anyway as he starts to file new stories. He's in Somalia but will work his way to Afghanistan and, later, Iraq. Continuing to report from so-called post-conflict zones when, in reality, all three have active on-going combat. We didn't part on very good terms. No fault to assign. Before you ask, no thank you, there's nothing you can do. So I'm afraid for myself. I was finally in a giving, loving relationship. Don't want it to be over. Even more, I'm afraid for Tom. I want him back, back whole in body and spirit. This stuff does things to him. He doesn't have internet access. So he can't contact me even if he wants to. Sorry to ramble. It's not like the self-sufficient me I've become. I need your support more than ever. Please stay in touch. Thanks, sis. Love you. Cassie

Date: Wed, 19 Nov 2003 10:46 EDT

Albert, hello from Mogadishu. I'm  researching a follow up article for *The Magazine* about the Canadian role in the 1993 Somalia incident and the subsequent inquiry. Still lots of interest. Internet access is only in the capital. Attached is e-mail conversation with Cassandra. Not sure of best approach. Should be talking with you not e-mailing but my assignment's expected to last several months.

My correspondence with Cassie is bound to make Bert think I'm paranoid. Or at least unstable. Worries me. Reminds me of the old joke that just because everyone really is out to get you, it doesn't mean you're not paranoid.

Had a vivid dream the other night. Working with a woman, though didn't seem to establish who. Could have started as Cassie but morphed into someone else as we started to get closer physically. Soon we were kissing and, well... you know, progressing. There're only two or three dreams in my life this vivid. I remember those to this day. As this one continued in full screen Technicolor, I maintained a sense it was only a visualization not real, Cassie wouldn't like the situation and it was just wrong. Action continued to the point of no return with me having an awareness I shouldn't allow it to go further but thinking I'm in control, I'll do the right thing and stop. Then, I shouted 'No!!', probably aloud and woke myself up. Realized it was only a dream but  was shaken. In my dreams, I'm usually an observer not a participant. Is that the source of my upset, conflicted? Am I nuts? Tom

Date: Thu, 20 Nov 2003 07:40 EST

Tommy, of course you're nuts! Have been as long as I've known you. Who else would throw away a safe government career for this war correspondent thing?

That's Bert, trying to buoy my feelings. Always been that way. Tom resumed reading:

I'm concerned. You took a big chance. You blew your cover to me. More importantly, you blew Cassandra's as well. You gave up information I didn't already know. Get rid of that correspondence now! I've deleted mine already.

Hard to tell over the net. But you may be suffering depression. You didn't mention it but probably sleep deprivation is the major contributor. Look after the sleep and the depression will look after itself. Tommy, please don't think I'm trivializing your concerns. Depression's very real and debilitating. You need to talk to someone. I can't imagine you'll find the proper professional help there. But your friends should have mental health contacts. Personally, you should consider coming home for a while. Let someone else chase the stories. You're no longer footloose. Now, you're enjoying Cassandra and her family far more than your adventurous life.

Easier said than done, but think about change. Speaking of your torture, why can't I have dreams like that? You wouldn't catch me stopping mid-dream. And, all your secrets are safe with me. Unless someone tortures me, of course! Take care, Albert

Hey Bert, the federal government has become so pervasive, insidiously enveloping my life. Maybe it's paranoia, or is that paranormal? Been on these assignments more than eight years. Don't I get to pull rank or seniority on something? It's okay, doc, I know when I'm ranting. Just want you to know I'm feeling edgy. But that could be a good thing, right? Thanks for listening, buddy. Tom

Tommy, just e-mailed a colleague to set up an appointment for you at the US military hospital in Mogadishu. Don't know the drugs available in Africa but the Yanks always have their own. Trazodone is a cyclic anti-depressant I recommend at low dosage to regularize sleep patterns in your fellow over achievers. Prefer it to prescribing sleeping pills unnecessarily. Should prevent your tired old brain from kicking in when you happen to turn over in your sleep. Prevent those thoughts from cycling and developing. But if you need to get up you'll be able to function. Downside is what's described as inappropriate or prolonged erections. For the life of me, how's that a contraindication? Although, I read of a case requiring surgical intervention. Not pretty... Keep in touch when you can. Happy sleeping, perchance to dream ... All the best, Albert

Hey Bert, I awoke this morning feeling an incredible amount of anger. Inappropriately directed, I'm sure. Immediately recalled hiking along a country road north of Cassie's place. Middle of nowhere country. Late September, beautiful, warm, sunny fall day. Whole forest canopy crimson and gold, contrasting with the green of the conifers. Suddenly I'm struck by the amount of litter in the ditches, both sides of the road. All seems bloody obsessive in retrospect. But I'll tell you anyway.

I paced out a two kilometre stretch, counting everything I found. Spent at least an hour. Twelve cars passed me. So, today I awake with that itemized list in my head. Sixty-three pieces of detritus. Three whisky bottles, empty of course. Six beer bottles or cans. Thirty-five Tim Hortons coffee cups, some fresh, some weathered. Nineteen McDonalds drink cups or coffee cups. Tim beats Mickey D almost two to one. But what appals me, the third place finisher, water bottles. Then a variety of Coke and Pepsi bottles and cans, almost five to one Pepsi over Coke. If I had internet time available I'd probably check comparative sales figures. I'm not alarmed to remember these details but I'm incensed about water bottles.

Remember meetings we went to in the seventies? Ice water in pitchers and glasses at strategic spots along the table. A few brought their own bottled water. We regarded them as left-wingers or out and out nutsies. How ironic water bottles should become such a pollutant.

Next I decided to produce a litter index. You know, fifteen point seven five litter items per kilometre or something like that. Could then define acceptable limits. I had to stop there and take a shower so I'd be on time for my appointment with Major General G.K. Simcoe.

Combination of things upset me. We saw litter along roadsides in Kosova. But there was neither infrastructure nor municipal services at the time. Very frustrating. But, you know, as services became available and personal pride was restored, littering diminished rapidly. Best to you, Tom

Tommy, I'm glad you made contact with George Simcoe. Guess I didn't explain he's a Major General. Didn't want to scare you off. But I'm willing to bet you got through base security without difficulty for an appointment with Dr Simcoe. His presence in Mogadishu's providential, there to train medical and support personnel in post traumatic stress techniques.

Of course, you may wonder why I'd suggest a PTSD specialist. First saw cracks in the old helmet when you were so agitated about anthrax hoaxes couple years ago. Those incidents really made you edgy (your word, not mine, but a good medical term). As your relationship with Cassie developed, I wasn't so worried. Then, after a while, you were unsettled about lack of resources to investigate your chicken gumbo virus outbreak.

PTSD is not only related to major battles. Life's little conflicts can be contributors. You encounter more traumatic situations than you write about. Progressive traumatic stress disarray. Good, eh? Just made that up. Same acronym. Battle fatigue's probably still the best descriptor for that contributory effect of episode after episode. Sometimes, patients with one major traumatic experience are easier to treat, one set of triggers, one set of fears, one incident where they've had trouble coping. Multi-episodic trauma is much more difficult. Firstly, because there's no one event to blame. Then secondly, there's no one event to blame. Conundrum, eh?

Love your magazine articles but what you don't write remains in your psyche, you think buried. Something keeps you awake at night, though. You need to talk. To say it out loud. Just like with your litter index. Which, by the way, we both know is not the problem. Since I'm nowhere near Mogadishu, I suggest you stay in touch with George while he's there. I'm here by e-mail or telephone whenever those modes are available to you. In the meantime, write it down and read it aloud. And, stop pulling punches. You know how to vent. Do it for *The Magazine.* Let the chips fall wherever they may. The little pink pills should help you re-adjust and regulate your sleep patterns. Barring fatal permanent erection, of course. Ah, side effects! Contraindications! Keep healthy, Albert

Subject: TOMMY
Date: Thu, 27 Nov 2003 14:25 EST
From: Albert Tindall
To: Keith Stephenson

Hi Keith. For old times sake I thought I'd drop you a line to say Tommy will be fine. As you mentioned, he has seemed a might spacey the last while. As a friend I can't be his primary physician but my diagnosis is depression and post-traumatic stress brought on by events he's witnessed. The key element is fatigue. When the three of us were younger, we always made it to work the day after some memorable benders. And sometimes we started again after work. No sleep for days! But our lives were not stressful.

This is different. Tom's not hearing voices or seeing visions.

Far from it! We both realize he's involved in things we can't know about. But he cannot continue. He needs to give that stuff up. And sleep would help! I don't know if either of us could influence him but I really believe he should come home for a while. All the best, Albert

# eight

## December, 2003
### *Mort!*

Camp Bondsteel, US Army base, near Ferizaj, Kosova. Cassandra waited in Security. She was glad Shpend had offered to drive her. She welcomed the trip through the snow-covered rolling hills as a chance to get away from the early winter mud of the city. She anticipated her conversation with some trepidation, though, having had no contact with Tom for almost two months.

"Ms Borden."

"Yes."

"Sorry for the delay, ma'am. Your telephone line's ready. We're connected with your party in Mogadishu. He has a secure line at our base there. Come with me ma'am."

"Thank you, corporal." Cassie followed her escort. He's so young, she thought.


"Hello, Tom?"

"Yes, Tom Stephenson here."

"Tom, it's Cassandra."

"Oh, Cassie. Didn't recognize your voice. Why the security?"

"We need a scrambled line. I have news…"

"Three marines came to get me from my hotel. No explanation. Sergeant just asked me to accompany them for a telephone call. All this for a telephone call?"

"Tom..." Not like Tom. Don't know what I expected.

"I'm sorry Cassie. I'm glad to talk with you, really."

"Tom, I have bad news."

"Oh. Okay."

"Agron is dead."

"Agron?"

"Yes. He died yesterday. Frank and I tried to have him airlifted but no airline would take him. They feared he was infectious. IMC was bringing in a special medevac plane from Copenhagen. But it was too late. It happened so fast."

"What was it? Why would they think he was infectious?"

"Diagnosis is influenza. High fever, chills, myalgia, arthralgia, maybe some neuralgia. He didn't complain."

"Frank... Why's Frank still around? The office is closed."

Didn't he hear me. I said Agron was dead, she thought. But she said "Frank's leaving at Christmastime. He's supervising the office closure. Helped Agron with chikungunya, too."

"You know a lot about him. You still doing those lectures for him?"

"No... we met for coffee a few times since you left. Nothing more."

"Why'd you say that? I didn't ask about anything more."

What's wrong with him? "Tommy, let's talk about Agron. This is not about us. Or Frank. We had coffee after Agron died. He asked me to tell you he now believes chikungunya could be a candidate agent for bioterrorism. When I asked for an explanation, he simply said you'd know." Cassie explained about the accidental exposure when the centrifuge tube broke.

"Not sure what he meant. So you meet for coffee often, then?"

"Tommy, I haven't even heard from you since you left. What are you thinking?" He doesn't have the right.

"No, Cass. Sorry. Just interested. Having trouble. Need to get my head together."

Something is wrong. Cassie felt the alarm flash through her.

"How'd you arrange this line? You must be in deeper than I realized."

"Desperation. Yes, I know who to call. I thought you should know about Agron. From me, not by official dispatch." Cassie tried to get him to focus on Agron's death. "Tommy, are you okay? Believe me, I thought this needed to be a secure conversation. Especially after Frank's comment."

"What comment?"

"That your theory's right." He and Agron were friends! He's fixated on Frank. This isn't the Tommy I know. She said, "I thought you'd be in Afghanistan by now. Wasn't that the plan?"

"I might go home. Just wrote a story about Frank."

"I saw it. Frank read it too. He was pleased."

"Okay."

Two days previously, Frank had taken her away from the hospital to Fellini Bakery for something to eat. She realized there was little more she could contribute. Flora needed the support of her own family and friends, her community, not foreigners.

"I can't believe Agron's dead," Cassie said. "It's so... so horrible... so sudden... poor Flora... how will she..."

"Let's have coffee, Cassie. How 'bout a sandwich? You haven't eaten, have you?"

Cassandra looked around absently. Everything fresh, clean and bright, this new Fellini Bakery location. Frank's a good companion.

Been a long day. She glanced toward the large dessert cases filled with delectable cakes. Could be anywhere. Vienna, Paris, even Ottawa.

"I am hungry. Hadn't thought about it."

"I'll just choose something," Frank headed to the counter to place their order.


"Agron's not going to make it," Frank had said when he phoned that morning.

"Whadda you mean? He only had a cold when I saw him Sunday." Frank's wrong. He's in the hospital? He's critical? Frank's wrong. He's not talking about Agron. Agron's a rock. What's he saying now?

"… facilities here can only provide simple supportive management. IV hydration, paracetamol for pain…"

"Paracetamol?"

"Yeah, acetaminophen."

"Then, we can't leave him here. He needs a medevac," Cassie insisted.

"That'll be difficult."

"Why?"

"Kosovar Albanians are not welcome in most of Europe."

"Get him to Canada, then."

"Very difficult, Cassie. We don't evacuate non-Canadians."

"But, dammit Frank. He works for our government. We both know how he's involved. Surely we owe him!"

"I'll see what I can do through the embassy. Meantime, you check commercial air possibilities."

"Everyone's afraid of influenza but we can provide barrier protection, can't we?"

"It's not influenza, Cassie. We'll talk later. We need to get to work now."

"What'll I call the illness when I talk to airlines?"

"Atypical pneumonia, non-infectious, safe to transport."

"But…"

Later that day, when she answered her mobile phone, Frank had said, "Cassie, IMC is bringing a plane from Zurich. We'll get Agron to a proper facility. Are you at the hospital?"

"Frank, it's too late. Oh, Frank, Agron's gone. Just a couple minutes ago."

"Cassie, I'm so sorry. Is Flora there?"

"I'm with her. She wants to touch the body. They won't let her near because they say he's infectious. She's so… so… distraught."

"I need to let IMC know. Cancel the airlift. I'll come to the hospital," Frank offered.

"I'll wait for you. Won't be useful here much longer. Their family and friends are starting to gather. Word gets around so fast here."

Now Frank passed her a waxed-paper wrapped long, flaky phyllo pastry roll filled with spinach and feta cheese. "I got you *burek,* Cassie," he said. "I'm going back to the counter for our lattés." He returned immediately with the drinks and two large slices of Fellini hazelnut torte.

"Thank you, Frank." Cassie picked at her pastry inattentively, distracted by her memory of the day. Poor, poor Flora. She was so sad.

"Do you want to go somewhere for a drink, Cassie?"

"You said it's not influenza. You sounded pretty definite."

"We had a lab accident."

"What? What're you talking about?"

"Last week. Tube broke in the centrifuge."

"Whoa! Back up! What were you spinning?"

"Chikungunya. Using the floor centrifuge."

"Not the mini-ultra with the shielded buckets?"

"It wasn't working. Waiting for parts. Only instrument available was the floor model. Without containment. We used it before. Never imagined a break."

"Dammit, Frank. You know better than that. What were you doing?"

"Agron thought we should try to purify some of the virus."

"What? You guys aren't experienced enough to do that!"

"Just to get rid of cell culture artefacts. It's my fault, Cassie. I accept blame."

"Except you can't." Cassie sat back, shoulders slumped as if exhaustion had finally grabbed her. "A consular official can't admit to having unauthorized access to a local laboratory after hours."

Frank's face was ashen, almost looked like he might faint. Cassie decided to offer a less public place for Frank to recover his usual self-assured demeanour. To her, he looked vulnerable, perhaps contrite. He'd been good to her whenever Tom wasn't around. She could return his kindness. She assumed he probably needed to talk this out.

"Let's take our desserts and get out of here, Frank. I've got a couple bottles of Vranac red at the apartment. I'm sure it'll go with hazelnut."

"What'll you tell Tom about the accident?"

"Tom and I haven't spoken for two months."

"Really?" Frank's surprise was evident, suddenly his expression less forlorn.

"We don't seem to have a relationship."

"Okay."

As they stood, Frank hugged Cassie, then grabbed her hand as they headed for the door.

Date: Sat, 15 Dec 2003 12:20 EST
From: Cassandra Borden
To: Albert Tindall

Hello Bert, I'm still in Prishtina. Until next weekend. Had a strange phone conversation with Tom this week. Don't know what you know of our relationship currently but it seems to be a non-relationship. This was our first contact in about two months. Called him because I thought he should know directly about the death of a colleague. Didn't want him to get second- or third-hand information. This is hard to write. Already seems disjointed.

Could you phone me? International lines are less busy since many projects have wound down. Five p.m. your time still works well. That's eleven here and most of the city has gone to bed by then. Thanks, Cassie

Shortly after she sent her e-mail, Cassie's apartment telephone signalled with its usual strident double jangle.

"Hi Cassie. It's Bert."

"Oh, Bert. Thanks for calling me. Glad you got through. You didn't need to be so quick."

"Cassandra, in the mental health business speed is important. May not always seem like that to an observer. Sounded urgent."

"It's Tommy."

"Okay. Before we continue, let me tell you something. I'm at the office. So I have a secure line at this end. Don't know this technology but I don't think it can affect your end. Am I right your line could be porous?"

"To say the least. Why's your line secure?"

"I don't know we will need it. But all government office lines are secure. I know there are official listeners throughout Eastern Europe, if you understand what I'm saying. My end of the conversation cannot be overheard. You don't need anyone else to know your personal details. Just think of it as protection of privacy. As much as possible I'll ask questions requiring only short answers. But first, please tell me your concerns in very careful language. Understand?"

"Yes."

"Good start. One word answer. You were able to contact Tom in Mogadishu?"

"Yes. You know where he is?"

"I do. We've had e-mail contact."

"I thought he didn't..."

"Easy, Cassie. You thought he didn't have e-mail access? If that's the question, he doesn't have easy or frequent access. Only for filing stories."

"But you've had a message?"

"Brief one, yes. Now tell me your concerns about Tom. No names, just pronouns. I understand you've had no contact for a while. His idea or yours?"

"You're correct. Not my idea. Didn't know I could." Why wouldn't he contact me?

"Okay. You're doing fine. You were told he wouldn't have access to phone or internet. I know that."

"Told him of the death of a colleague."

"Would I know of him?" Bert asked.

"I don't know."

"Let me try some names... Shpend, Agron..."

"Yes."

"Not Agron?"

"Yes."

"No! Not Tom's friend. Death unexpected?"

"By me," Cassie said.

"Cardio? Cancer?"

"Neither. Infection."

"Unusual organism?

"Don't know yet. Maybe, that's what T… what he thinks."

"You?"

"Perhaps seasonal respiratory."

"To cause death, probably a viral pneumonia, likely influenza the primary disease?"

"Yeah… yes."

"You hesitated. You aren't satisfied with influenza as cause of death. Would I find current reports of influenza for the Balkans on the WHO website?"

"Yes. Another one is ill as well. Both subjects immunized."

"Okay, okay, some reason for doubt. You would know they were immunized?"

"Came up in conversation. Over coffee."

"We wouldn't be talking if you had a satisfactory conversation with Tom. Was he okay?"

"Distracted. Unfocussed. Argumentive. Maybe jealous."

"Jealous of your relationship with this…?"

"Maybe."

"Good friend of yours?"

"Yes."

Cassie felt some irritation with Bert's questions. But I initiated this, she thought.

"Must be difficult not knowing where you stand with Tom."

"I'm okay, Bert."

"When you're home at Christmas, we can talk in person. Face to face is better. Come see me in Ottawa. First, though, you have kids and family to be with."

"He said he might go home."

"Tom?"

"Yes."

"A problem for you?"

"No, I'd love to see him. You know, Bert, I love him. I'm concerned about him. He's usually so strong. Do you think he's depressed?"

"You know PTSD?"

"Post traum…"

"Don't say it. I think you know the acronym."

"Him?"

"As a friend, I'll say that's my suspicion."

"But he's not involved in battle."

"You're both witnesses. You to chaos. Tom listening to first-hand experiences. You know he doesn't write everything he encounters. It affects him personally. He bottles it inside. He's in trouble."

"I wish he would go home."

"Yeah, Cassie, me too."


Date: Sun, 16 Dec 2003 13:22 EST

Hello sis, looking forward to flying home Saturday, arriving Sunday afternoon. Hope we can all get together at Christmas. Right on the day doesn't matter to me, but during the season. Marianne will come home this year, which is wonderful. And spending time with Jeremy will be great, as well. Though he may want to spend time with friends. I'm okay with that. Hi mom, how are you? Can I have the car? Actually he has his own vehicle, doesn't he? Sorry, I'm rambling.

I was in touch with Tom this week. Not sure I see a future for us. Needed to tell him a friend died. Probably influenza. Tom sounded jealous and argumentive when I told him Frank from the Canadian Office had helped me try to arrange a medevac. Probably a mistake to say Frank and I had coffee on occasion. He couldn't seem to focus. Didn't even seem to listen. Frank was good to me, very supportive. Mainly we would have coffee at different cafés and restaurants.

There's more but it's not for e-mail. I'm hurting, kg. I hurt so badly. I miss Tommy, the old Tommy, the one I've known for so long, my best friend. I feel like he's the one who died. Don't worry. I'm better just writing this. If I can't share feelings with my sister, who could I unburden myself to? Thanks for listening kg, Cassie

Date: Tue, 18 Dec 2003 08:50 EST

Hi Karen, I've changed my flight home – leave for the airport in two hours. I will arrive in Ottawa tomorrow two-forty. Please arrange to pick me up. I'm suffering arthralgia in my fingers and knees. No other signs yet. Frank's sick too. He's serious and has been airlifted to Vienna. Probably home from there. I'm worried I could have what Frank has. Can't chance being stuck here sick. I need to get out before I'm too obviously ill. I don't want to be blocked from flying.

Mogadishu, Somalia, Tuesday afternoon.

Tom was puzzled why he'd reacted to Cassie the way he had. He hadn't tried to contact her because he only felt like arguing with her. He wondered when that change had begun. She was simply the bearer of bad news, he thought. She didn't deserve my attitude. Agron. Influenza? That just can't be. We were all immunized. The good stuff. From home. Brought it myself. Special blend with extra subtypes. Can't be influenza. These anti-depression drugs! Felt better before this prescription. Dull, dull, just feel dull. Should go home.

Influenza? What did Frank say? Cassie said lab accident. No, no! Dammit! No! Agron, you had no lab training. Frank, you only had student experience. You should've known better. No, I should've known better than to allow you guys to become so involved. My fault. Dose related! Must be dose related. Died so quickly. Inhalation route.

Tom's telephone rang Wednesday afternoon.

"Tom, it's Dirk."

"Yeah."

"I have some bad news, Tom."

"Agron?"

"Oh, you know about Agron. Sorry, didn't know anybody would know how to get in touch."

"Yeah, Cassandra."

"Oh, I thought…"

"You thought what? We weren't in contact? How would you know that?'

"Sorry, Tom. I thought nothing. Don't know your personal life. I need to tell you Frank MacGregor isn't expected to live."

"Frank? What… *why*?"

"He was airlifted home from Vienna. It's influenza like Agron but he's not responding to treatment. He has maybe only a day or two left."

"No, we were all immunized. I brought it over myself. I wanted to be sure we'd have immunity. It's not influenza, Dirk."

"Also, I've made your Afghanistan arrangements. You leave the twenty-seventh."

"Jesus, Dirk. Listen to me. Agron and Frank. It's not influenza," Tom exclaimed. "I need to come home."

"Before you go to Afghanistan? That'd be easier to arrange. Delay your arrival."

"I probably need two or three months."

"You're kidding, aren't you?"

"No, I'm sick."

"You need to be evacuated?"

"No, just my head. Mental problems. Dammit. Depression."

"Oh... Okay, Tom. I'll get you a flight. Tomorrow okay?"

"Thanks, Dirk."


In Ottawa, about ten days later, Tom followed up with Albert Tindall.

"We've got you off that *mélange* of drugs. I'm sure you feel different. Now we need something simpler," Bert said. "Never really believed in scattergun treatment, myself. Sometimes a patient needs a second drug but seldom a third. I'm surprised George would have you on three. Your mental acuity must've taken a kicking."

"You're criticizing another physician. Thought that was against the oath." Tom. laughed

"Hey, you're already responding. That's the first wit you've shown since you came home. Thought maybe George's cocktail dissolved the funny bone. And, by the way, those comments aren't for public consumption."

"Yeah, Bert. I know the old privileged conversation drill. I do feel better being back home." Tom looked around Albert's austere office. At least he has family pictures hanging. Otherwise it's no better than the offices in Kosova. Well, he does have heat. Probably running water as well in that handwash sink.

"Have you talked with Cassie yet?"

"No."

"Any reason?"

"No. Thought I'd let her enjoy her family over Christmas. Our relations have been pretty stormy. She doesn't need that right now."

"Afraid to see her?"

"Maybe. I've known her almost thirty years. We were always good friends. Got along amazingly. We became lovers, and well, you know what they say about becoming lovers and destroying a friendship? That didn't happen. Everything was still great. For almost two years anyway."

"What do you think happened?"

"I'm aggressive. Everything she says hits me wrong."

"Why's that?"

"Bert, I don't know." Tom's exasperation tainted his voice. "Cassie's my ideal partner. I'd do anything for her."

"Except get along with her."

"Yeah, do anything for her as long as I don't have to talk with her."

"She'd love to see you."

"How would you know that?"

"I just know."

"Have you two been discussing me?"

"No, Tom. You know I wouldn't do that. Is this the aggression you're describing?"

"What?"

"How you're reacting to me. Even mentioning Cassie has you defensive. Anything you need to tell me?"

"About what?"

"Anything. Affairs. Any reason for a guilt trip?"

"No. Nothing. Not for me. Can't speak for Cassie."

"What d'ya mean?"

"Well, Prishtinë can be cold and lonely. Most of her friends had left. Except Frank."

"Did you have affairs when you were cold and lonely in Prishtinë? You bodychecked and deflected all my enquiries about women."

"No, not me."

"Then, why would Cassie? Because she's a woman? Not able to withstand the advances of available men?"

"No. You know I've always gravitated to strong women. Just like you. Maybe I just need to ask her and clear the air."

"To clear the air?"

"Yes."

"No, no, no, no, no. Wrong. Please don't ask that, Tom."

"Because you suspect or know something?"

"No, it's inappropriate. Specially if you want to rekindle your relationship. It's an invasion of her privacy."

"Will I be okay, Bert? Am I capable of getting back with Cass?"

"You need to understand PTSD. It's a disorder, a disease process. We're still learning," Albert explained. "Trauma doesn't need to be battle related."

"I don't know my trauma."

"It's cumulative. Things didn't necessarily happen to you. But you're a witness to man's inhumanity to man. That's always bothered you. Tommy, we've talked about this for years. Honestly, it's going to be a hard grind. Because we don't have a single event to focus on."

"Yeah, I see, I think. You said that before. But why the anger?"

"PTSD is like grieving. Same steps. You've passed through sorrow and disbelief. Still paranoia and anger to deal with."

"So, will that pass?"

"I think you're stuck on anger. You can't deal with it without downtime. You can't wander around or write all night if you don't sleep some other time."

"Okay, so what do I do? Just hang around all day, all night?"

"I think you know why I can't be your primary care physician. We're too close."

"So you're just going to hand me off to somebody?"

"There's an excellent program I can refer you to. It's residential."

"Meaning?"

"Once you check in, you're there for the duration of the program. Maybe a couple of months."

"You think I need that, Bert?"

"Yes, Tom, I do."

# Part 5

# January – March 2004

one

# January 2004
## *Nuk punon*

Church Hill, Ontario, a quiet Sunday afternoon at Cassie's house, the two women sat drinking coffee. Warmth emanated from the crackling logs in the open fireplace. Winter sunlight brightened the room, a welcome bonus after a week of dreary, grey days. Cassie knew sunshine always cheered her. She embraced the recovery of her sense of well-being, a feeling she'd been missing since she came home. She thought she'd weathered the Christmas season well, calmed by the presence of family and friends. No one had pressed her about Tom, accepting her explanation of his changed assignment. She'd come to relish a well brewed pot of coffee and shared conversation, this time with her sister. But now, Cassie needed to talk of other things. Personal things.

"Thanks for all your support, sis." She reached across the kitchen table to grab her sister's hand. "Oops, sorry," she whispered as she jostled Karen's coffee mug with her arm.

"That's what sisters are for. Heck, that's what families are for, Cass."

"Families still do that?"

Karen smiled and shrugged. "Nah, not really," she said.

"Well, kg, I'm seriously grateful for your help. And for being available for me and for Jeremy."

"Mom was the one doing that for Jeremy."

"But you were always there for him. Believe me, he appreciated that. And I couldn't have been away otherwise."

"Not a problem."

"I'm glad we could talk frankly about me as well. You know I'm sitting on a piece of scientific information I can't disclose. Ironic, eh? It's in Tom's scientific interest I disclose what I know. But in my personal interest I don't."

"You're so certain you had chikungunya. There's no lab able to test for it."

"Agron and Frank both died of chikungunya. I'm convinced of that. They both worked with Tom before he was reassigned to Somalia."

"Frank's symptoms were consistent with influenza."

"What about mine? My influenza testing was negative."

"You were subclinical. You only developed mild arthralgia." Karen sounded insistent.

"I don't buy that. Arthralgia's not subclinical. Maybe not much of an immune response, but it's an immune response. Besides arthralgia is not normally a symptom of influenza."

"No. But you said mild. Just some stiffness. Sometimes patients can't differentiate joint stiffness from muscle stiffness."

"Well, you're the doctor..."

"Yeah but you know better than I, Cass, there could be different circulating types of influenza in Kosova. Different from what's being tested for in Canada. You don't usually jump to unsubstantiated conclusions."

"Maybe it is a stretch. Tom didn't seem to understand what I was talking about when I passed on what Frank had told me."

"You've seen Tom?"

"Talked on the phone when he was still in Somalia. That's all so far. That's something else I want to discuss."

"Yeah but let's talk this other out first."

"You think I'm disorganized, don't you, jumping to new topics... "

"No, Cass. That's normal conversation. But you said you needed to talk about Frank."

"Not Frank! Chikungunya virus!"

"Okay, okay."

"Sorry. That's why I can't be with Tom. We'd be jumping down each other's throats. We're both just a little sensitive," snapped Cassie. Right now, can't be with him right now.

"You're grieving for Frank. You're still upset about Agron but you're grieving Frank's death."

"I am. Didn't see that, though it shouldn't be a surprise. Told Bert I was upset but not... can't think of the word. Probably just said not grieving, we weren't that close."

"But you were close."

"Yeah, Frank and I were close. I'm grieving for Agron and Frank but I'm more concerned about Tom."

"Complicated, isn't it?"

"Sure. All things considered, it's Tom I miss most."

"I think you're missing Frank, as well?"

"I know. I've been in double denial. Of Frank's death. And Tom's deterioration. Denial and hopelessness. I'm stronger now. Thanks to you, sis."

"You've healed yourself."

Cassie got up for more coffee but instead moved to the window, her attention focussed on her birdfeeders, the bluejays standing tough chasing other birds from the platform. They're so aggressive. There's enough food for everyone and, with three feeders, plenty of space, but the jays are not content to share food or space. They argue noisily and chase birds and squirrels away. Everything an argument. Even with Karen. Even while she appreciated everything she did. The anti-inflammatories she'd prescribed had looked after her physical symptoms but Cassie realized she was still into a bit of a psychological quandary. She turned back to Karen who'd been quietly watching her. "I've had some good conversations with Bert. Helped me focus."

"Does he discuss Tom with you?"

"Only as far as his behaviour, or his condition, I guess, affects my progress. He's not treating Tom, you know."

"Oh, so what's happening with him?"

"Bert got him into the military unit at the Royal Ottawa. It's a brand new facility."

"How'd he place him into that treatment program? Tom's a civilian."

Cassie poured two coffees from the carafe on her tea trolley knowing she needed to recover from her slip of the tongue. She quickly decided the direct approach would limit the damage. "Sorry, Karen. I've said more than I should've."

"Whoa. When you start calling me Karen I know I've hit a nerve."

"No, kg. Not so serious."

"You're into something not for public consumption, aren't you? This chikungunya stuff?"

"Let's leave it. My guard's down. I said too much. Please let's keep it between us."

"Some sort of security clearance needed?"

"Yes."

"Oh, this is exciting... I'm sorry, Cass, I'm teasing. It'll go no further. Why don't you go back to your science conundrum?"

"If we know Frank and I both had chikungunya infection, the virus can be transmitted by close personal contact. Listen to me, kg, I'm talking in euphemisms. Close personal contact. I slept with the man! That's how the virus was transmitted. Only one weekend because after that he was sick. He made me feel good. As kind and gentle as Tom. I needed that." And I make no apologies.

"No condom?"

"It... I... I don't know. Totally unplanned. Just happened. After the first time it didn't seem to matter. I wasn't thinking."

"I had HIV testing done," Karen said.

"What do you mean?"

"Your specimens. I requisitioned HIV testing."

"Karen! Without my permission?"

"Cassie, calm down. You know this stuff better than I do. You told me that more than ninety percent of all people infected with HIV don't know they're positive."

"But, Frank…"

"I know he was kind but did you really know him? You think you caught chikungunya from him. Wouldn't something else be possible? Test was negative, by the way."

"Sorry, kg. Sorry for reacting like that. You scared me. Thank goodness it's negative."

"Yeah. Guess I've interrupted your chikungunya story. Wanna go back there?"

"Sure. Just wanted to say chikungunya is transmitted by insect bites. There's no published evidence of person-to-person transmission."

"What about accidental injection of infected body fluids? You know, like needle-sticks?"

"Don't know. Theoretically, I guess. But that's not what happened with me."

"Yeah, we're off track."

"And it was November."

"Okay. November?"

"No mosquitoes. Just like here."

"I see your problem, sis. Lose the science or betray Tom."

"We're not together. I don't know what to think."

"Of course it's only one case. And without proof of chikungunya infection in both you and Frank, it's highly speculative."

"Actually, sis, the more we talk about it, I'm starting to think it's not that earth-shattering. I don't have enough data. You're right it's speculative."

"Well, Cass, things are different when you gain distance from them."

"Thanks, kg. I've probably personalized this too much."

"That's easy to do. It happened to you. But, Cass, let's stand back and take stock. There were two deaths we know of and a bunch of other cases that left people with arthritis. That happens with many viral diseases."

"And Agron and Frank were exposed to massive quantities of virus. Me, as a secondary case, only mildly symptomatic. Obviously person-to-person spread couldn't be highly effective. And the other cases probably arose from animal contact."

"Don't diminish the outbreak completely, Cass."

"I won't, kg. It was contained. I don't need to tell Tom anything about me."

two

# February 2004
*Nesër*

Cassie reached quickly to answer her telephone.

"Cassie, it's Bert. How're you doing?"

"Hi Bert. I'm doing well thanks. Really quite well."

"Good. I'm going to visit Tom tomorrow. Strictly social. Just wondered whether you'd like to come with me?"

"Whew! You've thrown me for a loop. How... what... do you think Tom would like to see me?"

"Absolutely! He'd be delighted. Question is do you want to see him?"

"I do, of course. But, I... sorry if I seem hesitant. Gotten used to not expecting to be with him."

"It's okay. We could do it another time."

"No, no. I want to see him. I just want to see the Tom I remember."

"You know, Cassie, can't guarantee anything."

"How's his treatment going?"

"I'm not involved, you realize. But I visit at least once a week. Keith sees him often, too. He seems pretty normal to me."

"Okay, I'm good for it. So, tomorrow..."

"Sure, how's four o'clock? I'll slip away from the office a little early. Meet you just inside the main entrance. That's the new building, centre entrance off Carling Avenue."

"Okay, see you then. Bye Bert."

Cassie tried to steady her trembling hand with the other one. So much going through her mind so quickly... Tom... Frank. I need to stay calm. Far too early for decisions. I need to see Tom first. Gauge his reaction to me. And, maybe more importantly, gauge my reaction to him.

Cassie was gratified by Tom's immediate broad smile when she arrived with Bert. The three of them chatted easily in the day lounge over a cup of tea. After a while, when Bert inclined his head toward the door to signal Cassie his intention to leave, she indicated with a slight shake of her head she was staying put.

"It's so good to see you, Cass. Thanks for staying behind."

"I'm happy to see you too. Nice of Bert to break the ice."

"Nice of him to leave."

"Tom!"

"It's okay, Cass. I'll see him again. He'll be back tomorrow. He'll want to know how things went with us."

"And?"

"All I can say so far you're the best therapy I've had."

"We haven't even talked yet."

"I know. We don't need to talk."

"You look good."

"Thanks. I'm quite well. Graduating to an outpatient program in two weeks."

"That sounds good. Here?"

"Yeah, here. Or they could transfer me to Toronto if I wanted."

"Which would you choose?"

"In Toronto, I'd have my own place, but this program's great. I don't really feel like starting anew."

"Yeah. What will you do if you stay here?"

"Keith's offered. Start there maybe. But I don't want to impose. Maybe get a room or something close-by."

"You wouldn't need to live around here."

"You don't know, I guess. They took my license. Can't drive until I'm certified okay."

"How would you get to Keith's?"

"Bus. OC Transpo. Little over an hour all told."

"What about my place?" Cassandra surprised herself with her offer. Just slipped out of my mouth. "It's only an hour away."

"I can't drive, Cass. But thanks."

"I could drive you."

"You… what, you'd…"

"Yes, I would."

"But, it's an hour each way. Each session's two hours. Three days a week. You can't do that."

"I can do that, Tom. It'd be my pleasure."

"What about Kosova?"

"Nothing planned so far now Canada's no longer directly involved. EU has offered a contract. But not yet. I need to renew my UK passport first."

"Strange, isn't it? You're eligible for a passport when you've never lived there."

"Maybe, but it has worked to my advantage. What're your plans, Tommy? I mean when you're finished treatment."

"Still have a contract for stories from Afghanistan. Maybe Iraq. I'm a little nervous but, heck, guess that's what I do."

Cassie silently contemplated this information. She'd no idea Tom was willing to return to the stressors he'd just now escaped. I don't know if I can cope with that. I don't know if this relationship can go anywhere.

"Cass, you've slipped off somewhere. I hoped you'd accept me as I am. But it's okay, you've made no commitments." Tom considered telling Cassie about his conversation with President Rugova, how the president had asked him to keep his job offer in mind:

"Would travel to Europe and North America be a problem then?" Rugova had asked.

"Not if Cassandra could travel with me," was Tom's reply.

"We would be willing to pay for her travel as well."

"No, Mr President, that wouldn't be necessary."

"Oh, but it would, Tom. You will be paid at Kosova rates. You could not afford air travel."

"Thank you, Mr President. I need to discuss this with Cassie," Tom had said but that discussion had never come about as their relationship crumbled...

"Tommy, please come to my place. We'll have time to talk on those journeys."

# three

# March 2004
## *Mirupafshim*

As they travelled toward Ottawa, they rode in comfortable silence as they often did, content to be together. Tom had lost track of the number of trips.

"I enjoy our drives, Cass. I really appreciate all you've done for me. Should find out today how much longer. I feel completely better."

"It's been great for me too."

"I've felt badly about the amount of time you've spent driving and waiting."

"You know that's not a problem. You've no idea how much work I've done in the medical library."

"Well, it may only go one more week. If they consider me sane." Tom laughed.

Cassie knew they'd been skirting any discussion of their relationship so she was unprepared for the rest of the conversation. Tom asked about her sense of where they were going. But then, before she had a chance to respond, he asked whether she'd thought about marriage. She felt ambushed, needing time to regroup, to collect her thoughts.

"I'm really enjoying being with you, Tommy," she replied. Unsure how else to respond, she then added, "Let's talk about it at dinner."

She watched Tom's reaction. He squeezed her hand and responded with a grin, unfazed.

"Sure," he said. "Dinner."

THE END

J. STEPHEN THOMPSON

# Glossary of Albanian Words and Phrases

| Shqipe | Anglishte |
|---|---|
| *Asgjë nuk punon* | Nothing works |
| *Birrë e Pejës* | Beer of Pejë (literal translation) |
| *Çfare një surprize* | What a surprise |
| *Ditën e mirë* | Good day / have a good day (as goodbye) |
| *Do të ketë* | There will be |
| *Është ditë e bukur* | It's a beautiful day |
| *Falemnderit* | Thank you / thanks |
| *Gëzuar!* | Cheers! |
| *Gjashtë vezë* | Six eggs |
| *Gjithçka punon* | Everything works |
| *Kafe* | Coffee / brown |
| *Mbaj vesh* | Listen / listen up / pay attention |
| *Më falni një moment* | Excuse me a moment |
| *Më takon* | It's my turn / it belongs to me |
| *Mirëdita* | Good afternoon / good day (greeting) |
| *Mirë, falemnderit* | Fine, thank you |
| *Mirëmëngjes* | Good morning |
| *Mirëpo, nesër* | However, tomorrow |
| *Mirupafshim* | Goodbye / 'til we meet again |

| | |
|---|---|
| *Mjet komunikimi* | Communication tool |
| *Mort* | Death |
| *Natën e mire* | Good night |
| *Në befasi* | By surprise |
| *Nesër* | Tomorrow |
| *Në të vërtetë* | Indeed / really / truly |
| *Ngase ne jemi të lirë* | Because we are free |
| *Ngase ne e kemi lirinë* | Because we have freedom |
| *Një bukë* | One (loaf of) bread |
| *Nuk punon* | Doesn't work |
| *Nuk të kuptoj* | Don't understand it |
| *Paralajmërium* | Admonition |
| *Pasnesër* | Day after tomorrow |
| *Po* | Yes (affirmation) |
| *Rrymë* | Power / electric current |
| *Shumës si jeni* | How are you? / How is everybody? |
| *Si jeni?* | How are you? |
| *S'ka persë* | No trouble / you are welcome |
| *S'ka punoj* | Doesn't work / doesn't function |
| *S'ka rrymë* | There is no current (as electricity) |
| *S'ka problem* | No trouble / no problem |
| *S'ka ujë* | There is no water |
| *Të dua* | I love you |

| | |
|---|---|
| *Të dua shumë* | I love you very much |
| *Të falemnderit* | Thank you |
| *Telefonatë* | Telephone call / phone call / call |
| *Tung* | Hello / hi /see you/ *ciao* |
| *Ujë* | Water |